For the myths and monsters who fuel my imagination.

THROUGH THE BLUR

YOLANDA SFETSOS

ANUCI PRESS

yolandasfetsos@yahoo.com.au

First paperback edition March 2024

Anuci Press edition March 2024

www.anuci-press.com

Cover Design by Adrian Medina

fabledbeastdesign@gmail.com

Internal Formatting by Sam Richard

Edited by Katarina Yerger

katraeyerger@gmail.com

Another excellent job!

ISBN 979-8-9898048-3-2 (paperback)

ISBN 979-9898048-4-9 (ebook)

"And while a deep sleep held the snakes and herself, he struck her head from her neck. And the swift winged horse Pegasus and his brother the warrior Chrysaor, were born from their mother's blood."

— OVID, METAMORPHOSES BOOK IV

CONTENTS

Chapter One   9
Chapter Two   17
Chapter Three   27
IN THE BLUR   35
Chapter Four   41
Chapter Five   47
IN THE BLUR   57
Chapter Six   61
Chapter Seven   71
IN THE BLUR   81
Chapter Eight   85
Chapter Nine   93
Chapter Ten   103
IN THE BLUR   111
Chapter Eleven   119
Chapter Twelve   129
IN THE BLUR   137
Chapter Thirteen   141
Chapter Fourteen   151
Chapter Fifteen   159
IN THE BLUR   169
Chapter Sixteen   175
Chapter Seventeen   179
IN THE BLUR   193
Chapter Eighteen   207
Chapter Nineteen   213
IN THE BLUR   223
Chapter Twenty   227
IN THE BLUR   231
Chapter Twenty-One   235
Chapter Twenty-Two   241
FREE FROM BLUR   249
Chapter Twenty-Three   255

Acknowledgments   265
About the Author   267

CHAPTER ONE

2013

"Yep, you're definitely going to die," Peg Ceto said, trying to inject as much doom and gloom into her voice as possible. She enjoyed doing card readings for her classmates, but what she liked even more was messing around with them. This way, she could make someone else feel miserable for a change.

"What?" Eve's hazel eyes widened and her smooth brown skin turned a sickly pallor. The apple charm hanging from her golden necklace sparkled. Even her hot pink sweater seemed out of place. "That answer has nothing to do with my question."

Peg shrugged, staring at the cards spread out on the desk instead of at the girl who tried so hard to fit in. "What was your question again?"

"Am I going to find what I'm looking for?"

"And what is it that you're looking for?"

"It's personal." Eve narrowed her eyes. "Besides, I'm not supposed to give you any clues, right?"

"Probably not." Peg glanced at the cards laid out between them before turning her head so she could focus on the field outside the classroom window. The clouds hung gray and heavy, ready to unleash a downpour which was probably waiting until the final bell. According to the clock above the whiteboard, that was fifteen minutes away.

Can't wait to get out of this school.

Not only for the day, but forever. Minerva High was a place she couldn't wait to leave behind because walking these crowded corridors and sitting in these dreary classrooms reminded her of her sister. Attending every day widened the open wound she desperately wished would become a scar.

"Do you really see death in my cards?" Eve asked, rousing her attention back to the spread.

"No," she said with a sigh. "I'm just messing with you."

"Don't take it personal. She does the same to everyone." The gossipy blonde sitting at the desk beside Eve rolled her big blue eyes and flicked a strand of hair behind her shoulder. While everyone else at least pretended to be minding their own business, or had skipped the lesson altogether because their teacher hadn't bothered to turn up, Lovey was scribbling in her open notebook. Didn't bother to hide she was listening in.

"No, I don't," Peg lied. But of course, she did.

"You've read for me five times and always start with the *'you're going to die'* thing, and it's not even funny," Lovey said while still scrawling all over the open page.

"Whatever." How could someone this beautiful and intelligent—almost perfect—be so annoying? No wonder Peg and Belle, her best friend, disliked her.

"Pretend all you want. But we both know it's true. You only have one trick up your sleeve."

"Whatever." Peg ignored her. "Eve, do you want to know what the cards say or not?"

"Yes, tell me." Eve's enthusiasm returned, once again making her features match the vibrant colors of her perfectly-coordinated outfit and necklace.

"Okay." She rested her arms on the desk and considered where to start. "You picked two black cards, so that makes the most basic answer to your question, no."

"Oh." Eve blew out a sigh that made the tight curls around her face swirl.

"But that's only if you're looking for a yes or no answer."

"A basic bullshit answer costs five dollars, but if you want her to give you the whole sad spool, she charges ten." Lovey met Peg's gaze as she spoke, her hand still writing away.

"Thank you, *Lovey*. Guess I don't need to hire anyone to do the marketing for me when I have you mouthing off my business."

A few kids snickered. Most were sitting around in groups, but now confirmed they were definitely listening in. Peg always drew an audience when she pulled out her deck of playing cards. She wished Belle was here, because she loved putting Lovey in her place and would give everyone a real reason to laugh.

Lovey winked before returning to whatever she was writing.

"I want the whole reading," Eve said.

"You must be looking for something very important."

Eve crossed her arms and shook her head. "Uh-uh, I know enough about tarot readings to not offer anything that might give you clues."

"I'm not a tarot reader."

"It's called cartomancy, and just because you use those crappy playing cards instead of a tarot deck doesn't mean that's not what you're doing."

"Once again, thank you for contributing when no one asked for your input."

This time Lovey gave her the finger.

Peg couldn't help but laugh, and snuck another glance at the clock. Ten minutes to go, if she didn't wrap this up soon, she'd have trouble shaking Eve and she didn't want to miss her bus.

She caught a shadow shift from the corner of her eye and when she chased it, the familiar sense of gloom crawled over the walls and curled around the clock. She hated when this happened, but the darkness was always waiting in the peripheral. She shut her eyes for several seconds and when she opened them again, the obscurity was gone and her gaze landed on someone watching her from across the room.

The new kid.

She couldn't remember his name, but the guy mostly kept to himself because the others didn't feel comfortable befriending the teacher's son. Still, he always found time to stare at her. If her sister was here, Chrysa would already be teasing Peg about this guy having a crush on her. But she wasn't, and now wasn't the time to concentrate on shifting shadows or lost sisters.

"Hey, are you okay?"

Peg blinked and found Eve's hand on hers. She concentrated on the fingerless gloves she'd chosen to wear today because this pair was one of her favorites. The ones with red and black lines and white skulls.

"Is everything okay?" the girl repeated.

She nodded. "Everything's fine."

"Ooh, I like your bracelet, it's so pretty."

Peg glanced at the silver snake coiled around her wrist. The end of the tail was hidden under her glove, but she'd rolled up her sleeves so the head was showing. She concentrated on the onyx-jeweled eyes, trying not to think about her sister never being able to wear hers again.

"Yeah, thanks."

"Where did you get it?" Eve's eyes were shiny.

"It's a family heirloom." At least, it was according to her mother. She'd given matching bracelets to her and Chrysa when they were younger, and insisted they wear them all the time for protection. She still didn't know what protection this piece of jewelry supposedly provided.

"Oh, that's awesome." Eve wrapped her fingers around the golden apple charm. "So's mine."

"Okay." Peg turned back to the cards. After all, these readings were a way of deflecting attention away from herself. "Uh, you picked ten of clubs, eight of diamonds and eight of spades."

Eve sat forward. "And what does that mean?"

The classroom darkened around Peg, pressing against her shoulders until she thought the walls were closing in on her. But she was used to this feeling, it happened every time she did a reading for someone. She took a shallow breath and exhaled slowly.

"The first card symbolizes the past. Clubs mean that you've traveled or moved recently, and the number ten is about you carrying a burden or secret responsibility."

Eve kept a safe distance but Peg could sense her uncertainty.

She had a way of knowing if she was on the right track, and this nervous tick meant she'd hit the truth.

Peg let her mind fill with all the possible meanings and rolled with the rest. "The second card is eight of hearts and represents the present." She traced the worn edges of the cardboard. "Hearts means you're trying to connect with someone or trying to share info you think is important, and the eight means you're waiting for the right time to strike."

Eve avoided her eyes, instead glanced out the window as she nibbled on her lip.

With less than five minutes to go, she had to hurry the rest. "And the last card—eight of spades means your regret and fear will probably work against you. That means you'll make yourself even more isolated and powerless than you originally were."

"Wow, what a chipper reading," Lovey whisper-hissed under her breath.

"That *does* sound bad." Eve's brow was furrowed, and seemed to be pondering something she probably didn't want to share.

Peg shrugged. "Sorry, I only read what's in the cards."

"But strangely, I think I know what you mean..."

"That's good, so it's not all bad, then." Her eyes swept over the cards as her mind rushed over everything she'd revealed and, in a flash, the conclusion came together.

"Well, thanks." Eve reached into her pocket. "I guess." She pulled out a ten-dollar bill but Peg held up a hand.

"I'm not finished yet."

"Oh." She kept the bill poised between them.

"This is like a science experiment," someone said to their left. "You get a conclusion as well."

Peg ignored the latest, and very immature, interruption. These guys were in their last year of high school, most mere months away from turning eighteen, and were supposed to be showing some sign of becoming functioning adults by now.

"You recently moved, hoping to carry out a secret mission by connecting with someone because you want to tell them something important." Peg sighed. "But maybe you're being too pushy and that'll work against you. In the end, you might regret you ever reached out."

"I thought you said it wasn't all bad." Eve's mouth was as wide as her eyes and she seemed horrified.

Peg yanked the money from the girl's fingertips and shoved the ten into the back pocket of her jeans. "Maybe you should stop trying so hard to find things you're not supposed to."

Eve shook her head. "I—"

"Hey, why don't you read me next?"

Peg looked up to find a tall, good looking guy with dark hair standing beside her desk. She still couldn't remember his name, but this was definitely the new guy she'd caught staring at her only minutes ago.

"Only if you tell me why your father didn't bother to turn up to class today." Considering Mr. Danae had only transferred to Minerva High at the start of the new school year, it seemed a bit strange for him to take so much time off. Especially when his son always turned up.

"He's not my—"

The bell rang.

"Sorry, but we're out of time." Peg stood and scooped up the well-worn cards into the palm of her hand. Without thinking about what she was doing, she shuffled the deck and the energy garnered from Eve's reading fell away like sprinkles of dust only she could see.

"Isn't it a bit strange that you use playing cards instead of what every other hack uses?" the guy asked.

Before she could reply, the oxygen was sucked out of the classroom and the familiar strain against the backs of her shoulders returned. She collected herself enough to snort-laugh and find her voice. "Yet, you wanted me to read for you."

He shrugged. "Maybe next time."

Peg pushed the chair back with a screech. "Probably not."

Eve was studying the scarred desk, as if she could still see the three-card layout in front of her. Lovey was getting to her feet and when she pressed a hand to the other girl's shoulder, Eve jumped.

The reading gets them every time.

Everyone wanted rosy revelations, or expected her to create a jolly narrative to cheer up their day and make the ten bucks worthwhile, but she only read what she saw. What her mother, Ed Ceto, taught her to see.

Peg shouldered her backpack and tucked the cards into the front pouch of her hoodie, before rushing out of the stifling classroom and into the crowded corridor. She always left as soon as the last bell rang to reach the bus on time and get a good seat, but that guy held her up. A few minutes made a huge difference.

Her ride home was parked all the way across the other side of the school entrance so she hurried past the crowd of slow-moving kids, narrowly avoiding elbows to her side and fingers in her eyes. She'd even made sure she went to her locker earlier. And now she was on her way to being totally late because shoving past the giggling, chattering swarm of kids was harder than trying to hack through a hoard of shambling zombies.

When she finally reached the doors and was about to push through, someone tapped her arm.

She swiveled in time to catch the one guy she tried to avoid the most, yet happened to spend the most time with. He was somehow always there, and carried too many memories that reminded her of Chrysa. All the things she didn't want to dwell on.

"Oh, hi, Cal." She flashed him a half-smile.

"Want me to give you a ride home?"

"Nah, I'm good," she said, trying not to get jostled too hard by the students pushing past. "Thanks anyway."

"But it's supposed to rain."

"I'll be on the bus so it won't matter."

"But—"

Peg sighed and turned to face him. "I'm okay, all right? You don't have to look out for me and be everywhere I turn." She gritted her teeth. "You don't need to save me because you couldn't save *her*."

His eyes flashed as if she'd struck him. "I'm not trying to—"

"Yes, you are." She hated saying awful things to Cal because he honestly cared, but she couldn't take his constant intrusions. She stuck her hands into her hoodie's pocket and found comfort in the feel of her cards. "Look, I have to go."

Without another glance, she spun on her heel and practically ran out the doors. She took the stairs too fast and almost lost her footing. As she made her way to the bus, glaring at the dark sky overhead while trying to ignore the breathless pain Cal always roused inside her, Peg watched the yellow monstrosity drive away.

"Shit," she hissed. "That's just fucking great."

CHAPTER TWO

MISSING THE BUS WAS ALWAYS A REAL KICK IN THE BUTT. MISSING IT ON a day when the heavens threatened to bear down with the force of Zeus and Thor combined, made Peg's bad mood worse.

She kicked a rock on the uneven path in front of her and watched it roll into the long grass bordering the sides of the abandoned road.

If it hadn't been for that annoying Eve insisting on her reading. If it hadn't been for Lovey's interruptions. If that teacher's kid hadn't wasted even more of her time being obnoxious. If Cal hadn't stopped her at the doors when a few seconds made a huge difference.

Peg kicked another rock.

Blaming the others for wasting her time might be convenient, but it was her own fault. She'd even checked the windows and clock to keep an eye on her escape, but the creeping gloom was the real distraction. The crawling darkness was something she'd battled most of her life, but the invasive nature of it had gotten particularly bad since her twin sister disappeared.

Now that Chrysa was gone, she imagined the weight of the night sky pressing into the backs of her shoulders more frequently. Until her skin stung from the intensity, and the pressure against her chest became unbearable.

Her dreams weren't any better than her waking hours, but she always pushed past all the obstacles never understanding why these peculiarities were there. She'd confided in Chrysa once, but unlike Peg, her sister never seemed to experience the weirdness of the gloom. This was her own personal peculiarity.

"*Hello, can you hear me?*"

She stopped in her tracks. To imagine a creeping wall of black spreading from the corners of her vision was one thing, hearing voices was another thing altogether.

"*Can anybody hear me?*"

Peg peeked over her shoulder, turned back to face the thick trees lining both sides of the canopied path ahead. She'd long ago gotten off the main road—something her mother always warned her daughters never to do—but the other way home added an extra ten minutes. And she was trying to outrun the rain.

"*I can feel you nearby. Can sense your presence.*"

"Who's there?" At least her voice remained steady.

"*Why won't you help me?*"

The whispers came from everywhere and nowhere. Whoever this was could be trapped somewhere behind the scrubland and trees bordering this road. But no matter where they were, one thing was clear. Their insistent hissing pierced into Peg's brain, threatening to carve her skull in two.

She tilted her head to the sky, wondered if the whispers were coming from up above because she used to hear the heavens calling to her all the time when she was a kid. And would climb the tallest trees hoping to reach the stars. While her mother didn't provide any real answers about this compulsion, she *did* tell her to never give in to those whispers.

When Mom started telling her and her sister stories from Greek Mythology, Peg often thought maybe Mount Olympus was calling out to her. Which god or goddess wanted to get her attention? And how many times had Peg thought she'd actually had wings when leaping off the highest branches because she managed to land perfectly every time?

She considered the gray clouds and tracked their lazy progress across the sky.

"You're still here, but why aren't you helping me?"

"You're not real." She stomped away and didn't care that mud stuck to the soles of her boots.

She passed a copse of trees and the creak of wood made her pause, but when she turned, she found nothing there. The branches creaked on the other side of the shadowed road as well, and her pulse sped up.

Peg continued on, walked faster while trying to ignore the never-ending murmured whispers tangling together. Her head filled with the cries for help and her fingers toyed with the deck of cards inside her hoodie pouch. She instantly felt a sense of calm wash over her. The playing cards were more than a way to make a quick buck at school to help keep her family afloat. They also anchored her whenever the gloom or her anxious thoughts got the best of her.

The cards didn't erase the problem but helped to focus her mind and breath.

When she cleared the next lot of trees, she breathed a sigh of relief because the road ahead was uncovered by vegetation.

The sky still held the lingering weight of a downpour, so she quickened her step. But a ding made her pause.

Peg dug the phone from the back pocket of her jeans and narrowed her eyes to read the screen. A text from Belle.

Annabelle Ruffin was her best friend, and had been since they'd both started high school. Back then they'd been part of a trio, and Belle was the girl between the two sisters. A friend they shared until Chrysa found herself a boyfriend who became her world. That was when Belle and Peg got a lot closer.

hear u almost scard girl 2 death

Who told you that?

Lovey

Of course she did. :/

where ru btw werent on bus...

Missed it. Walking home.

better hurry or ull get caught in rain

Stop texting me, then.

:)

Peg couldn't help but smile as she put her phone away. Belle was the main reason why catching the bus was essential. She made Peg feel better about everything, would listen to her complaints, and tell her stories until they reached her stop. And she was right, if Peg didn't hurry, the rain was going to make this walk even more unbearable.

She took another step and a branch snapped to her left.

Peg turned to find no one there. Her pulse sped up and she quickened her pace.

Another branch snapped, this time on her right.

She didn't bother checking but with each stride, the undeniable sensation of being watched made her skin crawl. Every time she stopped, another twig snapped and by the time she turned toward the sound, it stopped. Only the scattered leaves confirmed her suspicions and when the crying started, she thought she was losing her mind.

Instead of wasting time, she ran. As soon as she made it past the clearing and entered the next canopy of trees, the rain started. Thin, long drops sliced through the leaves, falling steady and making the path ahead appear hazy.

At least she was thankful for the trees because the thick foliage provided some shelter.

Peg pulled the hood over her head and continued on her way

with both hands tucked into the pouch. She ignored the crying, but the awful sound unsettled her frayed nerves.

She desperately wanted to get away, but what if someone was hurt? Maybe an animal was wounded. Or a kid had fallen off the slight embankment and couldn't get up. This unlikely scenario happened to her sister years ago while riding her bike.

Peg stopped and the crying persisted.

She took a deep breath of the crisp air and it helped clear her mind, but the rain had turned icy. Even tucked away, her fingertips were frozen but her hands were warm in their woolen gloves. She sucked down the senseless fear and felt a slight pressure around her wrist as she stepped over the muddy dirt and approached the left side of the road. She pulled her hand out and glanced at her wrist, could have sworn the onyx eye on her snake bracelet blinked.

I'm really losing it.

She wanted to run home but had to make sure no one was hurt. She'd never forgive herself if she left an injured dog, cat, or kid alone in this weather. Her nerves hardened as much as her resolve.

All she had to do was take a quick peek over the side. If she was right, she would try to help. And if she couldn't help, she could call someone. Either way, she had to find out.

Her pulse thundered in her ears and the thrumming of the rain settled into comforting background noise. She swiped the long grass aside, sending beads of water flying all around her, but she was determined to lean closer. As she did, the world darkened. The edges curled and she convinced herself the gloom she'd encountered inside the classroom had chased her here, like it always did. The blackness spread but she ignored the weight of the darkness to focus on the intensity of the weeping.

"Hello? Is anyone there?" she called, but couldn't see anyone. "Are you hurt?"

The crying stopped abruptly. Piercing amber eyes appeared in the darkness, blinked and rose from the bottom of the ravine until the round orbs glowered from the tall branches above her head. Was that the sound of fluttering wings?

Peg almost lost her footing as she stepped back. Her heart slammed against her ribs when a loud honk echoed behind her. She stifled a scream as she turned around and recognized who'd scared her half to death. The familiar powder blue VW bug rumbled up beside her and the driver wound down the driver's side window.

"Hey, what're you doing out here?"

"Cal, what the hell? Are you trying to give me a heart attack?" Her heart was beating too fast and she could feel the glittering orbs still staring at her.

"Sorry." His gray eyes were as dark as the sky above. "I was on my way to see if you'd made it home all right when I saw you by the side of the road. What're you doing?"

"I..." She didn't know what to say. How could she explain a disembodied voice asking for help or the creepy amber eyes? It might be easier to focus on what he'd said. Even after telling him to stop looking out for her, he was still doing it. "Didn't I tell you I was fine?"

"Yeah, you always tell me you're fine, but I know you're not."

"Who died and made you my keeper?" As soon as the words slid from her mouth, she regretted them.

Cal's eyes were suddenly shiny. "You can be a real bitch sometimes, you know that?"

She lowered her head, because he was right, but it was her way of coping. The only way to deal with a missing twin and a barely-functioning mother who hardly left her bedroom.

"I'm... sorry, Cal." She sighed. "I know you're trying to help."

He nodded and wiped his eyes with the back of his hand.

Peg made her way around the front of the car, and noticed the hood was as rusty now as the day he'd bought the vehicle from Mom. After buying the rust bucket, he'd taken the car home to his old man and brother, who were both mechanics, and they got the damned thing working.

The Ceto and Ackley families had a symbiotic relationship—one provided the scrappy, dented and rusty frameworks, while the other fixed them. They helped each other and everybody benefited financially. Cal and Chrysa falling in love wasn't unexpected because there was always something between them.

The raindrops bounced against the curved hood and she focused on that instead of the familiar face of the boy she'd known forever. The one watching her silently through the windshield.

When she reached the other side, she tried the door but it was locked. "Are you going to open it, or what?"

"I think I've changed my mind."

"Come on, I'm *really* sorry." And she was, for a lot. Cal always listened when she needed to chat about Chrysa. They shared a pain only her mother could also understand. Belonged to an exclusive club no one wanted to be a member of.

He reached over and opened the creaky door. "You know it doesn't lock."

"But I can't get in unless you open it from the inside!"

He shrugged.

"Why don't you get that fixed?"

He shrugged a second time.

Peg climbed into the passenger seat. The same one she'd avoided for months because this seat belonged to Chrysa, not her. She should be in the back where she usually sat whenever the group went out together. Sometimes she brought Belle along, or whoever her latest crush of the week happened to be.

"Close the door, you're letting the rain in."

Peg took one last peek at the side of the road and thought she noticed the branches close over two bright amber spots, but she couldn't be sure. She slammed the door and was at least glad to be out of the cold.

"Thanks for stopping."

"What were you doing?" Cal put the car in gear and took off, tires sloshing in the mud.

"Thought I heard something."

He glanced at her. "Why would you take the scenic route home in this weather, anyway?"

"*Someone* made me miss the bus."

"Oh, really?" Cal squeezed the steering wheel. "Sorry about that. It's just... you've been avoiding me and I wanted to see how you were doing."

"You have to stop worrying so much."

"I can't do that. I've worried about you and Chrysa my whole life, and that's not gonna stop now because she's..." The unspoken truth hung between them, stealing the air from inside the car.

... gone.

... missing.

... lost.

... dead.

Cal could have used any of those words or a combination, but he often tiptoed around the obvious and she could understand why. Peg bit her tongue, even though she wanted to tell him how stifling his attention could get. She didn't want to hurt him any more than she already had today.

As the bug passed the *Golden Pegasus Scrap* sign that advertised her mother's business and marked the property, Peg finally said, "Do you want to come in and say hi to Mom?"

"Sure, I'd like that."

"Maybe we can watch something shitty on TV, or sneak in a movie."

"Sounds like a plan."

"Are you sure you don't have any homework?" she teased.

"You know I'm never in the mood for homework."

She couldn't help but laugh. The only thing Cal didn't have in common with his girlfriend but shared with Peg was how little he enjoyed school. Many times, Chrysa had to pair up with Lovey because Peg and Cal didn't care much about schoolwork.

"Hey, Peg, mind doing a reading for me?"

To that, she shook her head. "No way, you always get the same result."

"But it's been a while—"

"No matter how much time passes, it'll always be the same with you." She snorted and caught sight of a silver truck passing in the opposite direction. Peg couldn't be sure because of the rain and the foggy windows, but she thought she'd spotted her history teacher in the driver's seat. But what would Mr. Danae be doing on their property? Especially when he'd skipped the last lesson of the day.

They drove in silence down the long and winding unpaved driveway before Peg decided to pull out her deck of playing cards. She shuffled and fanned them out. "Pick a card, any card!"

Cal smiled, plucked one and showed her.

"Ugh, you got the five of hearts, what a surprise!"

"What does that mean again?" His eyes were shiny, filled with the rare mix of sadness and excitement only Cal had learned to cultivate.

"Loss and regret," she said. "This is why I don't like to do readings for you. Dude, you're totally depressing." *Worse than me.* She could tease him all she wanted, but this was just another thing they shared because her own personal readings were as sad as his.

"I am not!"

Peg ruffled his shaggy hair before he could stop her. She laughed the rest of the way to the house, almost forgetting about the weirdness she'd experienced on the road.

Almost.

CHAPTER THREE

THE PIERCING SHRIEK SLICED HER DREAM IN HALF AND THE SHARDS shattered inside her head, until she thought the pieces might cut into her brain.

Peg's eyes snapped open and for a split second, she wasn't sure if she was awake or asleep. Her eyesight was blurry and her lashes were stuck together, so she rubbed them with the back of her hand. The room was pitch black, which didn't make any sense when her bed was positioned against the window.

She wasn't sure if the scream had chased her out of sleep, or if she'd awakened because of it. Another cry carved through the silence and made her realize the sound was coming from outside the house. She couldn't help but think about the weeping she'd heard by the side of the road. Was this a new delusion? Wasn't the growing obscurity enough to deal with?

The wail started again, reminding her of an alarm because it started slow and reached maximum pitch in seconds.

Peg stared out the window and noticed a strange glow inside the barn. The windows were glowing an eerie green and light spilled out from between the open wooden doors. What was going on out there? Was someone robbing the place? Now that their dog Sword had vanished with Chrysa, there weren't any animals on the property. Sometimes, wandering goats and stray cats from nearby farms took shelter in the barn, or hid inside one of the vehicles abandoned on their many hectares of land, but this couldn't be an animal.

She kicked the covers off and jumped out of bed. Peg caught sight of her snake bracelet and gloves resting on the bedside table but didn't bother with either.

The wailing stopped abruptly and was replaced by the buzz of silence. She shivered and was suddenly glad she was wearing the pony onesie her sister gave her during their last shared birthday together. The silvery fleece was cozy and even after her bare feet hit the cold wooden floorboards, she remained warm.

A couple of strides later, the scream was back.

She raced out of her room and went to her mother's without bothering to knock. She might be mostly out of action lately, but Peg needed to force her to act like an adult and deal with whatever was going on. If someone was trying to steal or destroy their belongings, it was time Mom acted like she actually cared about their livelihood.

"Mom," she whispered, trying to stay quiet in case someone had crept into the house. She kicked something on the bedroom floor but didn't bother to look. *"Mom!"*

She didn't stir, so Peg closed the distance between the door and bed to find that it was empty. She kicked something else, but it was too dark to see. What the hell was all over the damned floor? She couldn't waste her time on this now. If her mother wasn't here, where was she? She rarely got out of bed and hadn't left this room in over three months.

Maybe she was already in the barn. Was that her screaming?

The screeching stopped, only to start up again.

Peg left the empty room and took the stairs two at a time, reaching the backdoor in seconds. She stepped out into the crisp night air and stuck her feet into the boots she kept by the door. Fall was already here, so nights were as chilly as the mornings.

As she trudged across the long grass, she wished she'd at least checked the time or called the police before leaving the house because she hadn't even grabbed her phone. The only thing in her pocket was a deck of cards.

The screaming halted but her pulse continued to beat fast. Whatever was going on made her skin crawl. Now that she was out of the house, she could also hear the commotion echoing from inside the barn, as if someone was flinging things around. When she reached the tall double doors, she paused and jumped when something heavy slammed the opposite wall.

She sucked in a deep breath, trying to steady her nerves, and rushed inside.

The barn was where her mother stored a variety of old advertising signs and vintage empty cans that were very popular with pickers who trekked through these parts on their many pilgrimages. There were also quite a few dusty and rusted out vehicles, along with old fuel pumps that fetched a pretty penny for those who liked a bit of restoration. With all of the metal packed into this space, as well as the shelving, Peg couldn't see anyone yet, but definitely heard them.

Someone was running between the shelving, while another person was in pursuit. She'd chased her sister and Belle through this maze many times, but the ground didn't usually vibrate. Things flew off the shelves, blocking the spaces between.

Peg hesitated, didn't want to get any closer. Maybe she should run back to bed. But like on the road, she couldn't turn away. What if Mom was hurt? People around here were notorious for owning rifles and guns.

The ear-splitting scream started up again and for the first time, she thought she recognized her mother's voice somewhere in that tragic wail.

"Mom?" The word slipped out.

The scream stopped.

Movement caught Peg's eye and for a moment she thought the gloom was back. She blinked, stepped forward and kept going until she found herself in the small clearing between metal shelves.

Her mother stood in the shadows near the closest shelf, with her back facing Peg. She noticed the rise and fall of her bony shoulders.

"Mom, what's going on?"

"Get out of here," Mom said, but she sounded raspy and odd. There was also something wrong with her hair, and Peg could definitely hear hissing. Was there a gas leak?

"Mom, are you hurt?"

"No."

"Do you want me to call the—"

"Go!"

"What? No, I want to—"

"Just go!" Mom screamed.

But Peg couldn't move. Her memory might be spotty, but she knew that when her sister disappeared, she hadn't done a damn thing about it because she didn't want to get out of bed. Peg refused to let the same thing happen to her mother. That night, months ago, Chrysa and Sword went to check the barn and were never seen again.

"Mom, what's going on?" She needed to see what had turned her inactive mother into a banshee.

Someone was scurrying up ahead, but she kept her attention focused on her mother, who was partially hidden in the shadows. The glowing greenish light returned as Peg advanced. She held her left hand in front of her in an attempt to calm whoever had spooked her mother.

The crazy yell started up again.

The green glow intensified, and she shielded her eyes with her other hand as she crept closer. Her mind stuttered and stalled when her mother spun around to face her.

Peg could only focus on the neon beam that suddenly filled her vision and totally immobilized her. She was nailed to the spot, forced to watch as a strange ray of light struck her left hand, squarely impacting with her open palm.

A chilling sensation swept over her fingers and all the way up her arm. When she blinked enough times to clear the shine of emerald from her vision, she found herself somewhere else. She was no longer inside the barn and was instead standing in the middle of a grayscale forest. Thick fog concealed the vegetation and the bottoms of the trees as static silence filled her ears.

The green beam had followed her here, and kept her arm caught in its dangerous radiance. She was horrified when she stared at her palm and watched a thick gray layer spread, sucking the color from her hand.

"Where am I?" The words felt gummy, were caught between her teeth. Her tongue refused to work properly and felt too big for her mouth. "Mom, where are you?"

Peg was rooted to the spot and when she looked down, she couldn't see her feet because the fog was swallowing her up. She put all her strength into lowering her hand, but her concentration faltered when tall silhouettes appeared between the trees. She couldn't see anyone, but knew a multitude of eyes were watching her.

Someone—many of them—were also approaching.

A current of fear tore through her body and the gloom coalesced around her. But it behaved differently, dripped like tar from the branches and vanished into the mucky fog below. But she still couldn't move, couldn't get away.

"Mom!" The pain emanating from her extended palm throbbed, but was nowhere near as excruciating as it had been back in the barn. Her aching hand fell to her side when she heard the voice she'd missed so much.

"Peggy, get out of here!"

Tears burned behind her eyes and the misty air stung. Only one person ever got away with calling her that.

"Chrysa?" It hurt to say her name, and her sister didn't respond.

Between blinks, Peg was back inside the barn. The screaming and greenish light were both gone. There was only sobbing.

"Mom!" The muddle lifted from Peg's brain and she rushed to her mother's side, who was curled up in the fetal position near the bottom of the closest shelf. "What happened?"

She didn't respond, only wept and covered her eyes with both hands. A strange memory flashed inside Peg's mind. The night

Chrysa disappeared, and Peg finally forced herself out of bed, she'd found her mother in the same distressed state.

"Mom, talk to me." Peg pressed a hand against her shoulder and nearly pulled away because her mother's skin was cold as ice. "What were you doing out here?" *What was that green light I could've sworn I saw coming from you?* But she couldn't articulate the question, and certainly wouldn't mention that she'd slipped into another place. Or that she'd heard Chrysa warn her away from *wherever* that was. She tried to clench her left fist, but the skin was too hard and taut, refused to budge.

Peg needed to get Mom back inside the house, where it was safe and warm. But first she decided to assess the area where she'd heard the scurrying, because whatever had stirred her mother into those unbearable wails had definitely been hiding in this corner.

After checking and not finding anyone or anything—only a mess she would have to clean up tomorrow—she made her way back to her mother.

"Come on, let's get you inside." Ed Ceto was a frail woman and Peg was deeply concerned about her mother wasting away, but the lightness of her weight helped get Mom to her feet. She wouldn't stop crying but Peg didn't stop. She guided her out of the barn and across the yard, then dragged her into the warm kitchen.

"He found me," Mom whispered.

"Who found you?"

"He found *us*."

"Mom, I don't know who you're talking about." When she didn't answer, Peg awkwardly locked the back door. "Do you want a cup of tea?" But Mom was already heading into the corridor. "Wait, I can help you to your room."

"No, I can do it." Mom kept her back to Peg, and the long strands of brown hair seemed to sway in the dim glow.

"What happened out there?"

She didn't respond.

"Damn it, Mom! I asked you a question."

Her shoulders rose and fell with a heavy sigh but she still didn't bother facing Peg.

"I need to know what's going on." Peg curled her fingers around her stiff palm and was at least happy the pain was gone. "Was that a disgruntled customer?"

Mom shook her head and the silky strands shifted independently in an unnatural way.

"Then what happened? Why were you screaming like that?"

"Don't worry about—"

"You woke me up because you were so loud, and I know there was someone out there." She almost mentioned the forest and hearing Chrysa.

Another dramatic sigh filled the space between them as the back of her mother's shoulders shook. Several thumps hit the floor, but it was too dark for Peg to see what her mother had dropped.

"Mom, please..." Harsh words weren't working and neither was an accusatory tone, so she tried to affect her maternal instincts.

"I'm very tired. I need to get back to bed."

Peg hung her head in disappointment.

"I'm sorry."

"About what?" *About keeping harmful secrets? About pretending Chrysa isn't gone? About retreating to your bedroom and refusing to come out all day? About forcing me to remove every single mirror in this fucking house to stop you from slitting your own wrists? Or maybe you're just sorry because you've become such a crappy parent, I have to take care of everything while you cry and feel sorry for yourself?*

"I'm sorry about your hand," Mom whispered before disappearing around the corner.

Peg was stunned. How did she know about her hand and why was *she* sorry? Now that she was back inside the house, she wasn't sure about what she'd seen. Where had that green beam of light come from? Peg was positive it was from her mother, but that wasn't possible. And now her hand was useless.

None of this made any sense. The only thing she knew for sure was that her mother was getting worse, a lot worse. She hadn't dared to contact the authorities or seek help from a doctor because she was still a minor and didn't want to destroy what was left of this pitiful family. Besides, her eighteenth birthday was only a few months away. Maybe then she'd get Mom the psychiatric help she desperately needed.

For now, she'd have to deal with this alone.

Or maybe, she could call her aunties. But Auntie Weirdo and Auntie Widow were busy living their own active lives. She'd already called several times during the past few months and both stated they would rush over, but never did.

Either way, Peg would decide when it was time. When she had nowhere else to turn. For now, she would provide whatever weak support she could manage on her own, while keeping the business afloat and the house neat.

Peg wasn't interested in going away to college, but had researched how to complete a business degree online. It was possible and definitely doable, even from a reputable college. Her teachers often attempted to convince her to aim higher and the guidance counsellor offered to help multiple times, but she wanted to do this on her own. There was no way she could face leaving this house. Or this property, or state... not until Chrysa was found. Or until her mother decided to start living again.

The responsibility lay on her shoulders and the thought made her skin itch.

According to the clock on the stove, it was three in the morning. There was no way she could get back to sleep now. Instead, she made herself a cup of tea and snuck into the living room to continue watching the trashy horror movie she'd started earlier with Cal but had to pause because he needed to get home for dinner.

As the masked killer sliced his way through all the youthful bodies with a machete and chopped the limbs off horny teenagers, Peg sipped on her tea and tried not to focus on the ominous clacking her palm made against the mug.

IN THE BLUR

CHRYSA'S BREATH CAUGHT IN HER THROAT.

She struggled to swallow enough air.

Her lungs stuck, felt like they'd shriveled and hadn't worked in years. She wasn't sure if they were working now.

Panic threaded its way through her limbs, but barely registered.

When her eyes snapped open, her eyelids were heavy. Almost completely crusted over.

She forced herself to blink once, twice, ten times before the blurred images crystalized into anything remotely coherent. She could only see what lay directly in front of her, because her head refused to move an inch.

Chrysa tried to open her mouth and was surprised her lips cracked at the corners, tearing her skin. No matter how hard she tried, words refused to come. All she managed was a series of weak, whiny moans. She was more animal than person.

The pressure of being watched made her skin crawl. She wasn't sure if she had real skin anymore. Nowadays, she was as stationary as a statue.

No, she *was* a statue.

The watchful eyes of the ones who kept her perpetually trapped inside her shell were always present inside this blurry place. Were *they* the reason she couldn't move? These creatures were nothing more than cloaked figures, always there when she managed to wake for several seconds at a time.

A sudden flash of green carved into the space between her and them.

And with it, the sensation of being watched disappeared.

Her eyesight cleared enough to work properly.

Chrysa's heart stuttered when the shimmer of emerald revealed the veiled creatures were but a step away. She'd never seen their full shapes this clearly. They were creepy leaden veiled cloaks hanging limp in the thick air. They didn't appear to have bodies, were only an outline—caricatures of ghosts made out of sheets.

She looked past these horrors and almost cried out when she saw someone she knew very well.

And the light... why did it seem so familiar?

The green tinge sparkled around her... *sister.*

The same thing had happened to her.

Somehow.

Sometime.

It was how Chrysa became a prisoner in the place she referred to as the blur, she was sure of it.

She couldn't stand by and let Peg suffer the same awful fate. Couldn't let her twin get lost in this frozen state, forever wondering if she was alive or dead.

Peggy shouldn't be here.

Chrysa refused to let her become another stagnant rock.

It took all the willpower she possessed, a Herculean effort she hadn't dared use since the first time she'd attempted to stretch an arm out and failed miserably. But now that the veiled were focused on a new target, she summoned all the strength she could manage into her closed fists.

The hard exterior resisted her efforts, but she refused to give up or give in.

This could be her only chance.

A crash echoed around the forest, loud enough for everyone to hear. Strong enough for her stone tomb to crack like an egg.

She had to break free because she needed to warn her sister.

Chrysa closed her eyes again, and this time when she attempted to open her hands the stone casing around her fingers split, connected to the crack already spreading. One small fissure had caused a deep hairline fracture that spread up both wrists. She extended her arms, shoved until the rock suffocating her smashed into smithereens.

I'm finally free.

She wiped the dust and rock fragments from her face and arms, didn't bother with her hair. Even her eyelashes were coated with specks of ground stone, but she could see well enough to focus on the threat.

"Peggy," she called from behind the shrouded figures.

Her sister raised her head but was focused on her open hand, seemed fascinated.

"Peggy, get out of here!"

"*Chrysa?*" Even though they were finally on the same plane, Peg sounded confused and far away.

At least she hadn't been claimed by this world yet.

The veiled blurred around the edges, reacting to her sister's intrusion.

As she prepared to call out again, Peggy vanished into the thick air.

Chrysa's heart ached but at least her sister was gone, had hopefully returned home.

That's all that matters.

She glanced down and saw her beloved and loyal companion, Sword, beside her. The golden retriever was sitting near her feet, transfixed to the spot. His soft brown eyes were the only part of him not made of stone and roamed around until he met her gaze. His pitiful wails reverberated through his stationary shell but he remained frozen.

She glanced over her shoulder and saw that the veiled were closing in.

Soon, they would be on her.

She wasn't sure what happened when people broke out of their shells, but she wasn't about to tempt fate. Couldn't stick around to find out.

"I'm so sorry, boy," she whispered and patted his head.

Sword whined, deep in his doggy throat and it made her want to cry. But she knew that for now, he'd be safer inside his stone casing.

"I'll come back for you. I promise." She kissed his cold head and ran headfirst into the fog, into the forest of trees. It wasn't until she was totally lost in the dense air of the blur that she realized how hard it was to breathe. She coughed and immediately regretted the action because she didn't want to give herself away.

Was the air toxic? Had she survived this long because she'd been encased in stone?

Another, rougher cough wracked her body hard enough to make her bones rattle.

Except she wasn't sure if bones worked the same way here.

Wherever here was.

She suddenly felt as light as a feather and wasn't sure if her feet were actually touching the ground. How had she ended up in this desolate place? A thread buried deep inside her mind teased her with the truth. Dangled in the recesses of her brain like a bookmark she couldn't grab. No matter how hard she tried, she couldn't grasp the truth.

The thread dissipated and she doubled over.

Another loud crash reverberated in the distance but she didn't know where it was coming from. All she could see was the thick fog, her monochrome surroundings.

She could feel the veiled approaching.

Chrysa had been trapped, a voyeur for too long, and refused to go back. How had these creatures changed her? She ignored the question as she straightened.

She dashed past the tree trunk in front of her and as she passed, something swept her off her feet.

No, *someone*.

Her feet dangled beneath her and a hand covered her mouth.

She whimpered, tried to kick out, but her legs were still too weak.

"Stop fighting, I'm not going to hurt you."

Said every serial killer ever. She'd watched enough movies and read plenty of books proving this theory. So, she continued to struggle.

"Fine, keep fighting and they'll claim you," a soft feminine voice whispered in her ear. "Or relax, blend into your surroundings and they'll pass us by."

Chrysa shut her eyes and stopped squirming.

When she opened them again, she watched wide-eyed as the ghouls who lived and ruled this foreign place floated past the ashen tree with their flowing robes.

There were so many, they seemed to pass by forever. And she hated the proximity of whoever was holding her steady like a useless child. Who was this person? And why did she sound familiar?

When the last one finally faded into the rolling fog, she released a breath.

"Are you going to scream if I remove my hand?"

Chrysa shook her head, surprised she could hear the voice so clearly.

The hand was gone as quickly as the grip, and Chrysa fell to the ground. Except, she didn't land on the colorless grass or the twigs, she floated on the cloud of fog that permeated the forest. The ground rumbled beneath her hands.

She raised them and watched the mist melt to particles of moist air.

"Where are we?"

"We're in Hades."

She looked up, but couldn't make out a face. "What?"

"Or the closest I've ever come to it, anyway."

"I don't know what you mean."

"Let's get to shelter before they return for another sweep."

"Who are *they?*" And who was this person who seemed to know more about the situation than she did?

A gloved hand appeared in front of her face. "Come with me and I'll answer as many questions as I can."

Chrysa didn't hesitate and took the stranger's hand.

CHAPTER FOUR

A LONG STREAM OF SUNSHINE WARMED PEG'S FACE AND PENETRATED past her closed eyelids. If it hadn't been for the intrusion of daylight, she might have slept all through the day and into the following night. But the heat was nice and helped chase away the cold beneath her skin.

As soon as she sat up a yawn escaped her. The sun disappeared and the chill seeped back into her bones. The choppy memories of what happened the night before circled her mind, but she pushed everything away.

She was surprised to find herself lying on the couch, wearing her onesie. Half of a throw blanket was on her, and the rest was trailing on the floor. Three empty mugs sat on the coffee table and the TV was still on, static on the DVD's main menu. She couldn't remember much about the movie because she'd been lost in her own thoughts.

Peg kicked the blanket off and stood. Her head was foggy, like she was hungover without having drank a drop of alcohol.

She dumped the mugs in the kitchen sink and noticed it was past ten. She'd already decided in the early hours of the morning not to bother going to school and texted Belle to let her know. After what she saw—or what she *thought* she saw—in the barn, and her mother's unstable behavior, she couldn't face those crowded hallways and classrooms.

The pain of loss manifested inside her chest with the familiar ache she hadn't been able to shake for months. She would have to keep an eye on her mother after her latest bizarre episode. The fact she'd slept for hours without checking if Mom was still in bed made her skin prickle.

Peg crept into the corridor, tiptoed up the stairs and slipped into her mother's bedroom. She found her lying under a heap of blankets, her breath coming steady. At least she was resting. She'd let her sleep for now, but her mom would have to eventually answer the many questions Peg was ready to fire away.

When she turned away from the bed, she slipped and caught herself on the doorframe. "Fuck," she hissed, glaring at the floorboards.

A shadow slithered past her, raced out the doorway. She didn't get a chance to catch what it was, but it reminded her of the snakeskins Chrysa and her used to find all over the place. But why would snakeskins move? She shook her head and convinced herself it was probably her imagination playing more tricks on her.

Peg left the bedroom door open and walked away, only to stop outside her sister's room. She tried not to linger for long but liked to keep an eye on things, to make sure the room didn't get too dusty during Chrysa's absence. The last thing she wanted was for her twin to return to a messy room.

If she comes back.

No, *when she comes back.*

Peg refused to give up hope. It was another thing she shared with Cal, and was why her resolve always melted away when dealing with him. She was always quick to point out how annoying he could be, but on the flipside understood his concern. And his grief. Girls weren't supposed to vanish into thin air. Weren't supposed to leave behind a shattered mother, a heartbroken boyfriend, and a sister who barely had time to mourn because she had to pick up the pieces of their daily lives.

She'd never believed Chrysa was truly gone, but after hearing her voice last night, she was convinced.

Her heart skipped a beat.

She'd heard Chrysa's voice. She had somehow slipped into a strange washed-out forest, and heard her call out. Had someone abducted her sister and was hiding her in the woods? But which woods? There were plenty of properties nearby and wooded areas between almost every single one.

Her hand itched, but she wasn't ready to inspect *that* yet. Instead, she pressed down on the handle, pushed the door open and stepped into her sister's bedroom.

"Chrysa, where did you go?" she whispered into the empty space.

No one responded.

Since the beginning, Peggy hoped to hear her sister's whispers inside this room, but it was a cold and empty shell. Only three months had lapsed, but it already felt abandoned. Isolation had washed over every surface, stripping away whatever remnant of coziness used to reside within these walls. The bed hadn't been made since her disappearance. The bookshelves were still crammed with her books and knickknacks.

Every day that passed without Chrysa made this space feel more alien. Soon—and Peg hated to consider this thought—she'd have to stop wandering inside because it would hurt too much.

Chrysa's sanctuary was a hollowed-out place with possessions that used to belong to a real girl who was now nothing more than a bunch of photos, and the memories Peg carried around of her. A girl who'd destroyed a boy named Cal, because he was obviously as stuck as Peg and refused to move on.

She regretted treating him like a pest, but the way Cal depended on her to fill the void Chrysa had left behind was too much. She had her own emptiness to deal with, because no one would ever replace her twin sister. Or heal the open wound her mother never attempted to disinfect when everything had fallen apart. Half the time she still couldn't remember the how and why of Chrysa's disappearance.

She was there one day, gone the next.

The local police came to the property to conduct an investigation, asked a lot of questions, promised to find her. They even organized a search party, but nothing was ever found. Her sister was nowhere.

Chrysa's disappearance broke Ed Ceto, turned her into a sobbing shell.

Chrysa's disappearance devastated Peg Ceto, turned her into a sarcastic mess.

Chrysa's disappearance crushed their happy family.

She ran a hand over her sister's desk, considered the planner still open on the day she disappeared. *Movies w/ Cal & Peggy + her new crush* was scrawled on the bottom.

Her breath caught. They did go to the movies that afternoon, to watch a scary movie Peg couldn't remember because she'd spent most of the time making out with some guy.

That was the day Chrysa went away forever.

No, not forever. For now.

She ran her fingertips over the imprint the blue pen had left on the page. Chrysa always pressed too hard when she wrote, it was something Peg teased her about. As well as using an actual notebook planner, when most other kids used their phones or tablets.

Peg had the same planner somewhere, because it was a Christmas gift from their aunties, The Sisters Weird.

She lifted the left side, thumbing the faux leather cover. It was bottle green and had the symbol of a snake carved into the front.

Her gaze snagged on the missing mirror that used to sit on her sister's dresser. Like the others, Peg had no choice but to remove it. There was only one mirror left in the house—the one in Mom's bathroom—and that was because the damned thing was fixed to the wall, but she'd taped cardboard over it. It wasn't safe to have mirrors because her mother might try to hurt herself, might break the surface and use the sharpest edge against her skin.

Yet, there was another reason why it wasn't safe to have mirrors anymore. She just couldn't remember what it was. But why?

Her gaze fell on her sister's silver snake bracelet sitting on top of the dresser. This was almost identical the one Peg wasn't currently wearing. And even though their mother insisted they wear this annoying piece of jewelry all the time, both sisters often forgot because it was an imposing piece to wear. The snake coiled around their wrists three times and the silver length was bulky. Chrysa did her best to wear it no matter what, but refused to leave it on while sleeping or in the shower. And Peg, she hated the silver snagging on her gloves, or how she could swear her snake's onyx eyes sometimes blinked.

Another delusion to add to the mix.

She contemplated Chrysa's collection of lipsticks. Her sister loved wearing lipstick, something Peg didn't because she was more a lip balm kind of girl. Since she'd been gone, Peg had made a habit of applying one of the many shades whenever she dared to venture into this room.

Peg smeared Chrysa's favorite pink shade over her lips and sat on her sister's bed. She pulled out the deck of playing cards from her pocket and shuffled them absently. She had become so accustomed to having a deck with her all the time that she often slept with the cards still tucked into a pocket.

After shuffling more than usual, she laid out the deck on the bedspread and plucked a single card. Her heart sank when she found the three of spades.

Heartbreak.

Separation.

Grief.

Her own personal readings were actually worse than Cal's. At least he alternated between two sad cards, but she always got the same one. She should remove this particular card from every deck.

As close as she felt to Chrysa whenever she visited her room, she was starting to feel the distance more each time.

She waited a few seconds before collecting her cards and getting to her feet. When she reached the doorway, she said, "I miss you so much."

The gloom coalesced behind her, weighing down against her shoulders until her skin itched. She shut the door on the trapped memories, and the darkness she was convinced would consume her one of these days.

Peg scratched her left palm absently.

She made the mistake of glancing at her hand and noticed what she'd dreaded the most. Her entire palm was gray, like the surface of a statue. She ran a finger over her skin and could barely register the sensation.

What the hell happened to me?

As much as this freaked her out, she wondered if the eerie green beam that struck her palm was the reason why she'd heard her sister last night. If this awful transformation would lead to Chrysa, she could bear it. But right now, she needed to have a shower, followed by breakfast and then a much-needed conversation with Mom.

CHAPTER FIVE

"Hey, Mom, I made you something to eat." Peg tried to sound cheerful as she stormed into her mother's bedroom with a saccharine smile.

"Oh honey, you shouldn't have bothered," she said, slurring her words. "I'm not hungry."

"But you missed breakfast, and it's way past lunchtime." Peg placed the tray on the portable laptop table she'd ordered online so her mother could eat in bed, and wheeled it closer. Mom rarely bothered to go to the kitchen anymore, and most days this was the only way of feeding the frail woman. "I made your favorite—a chicken and coleslaw sandwich."

"You really shouldn't have."

Peg stepped around the bed and noticed Mom was wearing the blindfold she started using after Chrysa disappeared.

"Do you have to wear that?"

"What?"

Peg sighed. "The blindfold."

"Oh." Her skinny fingers dragged on the shroud until it hung around her neck.

"You need to see what you're eating."

"I don't—"

"Is that a damn snake?" Peg's eyes widened. She couldn't believe she was suddenly seeing snakes everywhere.

"It's okay, don't worry about it."

"What? Don't worry about the snake on your bed?" Mom had taught her daughters not to be scared of snakes, but having them inside the house was ridiculous. "It could be poisonous."

"It doesn't matter, she'll be on her way now." As if her mother was a snake whisperer, the brown serpent slithered off the bed and vanished. "See?"

"Things are getting out of hand around here." As hard as Peg tried to keep everything clean and running smoothly, both inside and outside, she was only one person. "Anyway, eat your lunch." She positioned the laptop table over the bed, until her mother had no choice but to sit up.

"Honey, I told you I'm—"

"But I went to all the trouble of making your favorite!"

"I know you did, and I appreciate it, but I'm not hungry."

Peg scrutinized her mother's features. Her gaunt skin used to be sun-kissed and smooth, now there were deep shadows under the weary green eyes that used to shine with excitement rather than sadness. Her PJs were huge, a navy-blue pair Chrysa outgrew and passed on to their mother. But the worst thing was her hair. The strands used to be long and wavy, hung all the way down to her waist in a lush curtain Peg coveted so much she'd ended up chopping off her own. Now, the curls were uneven and hung lank around her shoulders, and there were bald patches everywhere.

Peg had offered to even out the ends many times, but Mom chose to hack at the length with blunt scissors whenever she got in a mood.

"Please, Mom, you have to eat."

She was quiet for several moments. "Did you add pickles?"

"Uh, of course I did." As disgusting as the addition was, she always included the pickles especially for her.

"Maybe I can manage a little..."

"Give it a try." Peg waited and watched as Mom glared at the food. "How're you feeling today?"

"I've got a pounding headache."

"Thought you might, so I added paracetamol for you to have after your sandwich."

"Couldn't I get something stronger, like ibuprofen or coke?" Her lips quirked in a half smile. "Even vodka or whiskey would do the trick."

"Don't joke about this, you'll feel better after you eat." A sense of déjà vu mingled with nostalgia flashed inside Peg's mind. Their mother used to say the *'you'll feel better after you eat'* spool all the time when Chrysa and Peg were kids.

When Chrysa disappeared, she took all the best parts of their mother with her.

"I'm sure I won't feel any better, Peg," she said, but her smile remained. "But I'll eat because you're a good girl and I don't want your hard work to go to waste."

"Do you mind if I open the curtains?"

Mom hesitated, took a sip of apple juice before nodding.

Peg slid the coarse fabric all the way across to one side, welcoming the patchy afternoon sun. She opened the window to let in some fresh air, and sucked some of the freshness into her lungs because the air tasted stale. If it wasn't for her, this room would be in disarray. She dusted every other day, picked up her mother's dirty clothes, and made sure the bathroom was clean. She even made Mom shower whenever she started to smell a bit ripe.

Nowadays, Mom didn't do anything without being pushed, and that scared the hell out of Peg. Watching her mother chop off her hair, or throw clothes out of drawers while she searched for some phantom piece and murmured incoherently, was tragic. But catching her own mother grabbing a piece of smashed mirror and pressing the sharp tip against her wrist had been even worse.

She released a breath, trying to shove all the sad thoughts out of her head. She glanced at the fingerless gloves she was wearing. Chrysa knitted this pair for her and they were chunky and too pastel, but did a hell of a job covering her palm. It was hard to stay positive, because like her sister's room, this bedroom was full of memories and only the bad ones surfaced.

Peg's room was the only one where she still felt comfortable and managed to take a real breath. Her sanctuary remained sanitized, because of Belle. Her best friend made her laugh when she was down, and always had a juicy piece of gossip to share.

"This is really good," her mother said between bites. "You always did know how to make a killer sandwich."

"Yeah, thanks."

She let her mind trail off as she stared out the window and watched the barn for a second, recalling the events of last night. Both her room and Mom's faced the back of the house, Chrysa's faced the front.

"Why aren't you at school?"

Peg turned away from the window and sat on the armchair beside the queen-size bed. "I couldn't get back to sleep after what happened in the barn."

Silence filled the room for several beats, thick and suffocating.

"Oh, I'm sorry about that."

She wanted to keep the conversation light, but had to know. "What happened out there, and why are you sorry?"

Mom raised the sandwich to her mouth and took the biggest bite she could manage. She followed this up with a long sip of juice, then sat back against the ornate headboard that always reminded Peg of old mythology books. The bedpost was black metal and consisted of intertwined snakes that formed an intricate design.

Peg watched her mother eat for a few more seconds. "Well?"

"An intruder broke into the barn and I tried to scare him away."

"By screaming like a banshee? Wouldn't it have been easier to call the cops?"

"No, no more cops." Mom shook her stringy head. "I've had enough of cops since what happened..."

Peg let the awful possibilities hang in the air.

... to your sister.

... when your sister vanished into thin air.

... when my daughter disappeared and destroyed me forever.

... when Chrysa left us because she died.

Peg hated doing this, but completing sentences had become a tick. A way for her brain to respond when anyone failed to conclude their thoughts. Before Chrysa disappeared, everyone was able to speak coherently, no one left words hanging like puzzle pieces she felt compelled to finish.

"The police didn't help before, so what would they do now?"

"About that, have they told you anything new?" Even though she was determined to press her mom for answers, Peg was grateful to have a diversion. She knew one of the officers called Mom every other week.

"Of course not."

"Not even one lead or a single witness?"

"You and I are the only witnesses," she said with a scowl.

"I don't remember much about that night." Peg shook her head. No matter how many times she tried, she could only tap into sensations—awful dread and pain. Besides, hadn't she stayed in bed during most of the commotion? "I wasn't a witness to anything."

Her mother considered her for a quiet moment, as if she was trying to read her. "You honestly don't remember?"

"No."

Mom shrugged. "It doesn't matter anyway, because the police aren't going to find her."

"That's not a very good attitude—"

"It's not an attitude, it's the truth."

"I heard Chrysa last night," Peg blurted out.

"What? When?" Mom leaned forward, rocking the tray and causing a line of juice to trickle down the side of the glass. She didn't seem to notice, and her shiny eyes dared to stare into Peg's, something she hadn't done in a while. "*How?*"

"Last night, or this morning, whatever... I heard her call my name."

"It's not possible." Mom lowered her gaze and added, in a barely audible whisper, "They never survive."

"Who never survives?"

"No one survives the stare of death." Her green eyes were suddenly shiny. She lowered her face.

"I don't know what that means."

"You'll never know what it means, unless it happens to you." She took a quick bite and munched before dropping the rest of the sandwich on the plate. Sunlight caught her face and she looked ghastly, a mere shadow of the woman she used to be. "Wait..." She closed her eyes. "Your hand. How's your hand?"

Peg instinctively tucked her left hand under her jeaned thigh. "It's fine."

"Let me have a look."

"No."

"Pegasus Ceto, give me your hand right now or I'll ground you for a month!"

She cringed at the use of her full name and snort-laughed at the threat. Mom had been an absent parent for months and thought she could threaten her with being grounded?

"What's so funny?"

"That you think you can parent now."

"I'm your mother and you will *not* speak to me like that!"

Peg rose to her feet. "I need to go and get the barn cleaned up, before tackling the online orders and clearing the washing off the line."

"No, don't go. Don't get upset with me."

"I'm not upset, I'm just sick of being kept in the dark." She headed for the door. "I thought you might actually talk to me this time. I was stupid enough to think you actually cared and would be honest for once."

"Peggy—"

"Don't call me that!" she snapped. "Only *she* gets to call me that."

"But, you're my sweet Peggy, you always were." The sob made her mother's voice crack.

"Not anymore." Her mother hadn't noticed, but Peg hadn't been sweet for years.

"I'm so sorry."

"Can you stop saying that? You keep apologizing but I don't know what for. Something strange happened in the barn and you're trying to pretend it was just another would-be thief. You're acting as if I find you yelling and sobbing on the floor every night."

"I'm sorry."

"I just told you I'm sick of hearing you say that." She paused in the doorway. "What are you sorry for, anyway? The fact you refuse to answer my questions? That you've decided to stop being a parent because you lost *one* child? That you don't care enough about *me* to bother getting out of bed in the morning?"

Her mother's eyes glistened and tears ran down her cheeks. "That's not true."

Peg blinked away her own tears because sometimes she thought being unkind might wake her up. Mom was an emotional void who didn't bother to live a real life, and Peg hated her for that.

"I didn't mean to hurt you, or her..."

"Do you have to keep talking in riddles?"

"You ungrateful little girl!" Her tears dried up, almost as if the faucet was suddenly switched off. "You come in here and butter me up with your food"—she flipped the table, sent the tray flying over the side of the bed—"and then try to tear me down with your words. How dare you? Do you know who I am? Most would wither at the prospect of a single glance from me, yet you barely cower."

"I don't have time for this." Whenever Mom started talking batshit crazy like this, the conversation was as good as done. "I have things to do."

"What you need to do is respect your mother, appreciate every-thing I've done over and over again to keep you safe from the one who hunts us like animals."

"Oh, yeah, I forgot about the mythical *hunters*." How many times had she heard this pathetic rant during the last three months?

"They're far from mythical—"

"Okay, Mom, I'm sure they aren't. I'll come back later to clean up this mess." Peg walked out and slammed the door on Mom's ranting. "I'll come back when you're sleeping because that's when you're the nicest anyway," she said to the corridor.

Peg's gaze blurred. She let the tears slide down her face as she strolled down the murky corridor, pretending the gloom wasn't coalescing on the ceiling, chasing her. She tried to keep her sobbing quiet. Didn't want to give her mom the satisfaction of knowing how much she'd hurt her.

She sat at the kitchen table and stared out the window before grabbing her phone and dialing a number she rarely called. She had no choice now. She had been dealing with this crap by herself for too long. It was time for adults to start shouldering some of the burden.

The dial tone echoed in her ear. It rang and rang, before voicemail kicked in.

"Hi, you've reached Rya. Leave your number and I'll think about calling you back," the husky voice murmured in her ear.

She didn't bother to leave a message and instead dialed her other aunt.

"Hello there, this is Eno and I can't come to the phone right now because I'm probably getting married, or engaged." Her voice was soft and gentle, even flirty. *"Leave your name and number, especially if you're a handsome, single young man looking for a new bride."*

Peg rolled her eyes, hung up and sent the same text to both. *Mom is acting crazier than usual. She's been screaming in the middle of the night and won't tell me what's going on. I need your help.*

Peg rubbed her palm, dumped the phone on the table and pushed the chair back with a screech she hoped disturbed Mommy Dearest.

As she stepped outside, she caught sight of Belle walking around the corner of the house.

"Hey stranger, how you feeling?" Her friend slid her oversized cat-eye glasses up the bridge of her nose, a habit Peg found adorable.

She faked a cough. "Not well."

"You're such a liar." Belle laughed. "I've got some homework for you and took photos of my math worksheets so you can catch up."

"Thanks, but you didn't have to." Peg shrugged. "I think I've learned as much as I'm going to in that class."

"But all of this will count towards our—"

"I know, and I don't care."

"That's the attitude," she said with a roll of her eyes. "Where are you going?"

"To clean up the barn."

"Mind if I come with?"

"Sure, but only if you're actually going to help this time." Belle's idea of helping was picking up one rusty piece after another and making up romantic stories about who owned them, why they got rid of the junk and where they would go in the future. Entertaining, but not helpful.

She pouted. "I always help."

"Yeah, right." Peg motioned for her to follow because if she looked at that cute pout for much longer, the last thing Peg would be thinking about was cleaning.

The sight of the open barn doors roused a chill down her spine, but she pushed it aside. She was here to tidy up and spend some time with her friend, not remember the freaky lightshow incident. Or what happened to her hand, how she somehow passed into the freaky woods for a brief moment, and heard her sister's voice.

She entered the barn and groaned when she considered all the work ahead of her. "I think some stuff fell off the shelves last night, and I'll have to—"

Peg didn't get the chance to finish before Belle grabbed a hold of her good hand, spun her around like they were dancing, and yanked on her arm until they were standing in front of each other. Before Peg could respond or get her bearings, her best friend closed the distance and kissed her.

Belle always tasted like grape gum, and Peg welcomed the warm connection her mouth provided. Her friend kept kissing her as she walked them backwards, until Peg's spine was pressed against the wall. Belle stepped even closer, and when their bodies were flush together, she slipped her tongue in for good measure.

"What... what was... that for?" Peg asked, coming up for air.

"You looked so sad." Belle ran the back of her fingers over Peg's face, along her jaw, and down the side of her neck. "So, I wanted to do something to make you happy." She lowered her eyes, still wearing her glasses. "You hardly ever smile anymore."

"And kissing will make me smile?" Of course it would.

"Well, you're smiling now." Belle's tongue poked out between her lips. "And it worked every other time, so I was sure it would work today."

"That's true." Peg's smile widened. "So, why did you stop, then?"

Another kiss was enough to melt all the chill from her body.

"Besides..." Belle whispered along her lips as she unbuttoned Peg's jeans and lowered the zipper with one swift move. "I've got other things in mind, too."

"Oh yeah, like what?"

Her best friend ran her other hand between Peg's breasts, down her stomach and slipped her long fingers inside her jeans. Belle's eyes were shiny behind her glasses. "Like this."

IN THE BLUR

"How do you know we'll be safe in here?" Chrysa asked, because she wasn't convinced anyone could be truly hidden from view inside this shabby creation.

"For starters, haven't you noticed that your voice sounds normal? No echo, no struggle to hear yourself, that kind of thing."

This person—who Chrysa was certain was a woman—had led her through the dull trees and scrub, and into a tepee-style formation made from brittle black branches. There were hand-sized spaces between the twigs and the leaves were too small to fully conceal their presence.

"Yeah, but—"

"The most important thing is that you can talk and move at all." She peeked between the sticks of the tent formation.

Chrysa was glad she could form coherent thoughts. She'd been lost in a tangle of surreal ramblings and dreams for so long, she'd started to doubt what was real and what wasn't. Before regaining consciousness, she'd resigned herself to barely existing. She got tired of trying to rise to the surface. Exhausted with the strength it took to stay still even though all she wanted to do was run.

But now she could move, and she was sure it was because of her sister.

Chrysa didn't know how Peggy managed to appear within the veiled, or even why, but she was happy she hadn't stuck around. She didn't want her sister to get stuck in the blur.

She considered her would-be savior. She wasn't sure she could trust someone who could sneak around the forest of statues and knew how to escape the creatures. Someone who was a head taller than her and was covered from head to toe in gray rags, somewhat resembling the veiled.

"Are we dead?" It was the only question she really wanted answered.

"Not exactly."

"What does that mean?"

"It means you're frozen in one place and trapped in another."

"Is this purgatory, then?"

"A sort of purgatory."

"Okay, I have no idea what that means either." An insistent throbbing struck the base of her skull. She closed her eyes and rubbed her neck, wishing the pain away.

"Someone must be thinking about you."

"What?" Her eyes snapped open.

"Around here, if your head hurts, it means someone is thinking about you. And if it gets so bad your skull feels like an eggshell ready to crack, that means they're crying for you."

Peggy.

Her twin sister would still cry for her. Would her mother cry too? For some reason, the thought of her mom roused anger deep inside her, instead of the ache her sister brought out of her.

And Cal.

He would *definitely* cry for her.

A hollow sensation tore through her chest because she missed him too. Had he gone on with his life and found another girl? Would it make things easier for him to find someone new? Did he still visit the farmhouse even though she wasn't there?

She didn't want anyone to hurt because of her.

If moving on brought Cal peace and freed him from the pain, she hoped he had. She wanted him to be happy.

"Can you tone it down a bit?"

"Tone what down?" Chrysa didn't understand.

"You're vibrating with love and it's much too bright."

"O-kay." She didn't bother to pursue whatever *that* meant and focused on something else. Anything else. "Are there other phantom pains I should know about?"

"Let's see... if you feel like someone is punching you in the gut, it probably means they're messing with your body on the other side. And if you feel as if your legs are broken or you can't move, your statue has been destroyed. If that happens, you're stuck here forever."

"Wait a minute, what statue?"

"You were a statue, right?"

She nodded and still wondered why this woman's voice sounded so familiar.

The fact she was staring at a hidden face, because the strips of worn fabric concealed so much, made her feel like she was talking to a mummy. But she recognized the only facial features she could clearly see—those sparkly blue eyes.

"Here, you're an extension of who you've become *there.*"

"This is too much." Chrysa tried to rub away the pain, and in the process desperately attempted to remember how she'd gotten into this god-forsaken forest in the first place. "So why can I move now?"

"Because you have people on the other side trying to figure out where you went, people who care. As long as you're not forgotten, there's still a chance for you." She looked away. "And when the others came through, it gave you the chance to awaken."

"What others?" She'd only seen Peggy appear and disappear. Only got the chance to warn her and no one else.

"One was your devoted sister. You don't need to worry about the other one, though I do."

"Why?"

She shrugged her shrouded shoulders. "It's my lot in life."

"Why do you sound familiar?"

"Probably because we know each other."

"What?"

The person who'd rescued Chrysa slowly unraveled the strands of fabric covering her face. A wave of platinum blonde hair escaped, filling the space with the only color she'd seen since the greenish glow with her sister. Chrysa felt as if she'd been struck by lightning when she recognized the pretty face and cheeky smile.

"Lovey?"

"In the flesh, so to speak."

"What are you doing here?"

"I came looking for you, and it looks like I got here just in time."

CHAPTER SIX

"You know that new guy?" Belle toyed with the cord of Peg's hoodie, avoiding her gaze. She always did this after, would try to deflect attention away from what they'd done. But the pink sheen on her cheeks gave away how much she'd enjoyed herself. How much they mutually enjoyed spending this secret time together.

"Yeah."

"He wasn't at school today either."

"So?" Peg rolled onto her side, winding her legs tighter around Belle's, glad they'd climbed to hide in their special spot in the eaves. Getting intertwined with her was venturing into dangerous territory, but she was still riding the high of their shared bliss.

"Are you sure you two didn't spend the day together?" She made a show of checking out the barn, as if Peg had hidden him somewhere in the eaves.

"Very funny, you know I don't even know his name."

"Well, he knows yours. He's always asking about you." Belle made a face, her way of letting Peg know she thought he was pathetic. It was how she reacted every time Peg chose to date a loser, which was quite often.

"You've never mentioned this before."

"Because I didn't want to creep you out."

"Are you sure it's not because you're jealous?" Peg couldn't help but tease.

They'd been kissing buddies since they were fifteen. Everything else the kissing eventually led to was something they'd shared for about six months. During one of their many sleepovers, after Chrysa fell asleep, Peg snuck a bottle of something into her room and got tipsy enough to end up in bed with Belle. That night, the alcohol and kissing provided a natural gateway into much more. Hooking up whenever they weren't attached to someone else became a delicious habit. On some level, that they both conveniently chose to ignore, this was probably why neither could keep a guy for longer than a few dates.

No one made Peg feel the way Belle did, but she couldn't bring herself to say this out loud.

"Well, are you jealous of something that isn't even there?" Peg asked, rubbing a strand of her friend's bubblegum pink hair between her fingertips. She couldn't take her eyes off how beautiful she was. The slim girl wearing an obscure band tee, a short denim skirt, mismatched socks and a black bandana.

"As if," Belle said with a snort.

"Just checking." Peg sidled closer and nuzzled Belle's shoulder. Her friend was adorable and often hid behind her glasses. But not now, not when they were lying around together with their clothes still in disarray.

"Do *you* get jealous when a guy likes me?"

"No," Peg said, a little too quickly.

"Oh, okay."

"Why would I be jealous when I know you'll eventually end up with me."

"Well, when you put it that way..." A small smile curved Belle's full lips.

Peg kissed Belle and rested a hand on her thin hips. They kissed some more, enjoying the feel of each other's lips and the easy rhythm their mouths always set. Peg had kissed a lot of boys and none even came close to Belle.

"I wish you would take these gloves off." Belle tugged at Peg's left hand.

"Well, I did, before..." Peg's body tightened at the thought of her friend figuring out the secret she was keeping.

Belle blushed. "Yeah, but you put it back on right away."

"Chrysa made these."

"I know she did." Belle sighed. "I didn't mean to upset you."

"I'm not upset," Peg said, avoiding Belle's eyes as she stood.

"Hey, where are you going?"

"We can't lie around all afternoon. I've got work to do." Peg smiled down at her, trying to lighten the mood she'd just ruined because she didn't want to admit that if they stayed like this much longer, she knew exactly what would happen again.

"But I'm enjoying this," Belle said with a toothy grin.

"Me too." Peg pulled up her jeans, then zipped and buttoned them. "But I *really* have to sort out this mess." She offered her right hand. "Come on."

Belle attempted to drag her down. "You always have stuff to do," she said with a pout. "Why can't you be like every other teenager and laze around all day?"

"Because, unfortunately, I'm not like other kids and have the responsibilities my mother chooses to avoid."

"Is that why you were upset before?"

"Yep."

"What did she do this time?" Belle asked.

"You know how she drives me up the wall."

"I know she does, but don't forget she lost Chrysa too."

"How can I?"

"Don't let it get you down." Belle stood and rubbed the back of Peg's hand. "You already deal with a lot, carrying your mom's grief is too much to add."

Peg sighed and pecked her friend's cheek. "You're so right."

"I'm right about a lot of things." They stared at each other for several quiet moments until Belle broke the tension with another kiss. A soft one full of raw emotion, and of promises to come.

Peg's heart sped up because these were the moments that terrified her the most. She could spend hours in the most intimate exchange with this girl, but the tenderness always hit her the deepest. She kissed her back with the same level of care, and their shared connection lasted a lot longer than it should have. But she couldn't pull her hand away from Belle's, didn't want to step back because she liked the way their heartbeats echoed each other.

Belle was the one who eventually pulled away. "Wow. That was something." She sounded breathy as she grabbed her glasses from the nook on the wall and adjusted the frames over her eyes.

"It sure was." Peg felt drunk on Belle, and wasn't sure how to deal with the overwhelming emotions.

"Come on, do you want help clearing things up or what?"

Peg nodded, followed her friend to the rickety stairs and climbed down from their secret spot high in the eaves. When she reached the bottom, she switched on the overhead light and her breath caught. She didn't remember the mess being this bad.

"Did a herd of elephants run through here?" Belle asked as she stood beside her. "This is going to take a while."

"You don't have to stick around, I've got this."

"No way am I letting you deal with this by yourself." She gave Peg's fingers a reassuring squeeze. "You deal with enough on your own as it is. Besides, you're not getting rid of me that easily."

"If you're sure..."

"I am. So, what happened here?"

"Someone broke into the barn last night and Mom stopped them."

"Did they take anything?"

"I don't know, and it's going to be impossible to figure out with all this junk."

"Speaking of that"—Belle dropped Peg's hand and turned to face her—"Teddy's coming home next weekend and wants to stop by to check out some of those rusty signs you guys have stashed away. He wants to dress up his dorm room with junk."

"That's what he said?"

"Well, he called it vintage or rustic or whatever, but I know he means junk."

Peg wrapped an arm around her shoulders. "Belle, promise me you'll never change."

"I'll never change, but I *am* going to regret offering to help."

"Let's get to it before you change your mind, then," Peg said with a laugh. "And you know your brother's welcome to go through all this junk any time."

For the next hour, Peg and Belle sorted through the shelving aisles and placed all the fallen pieces back into their rightful places. Having her friend's help made things easier for Peg. Not to mention fun because they laughed and talked all the way through.

That was the thing about Belle. The girls were friends and had been since starting high school, but back then Chrysa was part of their small group. The three did everything together. It wasn't until Chrysa started going out with Cal that Belle and Peg became best friends. By then, they'd already started this kissing game behind Chrysa's back. But no matter what, they were friends first and foremost. She could tell Belle anything and knew she'd keep her secrets, or try to cheer her up. Belle was a pillar of strength she could always lean on.

That was why Peg was happy with their arrangement. Make out when they wanted, but be friends always.

When Peg was in the furthest corner away from the barn doors, she noticed a coin on the dusty ground. She picked it up and was surprised by how heavy and old it seemed. When had Mom gotten her hands on this, and why was it in the barn? The coin was one-sided and tarnished to black, imprinted with the face of a monster with snakes for hair.

The biggest sign in the barn suddenly slid halfway down the wall, blocking her path.

"Great, just great." She pocketed the coin and attempted to lift the bulky metal nuisance back into place. She was about to call Belle for help, but the name froze on her lips when she spotted a strange wooden door. "What the hell?" Had this always been hiding behind the sign? She'd never noticed.

"Did you say something?" Belle asked from several aisles away.

"Uh, no."

"Okay, because I'm knee-deep at the moment."

Peg considered concealing her discovery and coming back later when she was alone, but the itch of curiosity was hard to ignore. She slipped behind the sign, trying to be as quiet as possible, until she found herself standing in front of a rickety door she'd definitely never seen before.

There were no visible handles and the wood was splintered, seemingly much older than the barn wall. Actually, it wasn't even made out of the same wood, and the edges were covered with moss. As she drew closer, she noted the edges were in fact mossy because of the stony doorframe.

What the hell is this?

She ran a hand over the uneven surface and gasped when a splinter got stuck in her finger. She bit back a curse and a small click was shortly followed by the door opening automatically.

Peg pushed on it, made sure not to catch her fingers again.

A rush of frigid air struck her face when she stepped into darkness. There was only enough light to see a staircase positioned in front of the door, which disappeared into the pitch black beyond.

She reached for her phone before remembering she'd left it in the house. Instead, she let her eyes adjust and couldn't believe there were no cobwebs or vermin, only strange symbols carved into the walls.

Peg sighed and took a quick peek over her shoulder before she decided to descend. How long before Belle came looking for her? For some reason, she didn't want anyone else to know about this. Not yet. There was something intimate about this place. Even more bizarre was the feeling of belonging. As if this chamber had begged to be found and was finally breathing a huge sigh of relief because she was here.

Figuring she had a few minutes before her friend noticed she wasn't in the aisles, Peg dared to continue down the rest of the stairs. She knew she'd reached the bottom when there were no more steps to take.

A strange itch began along her shoulder blades. She shrugged a few times, trying to ignore the strange sensation.

Peg sucked in a breath and when she exhaled, it misted in front of her. Peg took a step forward and was struck in the face by a long cord. She was about to flick it aside, when she realized what it was and pulled down on the length. The bright light took her by surprise and stung her eyes. She'd assumed a shaky bulb would light the way, but one fluorescent after another came to life along the tall ceiling.

She suddenly felt like she was standing in the middle of a massive warehouse. Her eyes were still dazed from the light, so she tried to blink away the disorientation. It wasn't until she noticed what was right in front of her that she cried out and stumbled back.

It was a statue. Statues were everywhere, placed at different intervals in every direction, like endless rows of a stationary army waiting to come alive. This was a museum full of art. There were all types— men, women, children, angels, couples and some she could only describe as monsters.

Peg took a tentative step toward the statues, but stopped when she came face to face with one that looked exactly like her sister. And at her feet was a dog—the golden retriever they called Sword.

She reached out and the chill coming off the stone tickled her fingertips. The compulsion to touch the surface and figure out why there was a statue replica of her sister hidden in this strange place took her breath away.

"Hey, Peg, where did you go?"

Her heart stuttered and she lowered her hand.

I can't let Belle find me here, or see this.

She backed away, haphazardly pulled on the cord and the fluorescents blinked out from the back to the front. She turned away from the army of stone and raced up the stairs, taking them two at a time while ignoring the pull of the strange basement. And how her shoulders itched worse than before.

As she ducked around the opening, she was glad Belle wasn't waiting for her. The door clicked shut on its own and she managed to pull the tall sign in front of the doorway.

Peg turned around in time to catch her best friend approaching.

"There you are! Where'd you go?" Belle asked with wide-eyed curiosity behind her cute glasses. She rubbed her arms. "Is it me, or did it suddenly get really cold in here?"

"It must be you," Peg said quickly.

Belle tilted her head and considered her. "What were you doing?"

"Just straightening some things." Peg absently pointed at the sign, hoping her friend didn't look too closely. "Do you want to stay for dinner?"

"It depends on what you're making."

"Toasted sandwiches—cheese and tomato." As much as Peg wanted to return to the cellar full of statues, she didn't want to rouse any suspicion. The fact her sister's statue was down there had to mean something. "With tomato soup, of course."

"And a sprinkle of pepper on said sandwiches?" Belle asked.

"Always."

"Then I'd love to." Belle swung an arm over Peg's shoulders and together they trudged through the narrow aisles and headed back to the house.

Halfway across the yard, Peg spotted her mother in the bedroom window. But she didn't resemble the waif of a woman she'd become. She looked more like a creature with greenish skin and writhing curls swaying around her face.

She shook her head and when she looked again, there was no one there.

"Hey, are you okay?" Belle asked, squeezing her closer.

"Uh, yeah, everything's fine," she said. "I'm just starving."

"Me too."

She opened the back door and motioned for her friend to enter the house first. She couldn't help but glance over her shoulder one last time, and wondered about the strange things happening inside the barn. Had she imagined the secret room and her sister's statue? She glanced at her finger and spotted the dark splinter still embedded under her skin. She winced.

"Hey, how did that happen?"

She looked up and found Belle staring at her finger. "In there when I was—"

"Let's get this splinter out before we do anything else." Belle took her hand and kissed her fingers lightly. "I'll have this out of you in no time."

"You really are spoiling me today," Peg said.

"And if you're lucky, I might make you smile again." Belle held Peg's stare as she licked her lips, cheekily.

Her heart sped up. "I really need to take more days off from school."

CHAPTER SEVEN

"Uh... hello?"

"Hi sweetie, it's your aunt. Is this a bad time?"

"Aunt Eno?" Peg rubbed her eyes and checked her phone. "It's midnight."

"I didn't wake you, did I? I know you kids love to stay up." She followed the ridiculous comment with a childish giggle, confirming this was Peg's cheekier aunt.

Good old Auntie Widow always picked up the slack because Auntie Weirdo couldn't be bothered. It wasn't nice to use these labels and Mom would get upset if she ever heard Peg calling them such names, but she couldn't help herself. And her mother didn't care about anything anymore anyway.

Chrysa and Peg had labelled the many aunts and cousins they had all over the world with odd names. Most were estranged, or plain strange, so they hardly crossed paths. Mom used to tell them that a quiet life on this farm was something she'd always wanted, and that they were better off without all the family baggage and drama relatives liked to dump on each other.

Too bad Mom never expected our own drama to cause irreparable damage.

"Are you still there, Peg?"

"Yeah, I'm here, but I *was* sleeping. I've got school tomorrow." After the previous night's fiasco, she'd decided to have an early night. Besides, Belle had hung around after dinner to help her catch up on the schoolwork she'd missed, before enjoying some well-deserved and very pleasing alone time. She couldn't stop smiling and could still see how gorgeous her friend had looked on this bed.

Now, she wanted to catch up on sleep and not have to skip another day of school. One day she could get away with, but two might create attention her family didn't need. As unbearable as things could get with the supposed adult in this house, she wasn't ready for outside interference. The help would have to come when Peg was ready. Ugh, who was she kidding? Hadn't she called her aunts already? She definitely needed help, just wanted to be selective about who to involve.

"Listen, we got your texts and want to know what's going on."

She sighed, felt a worm of betrayal weaving under her skin. "Mom's been acting stranger than usual."

"Oh sweetie, you know she's going to be messed up for a while. Losing a child is hard for everyone, but so much worse when you're the reason it happened."

Her heart fluttered. "What's that supposed to mean?"

"I, uh..."

"Seriously, Auntie, if you're going to keep secrets from me as well... I don't think I can deal with more of this crap."

"Peg," Eno said, her voice sweet yet firm. "We intend to be as honest as your mother should've been. Instead of letting that controlling woman convince her otherwise, Ed should've shared the truth with you girls from the start." Several beats of silence followed while someone murmured on the other end of the line. "We'll get to the bottom of this, but some things aren't meant to be spoken over unsecured lines of communication."

"Ask her about the screaming," Aunt Rya said, no longer murmuring secret instructions.

"Hi, Auntie Rya," Peg called.

"She says hi back."

Peg doubted that. Rya was quiet and reserved, a bit rough around the edges and the last thing she enjoyed doing was exchanging pleasantries. Which was probably why she kept whispering commands at Eno.

"In your text you mentioned that Ed was screaming?"

"We had what she likes to call another intruder in the barn and she lost her shit, was standing there screaming at nothing." Peg chose to leave out the green light incident, because she didn't want to bombard the aunts with everything at once. Plus, the beam reminded her of what was happening to her hand, and she definitely didn't want to think about *that*.

"Did you see who it was?"

"No, probably some neighborhood kid on a dare or something. It's not the first time that's happened." Peg sat up. The barn was another mystery she wanted to keep to herself for now.

"Maybe she was trying to scare them away," Aunt Eno said. "She was always a screamer, your mom. You should've heard her when she gave birth to you two."

An awkward silence followed.

"Tell her she's right, Ed was probably annoyed at being woken up in the middle of the night," Rya said, so close Peg heard every word. "We all know how defensive she is about her belongings."

"That's true," Peg said. "But she's been acting stranger than usual. I'm really worried about her and was wondering if you guys could come and stay for a few days." She sighed. "It's hard dealing with her on my own. She refuses to leave her room, barely talks and when she does, it's in riddles about hunters. It's getting hard to concentrate on my schoolwork."

"Of course, we'll come. We'll leave first thing in the morning."

"Oh, are you sure? It doesn't have to be that soon."

"By the sounds of it, it does." Aunt Eno seemed to be contemplating her next words. "What exactly is she saying about hunters?"

"I don't know, she says she's trying to keep us safe from the hunter who wants to find us. And last night she even cried because she's convinced herself that he's found us. I have no idea what she's talking about, but she gets all freaked out and cries uncontrollably—"

"Don't fret, sweetie. We'll be there before you realize it."

"Thanks."

"Make room for your aunties because we're going to stay a while. And by the way, if that sister of ours doesn't stop with all this crazy talk, I'll institutionalize her myself," Eno said. "You're much too young to be as soured as you sound."

"I'm not soured."

"Trust me, I know when someone's had enough bad cards dealt."

Peg reached out and thumbed the deck sitting on her bedside table.

"Why are you looking at me like that?" Rya asked.

Peg couldn't help but smile, could imagine the sisters sharing the phone without bothering to use the loudspeaker.

"If Ed doesn't wake out of this stupor and starts concentrating on what's worth living for, she's going to lose you. And we've already got more than enough separations in our family tree."

No wonder Auntie Eno captured the attention of men so easily. She had a way with words, a way of making you feel special, even if she wasn't making any real sense. And right now, after having such an absent mother, she found comfort in her friendliness.

Peg was glad she'd reached out. "Thanks, Auntie."

"Not a problem. Now, get back to your beauty sleep and I'll go and make sure Rya is all packed up and ready to go." Her other aunt called out an answer, but it was too low to hear. "See you soon, Peg."

"Bye," she said, long after the phone had disconnected.

As she lay back in bed, she felt better. Spending the afternoon with her best friend, and knowing her aunties were going to come and help out, made her happy. Maybe she wasn't as alone as she thought she was.

Peg stared at the ceiling and watched the gloom swirl past the moonlight filtering into her room. She tried to trace each one with her eyes, rather than letting her fear take over. Most of her life had been swamped by these swirls and whirls, but she'd never paid much attention. Always hated how scared this made her, but chose to blame every suffocating incident on her overactive imagination.

It's safer that way.

She closed her eyes when the moonlight was blocked out completely, and counted to ten while grabbing a hold of her cards. She shuffled quickly and pried her eyelids apart.

The room was back to normal. She gripped the cards and couldn't stifle a moan of pain when her rigid palm kept her from closing her hand properly. This was going to become a painful annoyance. Maybe she could trust her aunts with this secret. Eventually.

Thinking about her hand reminded her of the splinter Belle had removed with the tweezers. And this led to what happened much later, which filled her with a cozy warmth in her lower belly and a sense of belonging. Belle made her feel special, even though she didn't like to dwell on the fact.

She closed her eyes, hoped sleep would take over if she relaxed, but it didn't. All she could think about was how good she felt when Belle touched her, the delicious feel of her tongue, and their comfortable intimacy. She pushed those raunchy thoughts away and instead focused on how hard she'd tried to conceal what was going on with her hand. How glad she was to be right-handed.

Thoughts of Belle tried to slip in again, but she forced herself to think about the secret she'd discovered in the barn. All of those statues, the fluorescents and how the stairs sparkled like marble inside that hidden place. And what were those symbols on the walls? She'd have to take a photo and try to find out online.

"Damn." She slapped the mattress on either side of her prone body, spilling cards everywhere. She gathered all of them and tucked the deck into the side pocket of her pony onesie.

Peg couldn't get back to sleep now. After her aunt woke her and all these thoughts had a chance to start running wild, she had to face the fact that tonight was going to be another uneasy one.

Might as well do something productive.

As she climbed out of bed, a sparkling across the room caught her eye. She headed for her desk and considered the silver snake bracelet. The jeweled orbs called to her and she slipped it on, watched as the silver length magically molded around her skin. For good measure, she placed one of her older pairs of fingerless gloves on.

Peg left her room and stepped as carefully as she could on the floorboards, making sure to avoid the ones she knew would creak beneath her feet. The last thing she wanted to do was wake her mother. She'd already snuck into her room after dinner and was surprised to find that the mess Mom made had been cleaned up.

As she approached the stairs, movement on the floor caught her attention but by the time she looked, there was nothing there. Well, except for more of those pesky snakeskins. She really had to clear them away before the aunties got here.

Shadows lengthened along the walls like thin fingers trying to capture the entire house. She ignored the effect and continued down the stairs, walked past the clean kitchen and out the back door.

Peg stepped into her boots and wrapped her arms around her midsection. This time, the doors to the barn were closed, like she'd left them. Or at least, that's what she thought until she was close enough to find one was ajar.

Her pulse quickened. Telling her aunt about local kids sneaking into the barn was a convenient excuse to settle all their worst fears. While it was true that teenagers often tried to snag a rusty treasure they could brag about to their friends, it was usually during the day.

The sound of murmured conversation made her pause.

She sucked in a deep breath and let it out slowly, then stepped into the barn. The lights were off, but her eyes had already adjusted to the dark and the voices were getting closer. Was that her mother? There was only one way to find out. She walked down the middle aisle, followed the shelving until she reached the end.

Peg tried to get her bearings and thought the murmuring was coming from her right, so she crept closer.

"What're you going to do about it?" That was definitely her mom.

"There's nothing that can be done now," a woman responded.

"You have to do *something*. I'm not ready to move on without my daughter."

"I'm afraid she's lost forever."

"No," Mom said, and her tone was whip-sharp. "She can't be."

"This was all *your* doing, and because of what happened she will most likely not follow you into the next incarnation." The female voice was strong, obviously trying to remain calm, while refusing to bend to Mom's will.

"There must be *something* you can do."

"There's nothing, and we both know it."

A soft moan echoed around the barn. "Peggy told me she heard her sister, that means Chrysa isn't dead or gone completely."

"I don't know what to tell you."

"It can't end like this!"

"It's never ended this way, but there's a first for everything."

"You can be such a cruel mistress, Athena."

Mistress? Athena? Was this woman her mother's lover? Mom never seemed romantically interested in anyone, and had shunned many male suitors who'd tried to win her over. She'd never shown an interest in women either. She didn't even speak about their father and had dodged all their childish questions by saying he wasn't a good man, and had abandoned them years ago.

"Not as cruel as you are a mother," the mysterious woman said.

"What's that supposed to mean?"

A chuckle bounced off the walls like an actual physical presence. "I know what you've been doing, wallowing in misery and falling into oblivion while your other offspring is pursued by so much worse."

Whoever she was, this woman certainly knew what was going on around here. Mom might be oblivious in her grief, but this lady was right. Ed Ceto was failing as a mother, in every sense of the word. She wasn't even a caretaker, or the successful business owner she used to be.

Peg was itching to lean forward, to catch sight of this woman.

"What are you trying to say? Who's after Pegasus?"

Gosh, I hate that name.

"I can't tell you."

"You *have* to tell me who's after my daughter!"

"I can't help you. I'm afraid you'll have to figure that out for yourself."

The sudden burst of wails reminded Peg of the night before and she flinched. Her hand was covered by wool, but the stiffness beneath suddenly throbbed. And the words finally slipped past her sleep-dazed mind. Someone was after *her? Who wants to hurt me?*

She wanted to interrupt their conversation and demand they tell her what role she played in this charade. She might not know what was happening, but she was sure something big was going on. Otherwise, her aunts wouldn't have committed to coming when they'd stayed away every other time.

All of this had something to do with her mom's screaming and that greenish light.

"Tell me, please," Mom said. "She's all I have left."

"Then you better start acting like you actually give a fuck about her."

The sound of a slap echoed down the aisle and the other woman laughed.

"You were always stubborn, strong and determined, but blind to what's right in front of you. Have you forgotten your part in this endless cycle?" Silence followed. "Of course, you haven't, you knew it was a matter of time before he caught up with you. It always ends up in the same place, but still takes you by surprise."

"It's because I'm not ready."

"You never are."

"Tell me who it is."

"It's not a big town, you'll figure it out."

"Bitch."

"Takes one to know one."

This time Mom laughed, but it was a cackle. Nothing like the warm laughter Peg loved when she was growing up with a happy mother who played games, taught Chrysa and her things, and doted after her twins.

"Don't contact me again. You'll have to deal with the hunter, and everything else on your own." The voice was getting weaker. "Or you can open your heart and allow the ones who want to help to do so. I refuse to keep their memories locked away any longer."

"But that was your—"

The sound of flapping wings filled the barn and Peg ducked behind the closest shelf as a beautiful white barn owl with a speckle of golden feathers flew over her head. The bird zoomed skyward before fading away.

She tried to calm her breathing, wanted to hold on to all the strange details of the conversation she'd overheard, but sobbing caught her attention. In frustration, she thumped her head against the metal framing a few times. What was she going to do—pretend she hadn't stumbled on any of this, or help her mother? Her brain told her to turn away and forget about the cellar for now, and leave Mom behind to sort through her own shit. But her heart told her the opposite.

Peg stepped around the shelf. Her mother sat huddled against the closest shelf, crying.

"Mom, what are you doing out here?"

"Chrysa?"

Peg stepped into the light so her mother could see her short hair and face. They were identical, but there were plenty of differences. Differences only a mother could spot.

"No, it's me, Peg."

"Oh, Peggy, I thought you were your sister for a second."

She crouched in front of her mother and when the older Ceto made a move to close the distance, Peg took her into her arms and cradled her until she was all cried out.

"Come on, let's get you back to bed."

"I'm so tired."

"I know you are." In what seemed like a repeat from the previous night, Peg half-carried Mom across the barn and yard, guided her inside the house and settled her into bed. She made sure the mountain of blankets was piled on top of her. She even leaned in and kissed her cold cheek. "Good night, Mom."

"Can you stay until I fall asleep? Please."

"Of course." Peg pulled the armchair closer and snuggled into it.

After several minutes of silence her mother said, "I really miss her."

"So do I," Peg whispered.

"Athena has to be wrong," she said. "We're going to find your sister."

"Mom, who's Athena?"

But her mother was already snoring.

Peg left the room and instead of heading back to her own, she stepped into Chrysa's and lay down on top of the covers. With her hands wrapped around a deck of playing cards and a bunch of uneasy thoughts racing through her head, she fell asleep.

IN THE BLUR

"Lovey?" Chrysa repeated, still unable to believe her eyes. "What are *you* doing here?"

The other girl shoved the bundle of shabby fabric into a pocket on the dingy robe she was wearing. A girl who would never be caught wearing anything but colorful designer labels while walking the corridors of Minerva High was in the blur wearing rags. Chrysa couldn't wrap her head around any of this.

Not after being in stasis for so long.

And finally getting her sight back.

Not after seeing her twin sister.

And being able to escape.

Finding out her savior was the snobbiest girl in their grade, but one she often ended up being study partners with, was blowing her mind.

This revelation made her brain stutter, like Cal's old records skipping over the turntable.

Cal, she missed him so much.

She pushed the thought away, determined to concentrate on what was in front of her—or rather, who. She'd already spent enough time reliving all of the wonderful memories she'd shared with Cal while she was frozen in time.

"Hey, you said you would answer my questions."

Lovey sighed and crossed her arms. "I did tell you that, didn't I?"

"Out of all the people I could run into, I get stuck with you."

"You tried very hard to be my friend in school, I thought this would make you happy."

"I haven't been happy for a long time." Her cheeks warmed. It was true that Chrysa cared more about the social hierarchy than her sister. And although all she really needed was Cal, she did like to be on friendly terms with the popular girls. There was nothing wrong with being a little ambitious, even though her boyfriend teased her about it.

"Well, you have that in common with your sister." Lovey's eyes were shiny. "Then again, she's never been as chipper as you, has she? With those silly cards she carries around and the gloves that don't match her clothes. She's an emo reject."

Anger bubbled up inside her. "Don't speak about my sister that way."

"Oh good, an actual human reaction. I think you've been a gargoyle for too long—"

Chrysa shot across the small space and shoved her.

Lovey smiled. "That's it, come alive, sunshine!"

Chrysa barreled into the blonde again, shoulder-charging so hard the branches snapped behind her as they both staggered and landed outside their shelter.

"Crap." Lovey's voice sounded as if it was coming from a tinny tunnel.

Chrysa looked up and felt the stir instantly. The ground rumbled beneath them and everything was suddenly coated in that thick, cloying fog.

"I wanted you to get lively, not to destroy our safehouse."

"What... do... we do now?" The words were a struggle to voice.

"We have to get moving!"

"But—"

"There's no buts. Let's go." Lovey shoved Chrysa off her and jumped to her feet. She pulled the cowl attached to her shabby robe over her head and yanked the gray bandages out of her pocket. She started winding the scraps around Chrysa's head.

"What the hell are you... doing?"

"Relax and let me cover your face before they reach us."

"The... veiled?"

"Huh. Is that what you call them? Clever." She nodded. "But yeah, them. They're trying to steal all the oxygen from the air." When Lovey was finished wrapping her up, she took Chrysa's hand and dragged her more than led her in the opposite direction.

Her legs were sluggish, but Chrysa stopped completely when a crashing sound echoed from the distance. "What... is... that?" It was getting even harder to breathe.

"I don't know, that's not supposed to happen. Come on, don't stop!" Lovey kept running fast enough that the awful crawling sensation of being watched hadn't reached them yet. As they continued forward, Lovey picked up the pace.

The farther they got, the better Chrysa felt. Her breaths were coming stronger and fuller, she actually felt like her lungs weren't drowning.

"Watch out!" she called a second before Lovey collided with a shape heading right for them.

"Oh, hell no," the blonde said before she, and whoever she'd collided with, tumbled down an open hole that appeared in the middle of nowhere when the fog cleared.

Before Chrysa could react, she was dragged down too.

Down the rabbit hole we go.

CHAPTER EIGHT

"GREEK MYTHOLOGY IS FULL OF TRAGIC TALES," MR. DANAE SAID. HE sat back in his chair as he considered the class behind his wire-rimmed glasses. "After all, Shakespeare himself drew heavily from the most tragic of mythological stories of love, lust, passion and betrayal."

Someone scoffed from the back of the room and another kid whistled.

Peg rolled her eyes. The boys in her class were so immature and still reacted to words like *lust* and *passion*. She shared a quick grin with Belle, who was sitting in the seat beside her. Maybe girls *did* mature faster. She'd always considered the statement to be an excuse for people who expected more from the females of the species or wanted excuses for sexualizing young women, but high school males were such clichés.

"At the heart of all the drama, the ancient Greeks also had a lot of heroes." The teacher did a quick sweep of the classroom, his intense scrutiny burning into each student he made eye contact with.

Mr. Danae was a history teacher but he seemed to offer more mythology than facts in his lessons, which was fine with Peg. Mythology had more interesting stories than history, anyway. She considered the middle-aged man who'd only started teaching at their school at the beginning of the school year. He was tall and had wide shoulders, always dressed in blue jeans and a white dress shirt. He kept his hair longish and a bit of gray adorned his temples. He didn't bother shaving and wore glasses that suited his casual College Professor style. She'd heard he was the new kid's father, but didn't know for sure. They shared the same surname and not much else.

His son didn't take this class, but Peg noticed the new guy wasn't in any of the other classes either. She didn't care one way or the other, but since her friend mentioned him yesterday, she couldn't help but wonder what his deal was.

Peg glanced at Belle and admired her pink bubblegum hair. She liked the way it looked spread out over her pillow. Her cheeks warmed at the thought and when her friend caught her staring, she smiled.

"Who can name one of these heroes?" Mr. Danae asked the classroom. "There are plenty to choose from, so give me one name."

When no one volunteered, he pointed at someone randomly.

"Mr. Ackley, can you name a Greek hero?"

"George Michael," Cal said.

A few people snickered, most because they probably didn't know who George Michael actually was, and the others because Cal could be a real smartass. Peg laughed because Cal was an 80s music tragic, thanks to his father's extensive vinyl and cassette collections.

"That's very funny, Mr. Ackley. While he might be a hero to some, I'll have you know that George Michael was born in the UK." The teacher shook his head, trying hard to hide a smile. "Anyone else?"

"Bellerophon," Belle called out of the blue.

"Very good," Mr. Danae said with an approving nod. "And why is he a hero?"

Peg met Belle's eyes and stuck her tongue out at her. Of course Belle would remember the many times they'd flicked through Peg's mother's mythology collection. In one of those books, they'd once found reference to one particular myth about some guy called Bellerophon, and what struck both of them as hilarious was that the name of the hero and his steed matched theirs—*Bellerophon and Pegasus.*

It was why Peg despised her full name. Who called their kid Pegasus? Well, aside from a mythology nut. Her mother apparently had a bunch of history and mythology degrees she could have used to become a professor or whatever, and instead chose to sell junk.

So many things about Mom don't add up.

And now she had other crazy shit to add to the mix: random night visitors, intruders, a woman called Athena, the foggy woods, an owl in the barn. Not to mention the statue room. Was that something her mother even knew about? Maybe they'd bought the place from someone who'd collected statues like others collected toys. But the fact that one of them—kept front and center—resembled her sister made her doubt this theory.

"He's the dude who captured and tamed the winged horse," Belle finally answered. "He also defeated a bunch of other horrifying monsters."

"That's the simple explanation, I suppose." Mr. Danae scratched his stubbled chin, while absently staring into space before he made his way to the whiteboard, where he jotted down the name and Belle's quick explanation. He took a step back and stared at the wall for a second. "I actually like where this is going. Who can add to the list?"

"Hercules! Hera hated this dude, so she made him complete a bunch of crazy tests."

"Well done, Mr. Rhodes." The teacher added the details to the list. "But next time, don't call out. Follow the proper protocol like everyone else." Several kids already had their hands in the air and he gave each a turn.

"Achilles was a hero from the Trojan War who hurt his heel."

"Jason and the Argonauts went looking for the Golden Fleece."

"Prometheus stole fire from the gods and gave it to the cavemen."

"Theseus killed the Minotaur using the thread from a giant spider."

"These are all great and deserving heroes." Mr. Danae turned to face the classroom and stood in front of the impressive list. "But I think you've all forgotten one very important hero."

The answer was right on the tip of Peg's tongue, but for some reason she didn't want to put her hand up. Didn't even want to speak the name out loud. That's when she met her teacher's eyes from across the room and a slight smirk quirked his lips.

"Miss Ceto, do you know who that is?"

"Perseus," she whispered, and the answer scratched her throat. The name felt dirty against her tongue, made her taste grit inside her mouth and she couldn't explain why. A ringing started in her ears and the gloom collected in the corners above the whiteboard, creeping down the walls like tendrils of smoke searching for her.

"And what did *he* do?" The teacher's voice sounded far away, even though he stood only a few feet away.

She blinked a few times, but the room was still clouding over.

"Miss Ceto, what did Perseus achieve?"

She tried to shake her head but suddenly felt disconnected from her body, her mind and mouth refused to cooperate. She didn't want to say the answer, *couldn't*. Peg avoided looking at him and instead scratched at the ache on her left palm and wrist. The itch was unbearable and caused her breath to hitch. She snuck her other hand into the hoodie pouch and patted her playing cards, but even this action didn't help.

Her heart was beating too fast.

Counting backwards didn't calm her.

Peg's vision blurred.

And that's when she remembered the coin in the pocket of her jeans. She thumbed it quickly, feeling the grooves of the monstrous head. For a moment, she imagined the snakes were popping out of the surface to caress her skin.

She found comfort in the delusion, not fear.

"Peg Ceto!" Mr. Danae's sharp voice cut across the room, and every piece of the gloom exploded.

When she looked up, she was surprised to find him standing in front of her desk.

"What did Perseus do?"

Why was he pushing her? This was supposed to be a harmless discussion, yet she felt as if they were the only people in the classroom. What was he trying to prove?

"He, uh..." Letting the sentence drop was intentional, maybe essential.

... needed too much help to complete a task.

... was a coward for sneaking up on someone who was sleeping.

... killed an innocent woman.

... wasn't a hero at all.

The thoughts were so unexpected, they pulled her out of her stupor.

She opened her mouth to answer, but someone beat her to it.

"Perseus killed Medusa," Belle said. "Athena, Hades and Hermes helped him find and kill the Gorgon and he escaped on winged shoes."

Peg's body sagged, she'd become a deflated balloon and had no idea why. Her stomach sloshed, making the acid rise uncomfortably up her esophagus to coat her throat. She was queasy and wanted to throw up. This lesson had taken a turn for the bizarre.

Mr. Danae kept his gaze pinned on hers when he said, "Thank you, Miss Ruffin. But next time I would appreciate it if you would let your friend answer her own questions."

"Yes, sir."

The end of day bell rang.

Peg exhaled several rapid breaths, and tried to focus on letting the sickness pass.

When she thought the worst of the nausea had subsided, she collected her things and realized she hadn't stopped by her locker to grab her backpack yet. She'd been out of sorts all day, fatigued because her nights were now continually interrupted.

The teacher remained in front of her desk but spoke to the class. "I want a two-page essay about one of the heroes we spoke about today."

Several kids groaned, but she couldn't muster the energy to respond.

Why had she reacted badly to the thought of Perseus? He'd never been her favorite hero because his whole claim to fame seemed to piggyback on the wings of cowardice, but her reaction seemed... excessive. At least the gloom was gone. Then she remembered how it exploded when her teacher screamed at her and shivered.

"I need to have a word with you, Miss Ceto."

"Good luck," Belle whispered as she ducked out.

He hadn't been at this school for long, but Mr. Danae's intensity was something his students often talked about. She had to agree because his unprovoked scrutiny was unnerving.

Suddenly they were alone in the classroom and she wanted to be somewhere else.

"Miss Ceto, have you seen my son?"

"What?"

"Do you know where my son is?"

"Why would I know where he is?" *I don't even know his name.*

He studied her. "You're either a very good liar, or genuinely have no idea what you're a part of."

"Excuse me?" What was he talking about? Peg wasn't the smartest girl in any of her classes, but she got good enough grades to be considered an average student. And this teacher—whom she'd only met recently—was judging and accusing her of what, exactly?

Mr. Danae's look of distaste made her feel like she was a squirming insect caught between tweezers.

"One way or another, I'll find out the truth," he said.

"I have to go." Peg grabbed her things, headed for the door and didn't look back. By the time she left the classroom, the corridor was mostly empty with only a few kids loitering around. She headed for her locker and could feel someone watching her. Was it her teacher?

How long had she spent in the classroom with the weird Mr. Danae? And why ask *her* about his son? How would she know where he was?

She unlocked her locker and yanked her backpack out before

shoving her notebook, pens and a few other bits and pieces inside. And that was when she remembered her aunts, who still hadn't arrived. *Typical.*

Peg was about to slam the door when someone said behind her, "Hey, are you all right?"

She jumped and turned to find Eve. "Yeah, you just surprised me." She certainly was jittery today. Not getting enough sleep was messing with her head, and dealing with her mother's weirdness was starting to take a toll on her. At least she had the weekend to catch up on sleep.

"Oh, sorry. I thought you heard me call out to you."

"No, I didn't." She glanced up and down the corridor and checked the clock affixed to the wall. Great, she'd somehow lost twenty minutes and missed the bus for the second time this week. "Did you want something?"

Her phone beeped inside her bag, but she didn't bother checking.

Eve toyed with the strap over her shoulder and her golden apple necklace shimmered under the ugly fluorescents. "I've been thinking about your card reading."

"You shouldn't," Peg said. "It's a bit of fun, that's all."

"But you were so accurate, and I can't get what you said out of my head."

She shut her locker. "Look, it's no big deal."

"It's a big deal to me, especially since I'm hoping you were wrong." Eve's hazel eyes were wide. Her cute curls were like a beautiful crown and her well-fitting bright lime green sweater reminded Peg of a Granny Smith.

"I usually am."

Eve shook her head. "That's not what the other kids say. Everyone I've spoken to told me how accurate you always are."

"Don't listen to gossip." Peg started walking toward the doors. The last thing she wanted was to run into her history teacher again, or be locked in the school with this girl who wouldn't leave her alone.

"I don't think it's gossip." Eve kept pace with her. "Can you read for me again? I've got another question I want to ask you."

"I can't right now. I've already missed my bus and really need to get home."

"I can give you a ride. My car is parked in the lot."

She shook her head. "That's okay, I like to walk. It helps clear my head."

"Oh, okay." Eve sighed, seemingly disappointed. "Could you do the reading another time, then?"

"Maybe."

"On Monday?"

"Maybe," she repeated. What was up with this chick? Why was she so pushy? And why did Peg feel like she was a magnet for all the newbies? It used to be that people left her alone. But that was before her twin went missing, and suddenly she couldn't hide behind the better person.

"Thanks, that's great." Eve perked up instantly, as if she'd offered her a lifeline.

Peg pushed the door open and stepped out into the overcast afternoon she was becoming accustomed to. She considered the threatening clouds and winced.

"Are you sure I can't drive you home? It looks like it's going to rain again."

"I've got an umbrella," she lied.

"It's really not a problem..."

... I can't tear down your defenses.

... let me pester you until you say yes.

... I'll show you what a great girl I am.

She had to stop doing this. Finishing other people's thoughts was starting to make her feel neurotic and obsessive, in the worst possible way.

"I appreciate the offer, but I'm sure," she said. "Thanks anyway."

"Okay, have a great weekend!" Eve called.

"You too." Peg raced down the concrete stairs and didn't stop because she wanted to get away from everyone.

She really couldn't wait to leave this school behind forever.

CHAPTER NINE

"Seriously, if you keep turning up whenever I'm walking down that deserted road, I'm going to start thinking you might be stalking me." Peg teased, trying to lighten the mood. She wanted to be upset with Cal but he'd literally saved her from a drenching. And from all the freaky things she experienced again—the eerie cry for help, those freaky amber eyes and the swaying branches.

"I'm not stalking you."

"Just kidding, but I appreciate it. I really do." Thanks to him, she was safe and sound inside the farmhouse. Every time he dropped her off, she felt obliged to invite him in, and today she'd sweetened the deal with the offer of fresh baked cookies.

"You can thank Belle," he said with a smile.

"For making me think you're a stalker?"

"No." He chuckled. "She texted me to say you'd probably miss the bus because Danae held you back after class."

"How did you not know? You were right there."

He shrugged. "I ran out as soon as the bell went."

"So, you didn't hear the homework assignment?"

"Belle told me about that, too." He glanced her way. "What did he want?"

"He was asking me about his son." The reminder made her uneasy.

"What about him?"

"He asked if I knew where he was."

"Why would you know that?"

"I have no idea." She glanced at the darkened corridor and strained to hear any sounds coming from her mother's room. She secretly hoped Mom would one day decide to start acting like herself again, and after overhearing the strange conversation with the mysterious Athena, she'd foolishly thought things might change.

"How's your mom doing?" Cal asked. He was someone who remembered how Mom used to be but rarely saw her anymore. He wasn't aware of what she'd become because she never left her room, but he'd witnessed some of her deterioration after Chrysa's disappearance.

"As well as expected." Yet, no one else witnessed her mother's downfall as closely as she had. When Mom spent all day and night crying, driving to the local police station every chance she got until one day she decided it was best not to leave the property, and replaced her police visits with annoying calls. That was when she'd convinced herself that if she wasn't here, Chrysa wouldn't be able to find her way back home. As ludicrous as it sounded, the same thought had occurred to Peg more than once.

She'd taken several weeks off school too, not wanting to miss Chrysa's return.

This house and the surrounding hectares were the family's anchor. Where happiness bloomed and fun thrived until the day it suddenly didn't.

"So she's still bad, huh?"

"Yeah," Peg finally said with a sigh. "She never leaves her room and I have to force her to eat."

"That sucks."

She turned away, trying to hide her eyes so he wouldn't see the shimmer of tears. Most of her tears had dried up months ago, but still surfaced when she least expected. She concentrated on the oven until her vision cleared.

"The cookies are almost done." Peg turned the dial and switched the oven off, even though the timer claimed there were two minutes left. She'd baked these enough times to know when the cookies reached the perfect crunchy sides and soft in the middle state.

"I can't wait." Cal was already filling the kettle and setting up their mugs on the counter. He knew which one was Peg's and had one of his own. He had been in and out of their house for over a decade. He was practically part of the family and everyone had assumed Chrysa and him would get married one day.

Peg swallowed the lump in her throat when she caught him reaching for Chrysa's mug on impulse, before pulling back.

Months might have passed since she vanished, but the effects of her loss dwelled no matter how much distance time placed between the incident and the present. She wondered if anyone would ever get used to Chrysa's absence. She doubted they would—or could—because not knowing what really happened to her would haunt them forever.

Would finding her remains help everyone move on?

A chill ran down her spine and she felt the weight of the gloom press against her shoulders. She shrugged, trying to shake the stickiness before the chilling sensation could penetrate past her hoodie and beneath her skin. She pushed all the dark thoughts out of her mind and the weight dissipated.

"Hey, are you okay?" Cal asked while returning the kettle to its cradle.

"Yeah, fine." She rolled her shoulders. "By the way, you *really* need to stop asking me if I'm okay. It's irritating and makes me feel worse."

"Like I've already told you, maybe I will when you start *looking* okay again."

She bit back a bitter response. This awkward conversation would go around in circles if she responded, and she didn't have the energy.

Peg stuck her left hand into an oven mitt and went about taking out the two trays full of choc-chip cookies. She placed both near the sink to let the cookies cool down and loved the way the sweet aroma filled the kitchen.

"They smell delicious," Cal said.

"They do, don't they?" She took the oven mitt off and dumped it on the kitchen counter. As she turned to head back to the table, her hip bumped one of the trays. Without thinking, she reached out to keep it from falling and waited for the sting that never came.

"Damn, are—"

"Don't even say it," she warned.

"Did you get burned?"

"No, I'm cool." Truth was, she hadn't felt the sting. She did hear the disturbing sound of stone against metal, though. She glanced at her fingertips and they weren't even pink, because her palm had taken the brunt.

"Are you sure you shouldn't put your hand under the tap or something?"

"Nah." She sat across from Cal, thanking him for the cup of tea.

Silence filled the kitchen for a while, and neither seemed to mind.

The soft pounding of the constant rain continued outside, hitting the windows and causing rivulets to slide down the glass. Peg mentally traced the drops for a few minutes, absently sipping her tea although she should wait until the cookies had cooled.

"Have you ever thought of growing your hair out?" Cal asked, out of the blue.

"No, I like it short. It's less fuss." She yanked on the short ends of her shaggy cut, and couldn't help but smile. "Chrysa spent hours straightening and styling her hair. I like to have time to do what I *want* to do, not what my hair dictates."

"Yeah, but she always looked so beautiful." His laugh stopped abruptly. "I think you would look nice with long hair, too. Not that you don't look nice now—"

"Don't even bother, you're never going to sell me on the long hair thing." At least Mom had never been the sort of parent who insisted her twins look identical in every way. She'd never dressed them the same and even when they were too young to take control of their own hair, she'd always kept their styles varied. Chrysa and Peg both had long and short hair at different stages of their childhood, but never at the same time. It helped the twins grow to see each other as individuals.

"You're a stubborn girl, you know that?"

"Maybe," she said, pushing her chair back. "I think they should be okay to eat now."

Peg took her time divvying out a nice pile of cookies to share, as well as several for her mother, before returning to the table.

"These look absolutely delicious, and smell even better."

"Dig in, then." She wanted to joke about how someone had to pick up the slack for the girl who always ate too many, but she didn't. Conversations about Chrysa were always more comfortable when sharing happy memories, rather than bleak thoughts.

It was all the encouraging he needed. Cal hit the turbo button and devoured half of the pile while Peg was still enjoying her second cookie. She was a dipper and liked to use her tea to soften the cookies and spread some chocolate cheer inside her drink. He took two bites and was done. Chrysa and him used to compete to see who could eat more, faster. It used to make Peg queasy, but she'd always enjoyed the couple's easy and loving banter.

They were the sort of couple that made competition healthy, not toxic.

Cal and Peg were friends too, but the dark cloud hanging over their heads sometimes made her feel like they were getting farther away instead of closer. Other times, this was the only thing that kept their friendship alive.

"How about Danae, huh?" Cal said after polishing off the bowl and sitting back in his chair. *Now* he picked up his mug and started drinking. He liked to slurp his tea after major cookie consumption.

"Yeah, I don't like the idea of having weekend homework."

"Guess you annoyed him enough to punish all of us." He sighed. "Wish Belle hadn't told me about the essay and I could pretend I didn't know."

"She saved you detention, you should be grateful." Their history teacher handed out detention too freely. "Besides, maybe it was your George Michael joke that pissed him off."

"Yeah, I suppose." He snickered and considered his mug. "By the way, is it just me or was he a bit too aggressive about the Greek hero thing? I mean, the way he pushed you to spill about Perseus was strange. He was totally out of line."

Peg shrugged because she didn't want to get into this. "He's doing his job."

He slurped his tea, loudly. "Can you imagine having that guy as your father? If Ira wasn't as much of a jerk as Danae, I might feel sorry for him."

Her ears perked up. She hadn't considered asking Cal about the new guy because experience had taught her not to fall into that trap. If she mentioned any guy, a week later she'd find herself on a double date. Sure, she usually ended up making out with the boy and spending at least a few weeks as a so-called couple, but she didn't want anything to do with this Ira.

All Peg wanted to know was why her teacher assumed she would know where he was.

"I didn't know you were friends," she said, casually choosing her words.

Cal cupped his mug. "We're not friends, exactly. We have gym together and sometimes end up on the same team, so we're friendly. He mostly keeps to himself and even when we try to include him, he doesn't seem interested."

"That's strange, for a new guy." Since Eve arrived at their school a few months before Junior year ended, all she'd done was try to pester her way into friendship.

"He does seem a little strange." Cal considered the inside of his mug. "Maybe he can't be bothered because of his annoying father."

"I guess so." She dunked the rest of her cookie. "He could just be an antisocial jerk."

"Who knows? But he does sound like a bit of a snob. Could be because he apparently has a bunch of scholarship offers lined up."

"So why hasn't he been at school, then?"

"I think he has the flu, or something." His eyes narrowed. "Why do you want to know? Are you interested in him?"

"No."

Maybe she'd answered too quickly, or a bit harshly because a glimmer sparkled in his eyes. "I can introduce you if you want."

"You just told me you're not even friends!"

"I can still—"

"Never mind, I'm not interested anyway."

"If Chrysa was here, she'd already be trying to get his number to hook you up."

"Yeah, but she's not."

He focused his attention on his mug, his hands and the wall, anywhere to avoid her gaze.

Peg hadn't meant to sound rude or accusatory, but Cal somehow managed to press her buttons. She tried to ignore him and thought about the chamber with the statues, and how she was dying to get back in there but couldn't seem to find the right time. She needed to return soon, there would never be a *right time*.

Tonight. She would go tonight.

It was Friday and she didn't have to worry about school tomorrow, so she could sleep in. She pushed her chair back. "I'll be back in a sec," she said. "I want to take some cookies to Mom before they get cold."

"Sure."

As she left the kitchen with a peppermint tea and the small plate of cookies in hand, she caught Cal staring at a picture of Chrysa on his phone. He had a lot of them, both of the selfie kind and the ones he'd snapped. His wallpaper and lock screen were all about the girl he loved.

Mom's door was open, so Peg walked in. "I thought you might like some cookies and a cup of tea."

When she found the bed was empty, her heart fell. She was about to dump the cup and plate at the end of the bed, when she heard the flush of the toilet echo from the adjoining bathroom. Her mother ambled out of the small room and jumped when she saw her.

"Oh, where did you come from?" A hand flew to her chest and she snuck a quick look behind her. "You scared me!"

"Cal and I made cookies, and I thought you might like some."

"What? Cal's here?" She smoothed her unruly, knotty hair and glanced at the doorway, as if he was waiting outside. "If you're going to have visitors, you should tell me. It's rude of me not to duck out and say hi."

"It's okay, he knows you're not feeling well."

"Rubbish, I'm feeling better than I have in days." She grabbed her terrycloth robe—another hand-me-down from Chrysa—put it on and tied the cord around her narrow waist. She was wasting away quickly. "Come on, let's take this cup back to the kitchen and enjoy it together, as a family."

"Are you sure?" Peg couldn't believe her ears. She'd had Cal over the other afternoon, and even Belle, yet her mother hadn't shown an ounce of interest. And now she was beaming and seemed happy to entertain a guest.

"Of course I'm sure." She frowned and shadows played over her face. "You worry too much, Peg."

"Lead the way, then."

Mom headed for the door and as she did, Peg turned to glance into the darkened bathroom. She caught sight of something sliding along the tiles, but all she could focus on was the reflective surface of a small mirror sitting next to the sink.

The smile fell from her face and she felt numb. What was her mother up to?

"Peggy, are you coming or not?"

"Uh, yeah, coming."

Peg carried the tea and cookies down the corridor, trying to pretend there weren't more snakeskins than usual on the floor. When she reached the kitchen, her mind was racing. What if this sudden good mood was a way to throw her off the fact Mom was toying around with mirrors again? And what was skimming the edge of her memory? Something that overpowered the fear about her mother using a mirror shard to slit her wrists.

No, there was another reason why she might want a mirror, but she couldn't remember why.

With all the stuff filling her head, Peg could barely grasp one coherent thought, so she let everything go. It was best to concentrate on her mother's sudden interest in socializing and actually leaving her room.

As soon as Cal saw her, he leaped off the chair and hugged Peg's mother.

"It's so good to see you, sweetheart." She held him at arm's length to scrutinize him. "Are my eyes playing tricks on me, or are you getting taller and more handsome every time I see you?"

Pink splotched over his cheeks and his shaggy hair fell into his eyes. "I've wanted to pop in and say hello, but Peg—"

"Yes, she's very protective of her dear old Mother, but forget about all that. Tell me what you've been doing at school. You too, Peggy. I want to know *everything*."

The shock of her mother's sudden cheer and interest shook Peg, so she hurried across the kitchen to place the cup and plate on the table before she dropped them. Could this be the beginning of her mother's recovery, or a distraction? Personally, Peg believed it was the latter.

Maybe her aunts could help her figure it out, if they ever got here.

CHAPTER TEN

"THANKS FOR LETTING ME COME UP HERE BEFORE I GO. I REALLY wanted to leave this for her." Cal held an orange leaf in his hand with a heart carved in the middle. "You know, for when she comes back."

Peg nodded, didn't even have to ask whether he'd made it himself or not.

"No problem." It wasn't that she never let him come into Chrysa's room, she did. Most other times she left him alone to his memories and thoughts. She would never deny him this attempt to hold tight to their connection.

Seeing Cal this afternoon had sparked something in her mother, and even with all the other worries and questions, it made for a nice couple of hours chatting over tea and cookies. Everyone was careful to skirt over the important issues, but it was enough that her mother bothered to come out of the bedroom at all.

Maybe she's getting better.

Or maybe she was taking the advice that Athena lady gave her about reconnecting with her daughter before it was too late. Peg still couldn't believe or understand why anyone would be after *her*. Yet, no one had expected Chrysa to go missing, either. Had Mom done something in her past that was now affecting her daughters?

Cal placed the leaf on top of Chrysa's open planner.

"I miss her every single day." His shoulders quivered, and she wasn't sure if it was because he was crying or sighing.

"I do too." Peg didn't want to make him uncomfortable by staring at his back, and decided to give him a moment. She made her way to the dresser and eyed the lipsticks. The itch to grab the pink shade she'd been using took over, and she applied the color to her lips. She found comfort in sharing her sister's lipstick.

"I always wonder why she wasn't wearing this when she disappeared." Cal turned to face her and was holding the familiar snake bracelet in his hand. "She never took this off before, and then...."

"She didn't sleep or shower with it," Peg said with a shrug. Since she'd placed hers back on her wrist, she hadn't taken it off. And every time she thought about the silver snake, the length tightened against her skin.

Cal's eyes widened when he noticed the lipstick tube in her hand, and his mouth opened but nothing came out.

"What?"

He raised a hand and pointed at her face.

"Oh, yeah, the lipstick. It's a weird thing I've been doing." She suddenly felt like she'd been caught acting stupid or childish.

"It's her favorite color." His voice sounded strained, he seemed to be struggling to get the words out.

She liked the way he spoke about Chrysa as if she was still here with them.

"Yeah, I don't usually wear lipstick but this shade makes me feel closer to her."

"It suits you." His eyes grew darker.

Peg broke the stare and put the tube back. When she looked up, Cal was still standing in front of the desk holding the bracelet and staring at her a little too closely.

"What?"

"*You*... you look so much like her today."

She chuckled. "We're twins, we always look alike."

"Yeah, I know," he said with insistence. "But today, there's just something."

"It's probably because of the cookies and being in her room, and the stupid lipstick." She felt like such a fool and wanted to wipe it off.

"It could be all of those things, or maybe none of them."

"Wow, you're quite the poet this evening. First, you entice Mom out of her hidey hole and now you're coming up with romantic notions," she joked.

But Cal didn't smile or laugh. Instead, he walked toward her and didn't stop until he stood a bit too close. "Thank you for being here for me."

"Yeah, well, I'm not always—"

"But you are, and you don't even realize how much it means to me." His eyes were glossy with unshed tears. "If it wasn't for you, I wouldn't have been able to get through any of this. Seeing you every day reminds me of her, helps keep her in my mind so I don't ever forget. You're such a sweet and helpful person, and you don't even know..."

"I'm neither sweet nor helpful."

"Yes, you are." He reached out and rubbed the ends of her hair with his fingertips.

Peg swallowed. He was definitely too close. She needed to take a step back, but instead tilted her head back to stare into his stormy gray eyes.

When Cal leaned over and lightly covered her lips with his, she froze. She suddenly understood his comments about her hair, and why he was everywhere she turned. But this was wrong. Nothing about this kiss was right because she knew why it was happening— his grief. Cal was trying to cling to Chrysa's memory by finding comfort in Peg.

Peg's own muddled brain was shocked awake when he tried to sneak his tongue into her mouth. "No," she said, pushing him away. "This is wrong."

His eyes were dazed. "It didn't feel wrong."

"Cal, you're my *sister's boyfriend*, of course it's wrong!"

"This was bound to happen. You remind me so much of her and

we've found comfort in each other... How could I not want you?" He tried to cup her face but she stepped away. "And that lipstick."

"Are you listening to yourself? You don't want me, I'm Peg. The third wheel to your couple. The pesky sister who's always around and gets in the way." Her breathing was coming too fast. The guilt of what she'd done wormed its way into the pit of her stomach and made her feel ill. This was wrong on so many levels, and she couldn't help but think of Belle. "I'm the weird chick who carries a deck of playing cards with her everywhere—"

"Peg, there's a connection between us, you can't deny that."

"The only connection we have is Chrysa."

He shook his head. "That's not true."

"Cal, I don't know what's gotten into you today, but you need to snap out of it. You don't want me, you're still in love with Chrysa and you're projecting those feelings onto me. Don't you see that?"

"But you kissed me back."

"I did, and I'm sorry."

"If it's wrong, why did you kiss me back?"

Peg shrugged, decided it was best to be cruel. "Why do I kiss anyone, or rather, everyone?" It was true, her sister often asked why she seemed to have no scruples and kissed any boy who made a move on her. That wasn't entirely true, of course. She had turned down quite a few, but not as many as she'd kissed. Was it wrong that she liked kissing? Kissing made her feel good and special, wanted. It was part of the reason Belle and her started up. Peg was the one who'd initiated everything and was excited to find her best friend was into it too.

Now, she'd let herself fall into the same old trap, but it involved someone who was emotionally frail at the moment. How did she miss this? She should've seen this coming because Cal had suddenly appeared everywhere she went, and was always there to *rescue* her. She thought of their conversation earlier and how he'd asked if she'd ever considered growing her hair out. He was trying to substitute her into her sister's role.

"You kissed me back because I kissed *you?*"

"That's right."

"That's..."

"Messed up? Yeah, I know." She wrapped her arms around herself. "You're not the only one who feels the connection between us. Since Chrysa's disappearance, we've leaned on each other. It's how we communicate—through our shared sadness and anger. It was only a matter of time before everything got muddled into some sense of longing."

Peg took several steps back and sat on the bed.

It took him a few seconds, but Cal made his way over and sat beside her.

They sat in silence for a minute, an hour, the whole night. She wasn't sure how long, but it wasn't comfortable or uncomfortable. It just was.

"I'm sorry."

"You really have to start cutting the *are you okays* and *I'm sorrys* out of your vocabulary. You don't have anything to be sorry about, and can you stop worrying so much? I'm as okay as you are," she said. "Until we find Chrysa or she walks back into the house as if nothing happened, neither of us is going to be okay. But we're coping."

"I know you're right, about everything. But I feel lonely without her. I miss her, and when I see you... it's almost like you're the part she left behind." His sigh was long and loud, dragged out as much as his pain. "You know how much I love her."

"Cal, no one knows better than me how much you love *each other*." Peg took his hand, squeezed his fingers. Grateful he'd sat on her right side and not her left.

"Do you really think we'll get her back?"

"Yes." She wanted to wish this into existence.

"I'm going to go to the police station tomorrow," he said. "I want them to come back and search the property from top to bottom, to see if they missed anything."

Her heart skipped a beat, but she didn't release his hand, didn't give away how much this revelation affected her. "Why would they find anything new?"

"They must've missed *something*."

"What could they find now, after going through the whole place so many times?" The last thing Peg wanted was for anyone to search the barn too closely. Now that the sign had fallen and she didn't put it back properly, the authorities might spot the door. She couldn't let anyone go down to that cellar and find all of those statues, especially not the one that looked exactly like her sister. "You have to let them do their job."

"It's been over three months, and they still haven't got a clue about what happened to her."

"I know, but that doesn't mean they'll find any new clues here." She stared at the wall, trying to avoid his eyes. "Plus, you're just a kid, they're not going to run back to this property because you demand action. This isn't a movie."

"But this is where she disappeared." He stumbled over his words. "I'll threaten to call the FBI or CIA."

"The CIA doesn't deal with missing person cases."

"But the FBI do."

"Maybe, but the cops who've come through here so many times are still convinced she ran away."

"She wouldn't do that."

Peg shrugged. "Mom told the detectives, but it made no difference back then. I doubt it'll make a difference now."

"We have to do something..."

... to find her.

... before I lose my sanity.

... to make sure she's not dead.

"Don't let your grief turn you into an angry vigilante."

He leapt off the bed. "That's exactly what I should do, start an investigation of my own."

"What?" Peg couldn't let him go through with such an insane idea. "You're not a cop, and this isn't some amateur PI story where you get a flashlight and a magnifying glass and can suddenly solve the mystery."

"I have to do *something*!" He stared at the snake bracelet still in his hand. "I'm going out of my mind trying to figure out what could've happened."

"You *are* doing something. You're going to school and will never forget about the girl you love."

"I forgot about her tonight," he said. "Just for a second."

"No, you didn't." The way his eyes glistened tore at her heart. "When you kissed me, you were thinking about her, about *Chrysa*." She had to force this point, couldn't deal with any other reason for the kiss. Kissing Belle in secret was easy and made sense, but kissing Cal was too problematic. There was enough crap to unpack in her life without adding the boy who saw Peg as half of the missing piece he couldn't find.

He opened his mouth to answer, but shut it. Instead, he seemed to put all his concentration in placing Chrysa's bracelet back on the desk.

"I have to get home," he said.

She followed him into the corridor and down the staircase. At the front door, she placed a hand on his forearm. "Don't do anything silly, okay? I don't think Mom would appreciate a bunch of cops storming onto her property without her permission."

He hesitated before saying, "Okay. I won't."

Peg didn't like the way he lowered his gaze, and thought she'd caught a spark in his eyes. She had a feeling he might have already done something he shouldn't. People who were grieving and still madly in love could do some of the craziest things during such emotional turmoil.

She knew from experience.

Peg watched Cal walk over to his VW bug, so caught up in his own thoughts he didn't even notice the rain or the mud. She waved before he ducked his tall body inside. Her mind was racing. She couldn't believe what she'd done and wished she could erase their kiss.

She leaned against the doorframe and waited until his back lights were blurry red dots in the distance. As she turned to head back into the house, she realized he'd forgotten his container of cookies.

IN THE BLUR

It took Chrysa several moments of frantic blinking before the dark surroundings made any sense. Were her eyes damaged? Was she going to spend the rest of whatever life she had left trying to clear her vision? The thought turned her blood to ice.

Since waking out of her endless cycle of nightmares in blur, she hadn't been able to shake the cold. She inspected her arms and found the sweater and jeans that used to have color were now drab and stained with dirt. Was she inside a mud pit?

Her legs were tangled under what she thought might be thick roots, and it took several twists and turns before she managed to dislodge her ankle. She was sweating and breathing heavily by the time she was done, which confused her.

Chrysa pressed against the harsh dirt and the grit stuck between her fingernails.

"Ugh." She instinctively pulled her hands back when she touched something that squirmed under her touch.

A groan filled the space.

Someone shifted beside her.

Everything that had happened so far rushed to her head: waking up from her nightmarish stasis, seeing Peg for a split second, being saved by Lovey, falling down the rabbit hole...

Her body should be aching, but it wasn't.

Instead, she was pissed and possibly dead.

The rage made her turn too fast and a wave of dizziness struck, but at least she'd found Lovey.

The blonde's eyes were closed and the hood she'd thrown over her head had fallen off. She looked just the same as she did in school, minus the style.

"Hey, get up!" Her voice echoed around the dank hole, bounced before being sucked away. Were they inside a grave? Nothing about this gods-forsaken place made any sense. "Lovey, get the fuck up!"

"Lovey?" someone echoed behind her.

When she turned, she was surprised to find a dark-haired teenage boy sitting against the thick walls imprisoning them. "Who the hell are *you* and how did you get here?"

He rubbed the back of his head. "Someone knocked me into this pit." He gave her an accusatory glare. "And who am *I?* Who the hell are you?"

"Don't look at me like that, I didn't push you in here." Chrysa hitched a thumb. "It was her." Anger boiled inside her, turning her blood to lava threatening to overflow. She didn't want to answer this stranger's questions.

"Okay, but why am I stuck here with two cute girls?" He looked around, considering the packed dirt before gazing at the small stretch of sky above. "And where am I, anyway?"

"You're in purgatory," she said.

"Really?" He cocked an eyebrow. "Well, that's new. Wait till he hears about this. In all his teachings, he never mentioned they ended up in purgatory."

"Whose teachings?" Chrysa asked.

"My father's."

"Is your father a teacher, a priest?" The queasy sensation inside her stomach made her feel like she was about to collapse, but she kept her feet pinned to the muddy ground.

"He's the new history teacher in a crappy high school."

"Which school?"

"Minerva High."

"You go to Minerva High?"

"Unfortunately."

She vaguely recalled her favorite history teacher had retired recently. But recently didn't mean the same to her. She had no idea how long she'd been missing.

"So there's a new teacher and he's your father?" Why was she fixated on this? She couldn't explain, but wanted to know more. Maybe it was because she missed everything back home.

"Well, he's not my real father. He's my godfather, but he adopted me years ago." He sighed. "Mum was one of his disciples and followed him everywhere, believed all the crap he tooted. She was actually the one who found the freaks he's been looking for, which is why I'm here... When she died, he became my guardian. Not because he cared, but because he owed her."

The shine of tears in his eyes was hard to ignore, but Chrysa pretended she didn't notice. She also decided not to dwell on his insane response, even though she wanted to dissect every word this strange boy was so easily spilling.

"What freaks?" she asked. "And what do you mean she was his disciple?"

He shrugged. "He's a mythology buff, so he teaches crap in and out of the classroom."

"Lucky you." She didn't focus on the fact he didn't answer her other question.

"Why do you look so familiar?"

"If you go to Minerve High, you might know..." her voice trailed off. "You might know my sister, Peggy."

"Peggy?" He seemed confused. "Do you mean, Peg? The strange chick with the cards?"

"Yes, that's her! How is she? Have you seen her lately?" She felt like an idiot asking a complete stranger these questions, especially when she should've asked Lovey.

"This is so bizarre, I thought you were missing because of—"

"She can't remember what happened to her," Lovey interrupted. "She doesn't know anywhere near as much as you do."

Chrysa wanted to respond to her—to both—but for the first time, words failed her because Lovey was right. She couldn't remember how she'd ended up in the blur. She scratched her head, but the gesture did nothing to reveal the memories she'd been trying to recapture.

"Glad you finally woke up," was the only thing she managed.

"Chrysa, this is Ira Danae," Lovey introduced. "Ira, this is Chrysa Ceto."

"Oh!" He smiled at her. "I didn't recognize you, but I know all about your kind."

She ignored his cryptic comment.

Ira was still grinning when he started ogling Lovey. "Is this what you wear when you're not prancing around in tiny, tight outfits?" he asked in a singsong voice that dripped with condescension.

"Don't even try your arrogant crap with me. I'm not in the mood." Lovey glared at the wide hole above, where only the combination of ominous white light and tree branches could be seen. "We have to get out of this pit."

"I'm not going anywhere until someone explains what the hell is going on." Chrysa crossed her arms. "Someone better spill, or I'll keep dragging you both down until I get some answers." She glared at one of her companions, and then the other.

"You always were a bold bitch." Lovey shook her head. "But fine, I'll answer some of your stupid questions." She sat cross-legged on the packed dirt. "You want to know how I got here. Well, I'm one of the few who can travel between the living world and this one. And trust me, it's no party because every time I do, I end up owing some asshole a big favor. The kind of favor I like to pretend I don't ever have to pay up."

"That gibberish means nothing to me. You didn't answer anything." Chrysa couldn't believe her ears. "How did you find me as soon as I broke out of my prison?"

"What prison?" Ira asked, confused.

"You didn't come through as a statue?" Chrysa asked him.

"Uh, sure... but I broke out almost as soon as I got here."

"What?" Chrysa had spent who-knew how long inside the blur with those watchful veiled, and he'd broken out instantly? When were things going to start making any sense?

"Ira didn't become a full statue because the veiled didn't get the chance to catch him, right?"

He nodded. "And then I fell into this freaking hole, so I hope we're safe—"

"We're not safe anywhere."

"Why is that, Lovey?" Chrysa asked.

"Isn't that obvious? You've been here long enough to know that the veiled are dangerous." The blonde rolled her eyes. "Besides, the reason why I'm stuck here with you two is because of your boyfriend."

"What, Cal sent you?" Tears blurred Chrysa's vision and a ringing started in her ears. "How?"

"Take it easy, if you emanate too much emotion, they'll find us in no time."

"Okay, sorry." She sucked in a heavy breath and tried to calm her pulse. The air in this place was thick, but down here it was also freezing and felt like she was breathing in icicles.

"Cal is heartbroken over you, and decided to perform a ritual that's bound to get him in trouble." Lovey repositioned the bandages around her neck and face.

"A ritual?" She didn't understand. "Like witchcraft?"

"There are many different kinds of rituals."

"You honestly don't know anything about Minerva, do you?" Ira said with a snort. "It took my father years to find that town because your kind do such a great job at hiding who you really are."

Chrysa flashed him a dirty look and turned back to the other annoying person. The one she desperately needed answers from. "What ritual did he perform?"

"A love ritual. He asked for Aphrodite's help, and I tried to ignore him but he kept going and going." She sighed. "He wanted to find his lost love and I gave him the clues he desired. Led him to the location where he should be looking. It's why he keeps going back to the farm, keeps hounding your sister. If he's not careful, he's going to fall for her."

Ira laughed. "Tell me you didn't bewitch him into seeing this one in the weird sister."

"I did nothing of the sort." But Lovey's grin said otherwise.

"Don't talk about the people I love like they're objects." When the initial anger cleared away, Chrysa finally realized something that wasn't possible. "Hold on a second, are you trying to tell me that *you're* Aphrodite?"

The blonde's eyes were glowing.

Chrysa burst out laughing because this was too much.

"What's so funny?"

When she got her breath back, she said, "A girl I've known most of my life is the goddess of love?"

"Yes."

"Lovey, I want real answers, I don't need you to fuck around with stupid lies."

"I'm not dicking around."

"Sure, you're not."

"She really isn't," Ira added.

"And who are you, Hades?" she retorted, outraged at being treated like a fool.

"I wasn't that lucky."

Chrysa paced back and forward. "Are you telling me that Cal summoned a goddess who happens to be a teenager we both know, and you willingly came to help?"

"I didn't want to come. Trust me, I really didn't, but he wouldn't shut up and kept doing the ritual. I don't know where he got it from, his kind aren't privy to these sorts of things."

"His kind?" Chrysa's confusion was turning into a very sticky, tangled mess. If she couldn't wrap her mind around these answers, how would she ever get back home? "What's that supposed to mean?"

"Oceanids," Ira interjected.

"What?" She might be rusty on her Greek mythology, but she recognized the term and it was outrageous for anyone to suggest her boyfriend was an ocean nymph. Maybe there were toxins in the air that made these people delusional.

"It's true," he said with a nod.

"Don't worry about any of that now. There's a lot of stuff going on that you don't understand yet." Lovey's blue eyes shone unnaturally, lighting the pit like a lamp.

"Are you going to help me get out of blur?"

"What's blur?" Ira asked.

"It's really cute really, but she's given this place and the creatures who roam the forest names."

"Just answer the question, are you going to help or not?"

Lovey waited for several beats before answering. "I want to help, but I can't get you out."

"Then what *can* you do?"

"I'm here to make sure you survive until *she* can get you out."

"Who?"

"Your annoying sister is the only one who can get you back to the other side," Lovey said.

"Peggy?" On some level, it made sense. They were twins, and had always been close. Their mother raised them as individuals, but neither left the other behind. And Peg had caught sight of her before she was released from her prison.

"But only if she remembers who she really is and what she's supposed to do to save your family." Lovey stood. "You need to reach out to her."

"Is Mom in danger too?"

Her gaze sharpened. "Your mother is the reason why we're *all* in danger."

Mom and Peggy were in danger.

Peggy was the only one who could get her out of here.

Finding Peggy was the only way to get back home.

The air in front of her wavered.

"What the hell?" Ira looked up. "Shit." He scrambled into the shadows.

"They found us."

"Who found us?" Chrysa coughed, trying to catch her breath.

"The veiled."

Chrysa tilted her head and found the concealed faces of the veiled crowding the open crevice. An endless rush of tiredness swept over her and she yawned.

"Don't look at them!" Lovey yelled.

The roots Chrysa had been caught under when she'd woken up were now slithering out from the mud and wrapping around her legs. Running over her body like snakes, crushing her chest. She caught a glimpse of Lovey and Ira, and they were caught up in the roots too.

"My head hurts," she whispered. "All I want to do is sleep."

"The last thing you need to do right now is sleep."

Who said that? Miss Know-It-All or Mr. Annoying-New-Guy?

"Chrysa, whatever you do, don't fall asleep!"

She wanted to respond, but couldn't speak. Could hardly breathe.

When her eyelids drooped, every thought of love rituals, Cal, goddesses and Peggy slipped away into the sudden blackness filling her eyes and mind.

CHAPTER ELEVEN

EVERY THOUGHT INSIDE PEG'S BRAIN WAS TOXIC. *CONFUSING. NOT QUITE right.*

The secret in the barn. The gloom. The Groundhog section of road on the way home from school. That she kept missing the bus. Cal's preoccupation with her. Her very satisfying secret make-out sessions with Belle. That she'd kissed Cal. Her mother's erratic behavior. A mysterious woman named Athena. The disturbances in the barn. Her teacher's strange reaction. Calling her aunts.

All of it was bad. None of it made sense.

Kissing Cal tortured her the most. How did she allow herself to fall into the moment like that? No matter how hard she tried to find excuses for why they'd found solace in each other, her guilt wouldn't subside. He was her sister's boyfriend. She was semi-involved with Belle. There was no sugar-coating reality.

She'd allowed a moment of weakness, of shared grief, to make her do something really stupid.

Peg sat up in bed and pressed her back against the many pillows she needed in order to get a full night's sleep. Though she hadn't achieved that in days. And tonight was no different. She'd dozed off for a bit, but dreamt about the dark woods that threatened to consume her. And after waking, she hadn't been able to get back to sleep. Didn't want to.

So, she'd decided to wait out the fogginess before heading out to the barn. She'd waited long enough. Nothing was going to stop her this time. Not even the anxiety coursing through her. Or the nagging sensation that wouldn't go away. The one that kept teasing her with a memory she couldn't access.

Every time she felt as if it was there, ready to grasp... whatever it was slipped away.

She stared at the deck of cards she'd spread out in front of her and chose one. This reading required a two-or-three-word answer, nothing more.

Is going back into that chamber the right thing to do?

Ten of clubs.

Burden.

Responsibility.

A single card revealed a lot about what lay ahead. Even if she ignored everything else, this one card would be enough. Discovering a secret room underneath the barn was her burden to carry. Was *her* responsibility to pursue. She had to solve this mystery alone because if Cal was serious about hounding the cops to come out to the Ceto property again, she wanted to hide the entrance. Needed to make sure she scrutinized every inch of the place in case there *were* missed clues.

Maybe I should interrogate Mom for more information.

There was so much Peg didn't know, and even more that she couldn't remember. The one thing she did know was that she had to go back to the hidden chamber.

Her eyes blurred as she stared at the card with the intensity of a thousand scorching suns. The walls around her dribbled their gloomy fingers down the ceiling. The gloom threatened to close in and steal the oxygen from the room.

She concentrated on the card and nothing else. A sharp exhale forced everything back into the walls and up the ceiling in reverse.

Her room was back in focus.

She couldn't help but feel as if she'd reached a very important crossroads. The intersection of change she'd expected would come after finishing high school. The challenge of changing from twin teenagers, to two adults with different ambitions.

That time was *now*.

Peg collected the cards into a pile and shoved them into her hoodie pouch, then zipped it up. She hadn't bothered to change out of her clothes, because the last thing she wanted to do was get caught outside in a onesie or PJs. That had happened too many times already.

She snuck out of her room and slowly tiptoed down the empty corridor, careful not to step on any creaky boards. The thought of checking on her mother almost made her turn back, but she fought the impulse. It wasn't a good idea to accidentally wake her, especially since she'd had a few glasses of wine after Cal left. Red wine always made her sleepy, which suited Peg perfectly tonight.

Even remembering the hand-mirror she'd noticed in Mom's bathroom wasn't enough to stop her advance.

Slithering long shapes crossed in front of her as she cut through the corridor and into the kitchen. The shadows shifted fast and she almost tripped several times, but she assumed it was the gloom playing tricks on her.

Cool air hit her as soon as she stepped outside and into her boots.

The uneasy sensation of being watched made her skin burn. Too many ancient stories hinged on the power of moving forward and not looking back.

It didn't take long to reach the barn doors, and for once they were actually closed.

She opened one very carefully, to keep from making too much noise. If Mom heard even a squeak, she might break out of her drunken stupor and come outside to take care of the intruder. Or hunter. Who was hunting them? And was it the same person Athena claimed was after Peg? And more importantly, who the hell was Athena?

Peg traipsed into the dark, between the metal aisles her mother had installed years ago. There was plenty of illumination streaming in through the large windows. Moonbeams slipped between the clouds and helped light the way.

It didn't take long to find the faded, rusty sign barely concealing the hidden doorway. She ducked around the side and checked the surface of the door. Her eyes strayed to the small hole in the middle, which resembled a lock without a keyhole. Instead, something roundish and small could be slipped into the groove.

Maybe a coin!

She pulled the tarnished token from her pocket and wedged it into the hole. The coin fit perfectly. As she watched, the edges of the door started to fade into the wall and she pulled the relic out before it disappeared completely.

So, this was how to seal the passage? But how had the coin come off in the first place? That was another mystery to add to the list. She rubbed the surface of the keepsake and stuck it back in her pocket.

She slunk behind the curling-edge of the sign's metal frame and pressed her fingers against the door. It was funny how the wood on this side mimicked the barn's walls—faded, splintery and worn—but the inside was clean and new.

Peg was about to press her entire hand against the surface, but stopped when a cooing sound and the flap of wings caught her attention. She tilted her head to check for birds or bats, but there was nothing there.

A single white feather floated down to land near her feet.

She leaned over, picked it up and couldn't ignore the shimmery golden flecks. She added it to her pocket of treasures. Along with the blackened coin she now carried around everywhere, her cards, and her phone, she was starting to feel like a magpie. Carrying shiny objects was going to start weighing her down.

Running her fingers over the door made her feel as if she was taking part in some old and special ritual. When the prick of a splinter struck, she didn't even gasp in surprise. For whatever reason, this seemed like the only way for the door to open. Was it her blood? Or did the wood need a taste of her skin? Either option sounded obscenely unlikely, but lately she'd been experiencing a lot of strange things.

She pushed the wooden surface and stepped inside, decided not to close the door behind her. Felt safer knowing it was ajar.

Peg stood at the top of the staircase and her lungs filled with frigid air. The temperature was cool outside, but it was freezing in here.

Moonlight didn't reach this far so she pulled out her phone and switched on the flashlight app. As she descended the stairs slowly, she took a good look at the etched symbols on either side. She couldn't fight the claustrophobic sensation of descending into a crypt. The writing seemed to be Greek, but she wasn't sure how she knew that.

She snapped several photos, and even took one of the stairs she was positive were made out of marble. As weird and sacrilegious as this seemed, she wanted to use the photos to refer to her mother's many mythology books because asking her directly wouldn't get her anywhere.

Peg took the stairs one at a time, careful not to slip. When she finally reached the bottom, she instinctively pulled the cord and switched off the phone light. She still couldn't believe how many statues were hidden in this secret place, or that the rows of fluorescents seemed to go on forever in every direction.

She turned in a circle and nearly jumped, surprised to find there were as many statues heading in the opposite direction—towards the house—as there were in front of her. She chose to ignore the discovery, and turned to the one that interested her the most.

The statue of a young girl and her dog, the one that looked exactly like Chrysa. The color might be gray, but Peg knew Chrysa was wearing her favorite purple sweater and blue jeans. Was this the outfit she'd worn that night? And there was Sword, who'd disappeared along with her and gave the police ammunition to endorse the running away narrative. But Mom never spoke about him, pretended their trusty dog never existed.

How had she managed to hear her sister the other night?

The itch on the back of her shoulder blades was back. So sharp she thought something was trying to pierce past her skin, attempting to break out of her. She'd never experienced such a visceral sensation before.

She rolled her shoulders while ignoring the buzzing inside her skull.

Peg stepped closer and on the shiny floor, in front of where Chrysa and Sword's statues stood, she noticed an engraving etched into the marble. But she couldn't understand the words.

She focused on the statue and it was like looking into a freaky mirror made of stone. Her hand itched and without even knowing why, she pulled off her glove and held her palm up to the light. The life lines that used to crisscross across her skin were completely gone, replaced by the smooth texture of stone. Her fingers were still made out of skin and bone and she could wriggle them, but she couldn't make a fist because her palm was as stiff as a rock.

Peg lowered her hand and turned her attention to the other statues.

As she strolled across the expanse of this freaky chamber, she was surprised to find a multitude of children, women and men caught in varying degrees of motion. Yet every statue shared several traits— their arms and legs were caught in mid stride, their eyes were wide open, and the mouths caught in a haunting O.

Every static figure reminded her of characters in a horror movie. How victims reacted a second before the killer or monster cut their lives short. And these statues were forever frozen this way. As she tried not to dwell on the connection, she soon noticed the people became chubby cherubs, angels with massive wings and hideous monsters towering high into the ceiling. The farther she went, the bigger they became.

There was something that reminded her of a dragon, but had multiple heads. A large serpent with so many necks she didn't bother counting. A huge lioness and goat body mixed together with a snake tail. A woman with a bird's body. A large eagle with wings spanning wide enough to stretch out across four rows.

Other monsters had the bodies of people, mismatched tails and more than one head—three in most cases. She'd seen these creatures in books and knew most by name, but right now, she couldn't remember a single one. Or understand why they were here. Eventually, she barely skimmed the rows because her brain struggled to make sense of all the impossible limbs and bodies.

Who put them here, and for what purpose?

That was when she caught movement behind one of the larger statues ahead. This one looked like a horse with a man's body—a Centaur. That was the name!

Her pulse sped up. Was it possible that her mother had followed her after all?

She shook her head, concentrating on where she thought she'd caught the motion behind the Centaur. Nothing happened, and she damned the stupid gloom that followed her everywhere.

Peg turned back the way she'd come, trying to keep within the row and glad she had stayed on the straight and narrow instead of crisscrossing. It would be too easy to get lost. Just as the thought entered her mind, she realized something.

The disruption had made her rotate. She wasn't facing the same direction she'd come from, and now these rows and rows of statues had become a labyrinth.

Peg took a right, searching for the stairs. But they weren't there, they weren't anywhere.

Where the hell do I go? What the hell do I do?

She didn't stop, kept jogging until she ran into the bull thing and let out a strangled gasp. She recognized this one.

"Thanks Minotaur," she whispered.

The Bull blinked.

A scream escaped her and echoed around the chamber as she backed away. She bumped into another statue and this one swayed slightly. She reached out, hoping to steady the motion but ended up pushing instead. The statue tumbled to the ground and shattered.

"Fuck."

The many heads on the end of the snake-like necks were now

scattered on the pristine floor. What the hell was she going to do? Bring a broom and sweep away the evidence, pretend this never happened?

She leaned forward, pressed both hands against her thighs and sucked in shallow breaths through her nose and out of her mouth. Her eyesight was starting to slant and the last thing she wanted to do was pass out in this hidden space.

Peg shut her eyes, counted back from ten and opened them when something bumped into her foot. One of the heads rolled past, and the eyes were blinking.

"Holy shit!" Peg backed away. How had this museum become a room of horrors?

She kept moving, desperate to find the stairs to get the hell out. Why did she have to go and explore anyway? Why didn't she concentrate on the one person she wanted to see again in the first place?

As if she'd summoned her, there stood her sister and dog.

Peg sucked in several breaths and concentrated on her sister's face. She drew in enough breaths to calm herself and focused all of her attention on the barren cold smell of the place, and the familiarity of the statue's features.

When the anxiety subsided, she stood directly in front of Chrysa and raised her left hand. She pressed her stone palm against her twin's cheek and a jolt flowed through her when stone clicked against stone. She removed her hand instinctively.

Somehow, her graying palm and the statue had reacted to each other.

"Where are you, Chrysa?" Tears blurred her vision as she remembered their shared childhood.

"*Nothing will ever tear us apart,*" Chrysa always used to say. Yet, she'd gone and left Peg all along.

"Where did you go?" Peg's voice echoed around the chamber, and she thought she heard a crack answer back. All the loss morphed into anger as she tried to close her fist, but the skin was too tight and she couldn't. She bumped it against her sister's chest anyway. "Why did you leave us... *leave me?*"

Peg smacked her again but when Chrysa rocked slightly, she dropped her hand. Movement from her right caught her attention. The sound of something large rolling along the floor made her skin freeze.

Shit.

A thump echoed down the stairs.

She took one last look at her sister. "I'll figure this out, I promise."

Peg petted the dog's head and was about to turn to race up the stairs when she decided to snap a quick photo of her sister. She needed the evidence.

She raced up the marble staircase and when she reached the door, took a quick breath before sliding out. She left the sheer cold behind and shut the door, which sealed when she stuck her keepsake in the slot and then pocketed it.

Peg could still feel the presence on the other side of the door. Was it one of those freaky heads she'd broken?

Her phone dinged and made her jump.

It was a text from Belle. *is it ok 4bro 2come ovr sunday*

For a second, she didn't understand. Not until she let go of all the horror and wonder and remembered her friend's brother was in town from college.

Sure, she sent back.

A kissy smiley with a heart came straight back.

She waited a few seconds for a follow up. When none came, she pocketed her phone.

If other people were going to visit over the weekend, she had to completely conceal this door. She dragged the big sign in front, then added a few smaller ones, hoping not to draw attention to the area.

As she made her way past the aisles, flapping wings caught her attention.

She chased after the murky shadows, but all she found was a snake. Her initial shock withered away. What the hell was a snake doing in the barn as well? First, she'd seen one in her mother's room, and now there was one in here. She turned her back on the snake and headed for the barn door. Before reaching her freedom, she spotted the white and golden owl sitting on top of one of the shelves. It hooted and spread its wings. She thought it was going to fly away, but the action resembled a greeting.

Peg waved and felt like a fool.

"What do you want with us?" she asked.

The owl responded by vanishing into the night.

Peg added this encounter to every other weird thing she'd seen, and left the barn.

She trudged toward the house and couldn't help but wonder if she'd awakened something. Surely that wasn't possible. The head rolled on its own because it had shattered, and she'd imagined the blinking eyes because she was exhausted.

Peg needed to hide inside the sanctuary of her bedroom and hope for sleep. She wondered if she should call Auntie Widow and Auntie Weirdo again.

As she ran, she pretended not to see the hideous creature standing at her mother's window.

CHAPTER TWELVE

"What can you tell me about this?" Peg held out the white feather. The golden spots twinkled against the weak light trying to break into her mother's bleak bedroom. The air was stuffy again because Mom never bothered to crack the window open.

Mom sipped tea from her mug and sat back against the ornate snake headboard. She took her time before deciding to take a quick glance. "It's a feather. Where did you get it?"

"I found it in the barn."

"Show me." Peg handed it over and Mom inspected the feather with feigned interest, pursing her lips for good effect. "I don't know what to tell you. Like I said, it's a feather."

"Maybe you could start with the truth."

The blindfold was pulled down and sat weirdly around her mom's neck, but she still seemed determined to avoid eye contact. "We get a lot of pigeons and other birds nesting in the barn. I don't know what else you want me to tell you."

"Don't pretend you can't see the way it shines."

"I—"

"Mom, I'm tired of the secrets and the lies." Peg stood too quickly and the chair scooted back, smacking against the wall.

Her mother winced.

"Some very weird things have happened to me these past few days, and I know it's all connected to Chrysa's disappearance." She paced the floor between the bathroom and the end of the bed, trying to ignore the discarded snakeskins. "I need to understand what's happening to me because at the moment, I feel like I'm losing my mind."

Peg might have gotten her wish of dreamless sleep because she was exhausted after the previous night's events, but she couldn't shake the memory of the hidden chamber. Or the rolling stone head, and the uncanny sense of being followed.

"You're not losing your mind," Mom whispered.

Peg hated these awkward interactions and wanted life to go back to normal. Without Chrysa—or knowing what had really happened to her—nothing would ever be the same. Her life would forever be tainted by the loss of her twin.

"It sure feels like I am," Peg said. "Sane people don't imagine darkness closing in around them. They don't look at playing cards and read them as easily as if they were looking into a crystal ball." She shook her head. "People who aren't nuts know what happened to their sisters. And can talk to their mothers without getting a bunch of riddles in return."

"That's not what I do, or why I do it." She sighed. "And you can read playing cards because of your psychic intuition. I taught you how to focus all of the energy flowing inside you into the deck of cards. It's not something that singles you out as crazy or strange, it's a wonderful gift."

"It doesn't feel like a gift." Nothing about her life did.

"That's because you're not seeing the big picture. You refuse to open your eyes to see what's around you."

"My eyes are open, but you refuse to answer my questions."

"I don't refuse, that's not what I'm doing."

Peg stopped pacing. "Then what *are* you doing?"

"I'm trying to protect you." Her mom's eyes were wide, shiny. "I'm trying to push you in the right direction so you can really see and understand things for yourself."

"Yeah, well, it doesn't seem to be working."

"Why do you say that?"

"In case you haven't noticed, I haven't been sleeping properly. Between intruders in the middle of the night and visitations from strange women, I've helped you out of the barn and back into bed twice this week." Peg paused to collect her thoughts, to make sure she got the message across because her mother wasn't listening. "But this isn't new, during the past three months I've taken care of this place, and made sure all the online orders are filled. We had some pickers stop by recently who wanted to film a segment, but I had to say no. I know it would've been great publicity, but..."

Mom lowered her gaze, concentrated on the feather she was flicking with her fingertips.

"I can't do this anymore. I have to concentrate on school," Peg said. "But more than that, I'm sick of living in this house with a ghost."

"I'm so sorry." When Mom looked up, her green gaze glistened with unshed tears. "This isn't what I set out to do. The last thing I wanted was to alienate the only good thing I have left in my life, but it's hard. Losing Chrysa the way I did, it messed me up. I can't get over it. I can't move past that night. The screams, the reality of what I did, and accepting I was responsible for what happened tears me up inside every single waking moment."

Peg didn't want to interrupt the flow because Mom seemed to be caught in her own loop of admission, but she had many questions.

"And now I've put you in danger, too." Mom's tears dribbled down her gaunt face.

Peg stepped closer and sat on the bed beside her mother. She tried to wipe away all the resentment and anger bubbling inside. It wasn't that she couldn't understand why Mom was struggling, because she totally could, but Peg wanted to confide in her. To find consolation in the fact they were both mourning the same person and could help each other.

Their individual isolation was killing what was left of their close family.

Peg longed for happier days. When Mom actually listened to what her daughters had to say, and wanted to be a part of their lives. When her mother would teach Chrysa and Peg how to scrap and sell, tell them stories about heroes and monsters. How gods and goddesses toyed with mortals and demigods, and the many impossible quests that kept the twins entertained for hours.

"Mom, I can take care of myself," she finally said. "But I need to know what's going on."

"I have to protect you."

"Fine, keep some of the details to yourself, but I need something real. Throw me a lifeline, because I'm drowning." Peg was struggling, falling deeper into the murk every single day and needed help. Maybe her mother would finally realize that.

"As much as I want to, I can't tell you."

"Why?"

"There are some things only you can remember."

"I need you to tell me *something*, though," Peg snapped.

Mom considered the feather in her hand. "This belongs to an owl."

"I saw the owl."

"Did she approach you? Try to hurt you?" Mom squeezed the feather.

"No, just watched me."

"Did you feel different afterwards?"

Peg shook her head. "I don't know what you mean by that."

"Did you feel like you couldn't remember what you'd done?"

Every bit of what she'd seen and fumbled inside the museum chamber was still as fresh in her mind now as it had been when it happened. "No, I can remember everything I've seen, done, or discovered lately."

"That's good, I guess. She told me she wouldn't bind your memories anymore."

"An owl can bind my memories?"

"Athena is many things." Mom plucked at the feather, but no matter how violently she tried, the glossy stem retained its original shape and glow. "An owl is one of them. Usually, she takes that form to spy or eavesdrop."

"Wait a sec." Peg's brain stuttered because this sounded familiar. "There's an owl called Athena who can do the same stuff as the goddess from Greek mythology?"

Mom caught Peg's gaze and the tears still shone in her eyes. "Athena the owl is the same as Athena the goddess."

"But you were talking to her the other night."

"You heard us talking?"

"I heard snatches of a weird conversation that didn't make any sense."

Mom sighed in obvious frustration. "Then you know that you're in danger, but I won't let anything happen to you. The worst hunter, my biggest enemy, has found us. But I won't let him destroy us."

"You can't be serious right now." Peg couldn't believe her ears. "Are you trying to tell me that you know a goddess who can bind memories, and she's keeping an eye on us? Oh, and she hangs out in our barn?" She shook her head because she didn't even want to know what binding memories meant. "When I said I wanted answers, I meant real ones. I don't want you to spin some sort of bizarre delusion to get me off your back."

"That's not what—"

"If you were involved in a life of crime, drugs or prostitution before we were born and now someone has come for payback, you can tell me." Peg tried to keep her cool. "I'm old enough to handle that. But I'm not a child you can placate with fairy tales."

"Athena, the hunters, what happened to Chrysa—none of that is a fairy tale. It's our lives and you wanted to know, so I'm telling you." Mom held the feather in one hand and reached out with the other. She wrapped her fingers around Peg's, encircling them too tightly. "We're in real danger, and it's not from some pimp or drug dealer. It's from the hunters of gods and monsters."

Peg attempted to pull her hand away because her mother was

getting uncomfortably close to her stony palm. She didn't want to listen to any more of this bullshit. "We need to get you some help." The words tased awful, but had to be said. "I thought we could wait until after I turned eighteen, but it looks like we can't."

"No. We don't need any help." Mom's eyes were glowing emeralds. "If you involve anyone else in this, they'll institutionalize me. No one's going to believe the truth. Actually, most of Minerva will use it against me. Call me insane, lock me up and throw away the key. No one was happy about us settling here, but as long as we stayed in our own corner, most tolerated me. Besides, our junkyard is a spectacle no one counted on. It's good for the town, encourages visitors to spend money."

She was even acting paranoid now. What was wrong with her?

"I have to do something," Peg said. "I can't bear to see you like this. You're getting worse every day. You hardly leave this room and don't seem to care about anything."

"I care about you." She squeezed her fingers. "I care about your sister."

"And yet, she's gone."

Peg didn't expect the slap, so when it came, she was stunned. Heat throbbed up her cheek and her ears were ringing.

"I didn't—"

Peg was speechless, couldn't shape words. Instead, she forcibly pulled her hand away from her mother's and when she tried to grab her again, Peg stood and stepped away from this woman. The stranger she'd become.

"Don't go, Pegasus. This conversation isn't over."

"It is for me."

"No, listen, if you're noticing strange things then your mind is already waking up to the truth. Right now, what I'm saying might sound like gibberish, the delusional rants of a depressed woman, but it's not." Mom's voice cracked. "Please don't call anyone. We can get through this on our own."

"No, we can't," Peg said. "Besides, I already have."

"Who did you call?" Her eyes widened. "Give me a chance to deal with this myself before anyone else gets involved. I can't risk losing Chrysa forever."

Guess you don't mind losing me, though. The petty thought filled her mind, leaving her nothing else to focus on.

"*Who. Did. You. Call?*" her mother repeated, enunciating every word.

"You'll find out soon enough." Peg made her way around the room, avoiding her mother's gaze.

"How's your hand?"

The question made her pause, but she didn't answer.

"I asked you a question!"

Peg didn't bother to respond. What was the point?

"Can you see my snakes yet?"

She froze, but kept her back to her mom.

"If you can see them crossing in front of you, then at least I can rest assured you'll soon understand everything enough to believe me."

"I doubt it." Peg slammed the door and the screaming started. A yell so loud and screechy it stung her ears almost as much as the slap had.

Peg backed away, but didn't miss the line of green illuminating the doorway. What the hell was Mom doing?

As she headed downstairs, she tried not to dwell on her mother's mention of snakes because the creatures were everywhere. Was this a sign of madness? Was this a Ceto curse Peg wouldn't be able to escape?

IN THE BLUR

THE COLD STROKE AGAINST HER CHEEK JUMPSTARTED HER BRAIN.

Sent a spark flowing beneath her skin.

"Where are you, Chrysa?"

"Peggy, is that you?"

"Where did you go?"

"Peggy, where are you?"

"Why did you leave us... leave me?"

Chrysa wanted to tell her sister that she didn't leave, but how could she when she couldn't see past the blackness surrounding her at every angle?

"I'll figure this out, I promise."

"You need to find me," she whispered and the words left a buzzing imprint along her lips.

Chrysa put all the focus she could summon into opening her eyes.

It took every ounce of willpower she possessed, but thinking about her sister's voice and the touch to her face made her feel stronger. She fought against whatever was trying to pull her under, because she refused to go back to stillness.

She wouldn't allow the veiled to keep her stuck in a nightmarish world of her own making, while motionless in another.

"Lovey, are you there?"

Her eyelids had cracked enough that light filtered between her lashes.

"Ira..." She tried to turn, but found her head was pinned in place.

That was when she remembered the dark pit and the squirming roots.

Chrysa inhaled a sharp breath and even though it stung all the way down her throat and esophagus, it was enough to inflate her lungs.

Her eyes snapped open.

She was back in the middle of the eerie forest.

The trees stretched impossibly high, joined to become a canopy. The branches shimmered and warped before settling back into place. Everything about her body felt wrong. She wasn't touching the ground. She was in mid-air, inside a cage made of thick, black roots rising from the pit.

She flexed her fingers and toes. Was glad she could at least do that. Everything worked differently in this forest. Sound was filtered and sight hid behind a gauze able to leech all color.

"Lovey..."

"Be quiet, will ya?"

"Lovey?" Chrysa struggled, but managed to pivot her neck enough to catch a glimpse of her classmate. She was also encased inside a cage made of wood, but there was something not quite normal about her feet. "What happened to you?"

"We're trapped." Her voice seemed stilted, and it wasn't because of their surroundings.

"They've put us in cages and we're now suspended in the middle of nowhere," Ira added from her right. "I really wish *Dad* had warned me about this place."

"No one knows about... this place," Lovey whispered.

"Seriously, what's wrong with you?" Chrysa asked, concerned.

"She tried to cut her way out of the cage and it stabbed her through both ankles," Ira said.

Chrysa's shoulder ached as she struggled to catch a glimpse, and when she did a gasp escaped her. Ira was right. Both of Lovey's ankles were impaled by the ends of sharp branches and her broken skin was weeping. "That looks painful."

"Feels as bad as it... looks."

"But you're a goddess, right? Can't you break free?"

"Oh, Chrysa." Lovey chuckled and the echo sounded freaky as hell. "I'm a lot of things, but everyone is... on the same playing field... in this place."

"And that's what makes everything even stranger," Ira said. "Why did you even bother to come when you had a choice?"

"Why did you?" Chrysa snapped at him.

"I didn't have a choice. That freak looked at me and turned me to stone," Ira spat.

"Ira Danae, none of us... had a choice." The blonde sighed and followed it up with a wince. "When Cal summoned the goddess of love to bring Chrysa home... I resisted. So many times. For several months. But he was persistent... and I couldn't ignore such raw emotion." Lovey made a noise deep in her throat. "Even if it meant... protecting the daughter of the one who caused all of this. If not for *her*, this place wouldn't even... exist."

"I hope you're not bad-mouthing my mother again," Chrysa said. "Because she had nothing to do with this."

"Oh yeah, how do you think *you* ended up in here?" Ira asked.

"I can't remember."

"You got here the same way I did," Ira said. "After you looked into her eyes."

Chrysa scoffed. "I've been looking into my mother's eyes since I was a baby. She never sent me away to some unnatural forest patrolled by freaks in robes."

"You don't know who she is, do you?" Ira snorted. "Don't even realize who *you* are. If you think finding out Lovey is Aphrodite is weird, wait until you realize what you are."

"Ira!" Lovey's scream was whip-sharp. "Now's not the time."

"When will it be the right time, then?" he snapped. "I'm sick of playing games."

"After we're free of this... when we're closer to getting... back."

"I dreamt about my sister," Chrysa blurted.

Both of them went quiet.

"While you were unconscious?" Lovey asked.

"Yes."

"What did she say?"

"She... she wanted to know where I went," Chrysa whispered, yet the words wrapped themselves around the cage, made the roots creak. "Said she would figure everything out and get me back."

"Maybe she's onto something," Lovey said. "Your sister is a pain in the ass, but... when she gets something in her head..."

Chrysa smiled at the thought because Peggy was certainly determined.

"You better hope she is," Ira added. "Or we're doomed."

"Can't you go back and tell her what's happening?" Chrysa asked Lovey.

"It doesn't work like that," she said. "Besides, they made me bleed. The veiled know shedding my blood... makes my abilities null... in this forest. We're all stuck together."

Chrysa struggled to understand any of this. "What are they going to do to us?"

"I'm not sure."

"Where are the veiled, anyway?"

As if she'd conjured the freaks, where there'd been nothing but branches and mist a second ago, countless of veiled figures were suddenly floating in front of her—around the cage. There were so many, their flowing robes blocked her off from Lovey and Ira.

"I don't want to go back to being a statue," Chrysa said.

"You will become something much more useful now."

Their response was scratchy and spoken by a multitude of voices, and she wasn't sure if it was inside or outside her head.

It was enough to make her shiver with dread. "What—what's that?"

"Bait."

CHAPTER THIRTEEN

THE IMPACT OF HER MOTHER'S SLAP MIGHT HAVE WORN OFF, BUT THE effects simmered beneath the surface. Peg couldn't believe her mother had reacted violently when confronted with the truth. And what the hell was the screeching and the green light all about?

She considered her hand, recalled the emerald shimmer she thought she'd imagined the other night when her palm was struck and started changing. The same beam that somehow sent her to a foreign place for the briefest of moments. And when she returned, part of her hand had turned to stone.

Maybe I imagined everything.

Maybe I need more sleep.

Maybe my mother's insanity is contagious.

Who was she kidding? Insanity was hereditary, not contagious. And she was stuck inside a house where madness seemed to be closing in.

She'd lived here her whole life. This house and the surrounding hectares were supposed to be her sanctuary. Even when local kids snuck in and tried to steal pieces, or someone wandered anywhere near the barn and the many rusting vehicles, none of those incidents were anything like what was happening now.

Since Chrysa disappeared, everything started falling apart. As if their lives were built on a house of cards and everything was crumbling.

Peg pulled out her well-worn deck and shuffled, found comfort and ease in the action she could do without much thought. Sometimes kids at school seemed to go into a daze watching her shuffle, and she liked holding such power.

Mom claimed using the cards was her way of anchoring her psychic abilities, but she'd never felt like she could divine anything. Not really. Peggy mostly thought of herself as a charlatan. A girl able to read into the questions people asked.

She wasn't special.

Peg couldn't take her eyes off her hand and the cards blurred.

She sighed, spread the deck out in front of her and ran an index finger over her left palm. Even with the woolen glove between digit and palm, she hated the stony feel and the creepy smoothness. Her hand reminded her of the museum chamber—cold and sterile.

Pulling the glove off wasn't a good idea, but the compulsion was there. So, she yanked the covering off, placed it on her lap and stared at her hand. Was it her imagination, or had the gray surface spread? She couldn't remember the stone chasing all the way to the base of her fingertips. If she didn't figure this out soon, she was going to become as crazy as her mother.

The kitchen walls closed in around Peg as shadows dripped in murky tendrils with long, searching fingers. She held her breath, hoping the gloom wouldn't find her, but could feel the cool sweep across the floor. Closing in on her socked feet.

It wasn't until she heard a hissing that the approaching gloom paused. It didn't fade away, it simply stopped short of reaching her. Peg checked under the kitchen table and found a group of coiled snakes hissing at the approaching threat.

"What's happening to me?"

A single snake turned in her direction, raised its sleek charcoal-colored head and met her eyes with a familiar onyx shine.

Her stomach roiled. "What do you want with me?"

We want you to remember.

She wasn't sure if the reptile was speaking out loud or inside her head.

"You want me to remember what?"

We need you to remember what happened to her. The snake reared its head, eyes stuck on hers. *Otherwise, you will never get her back.*

"I can't get her back." Why was this snake trying to insinuate that she could somehow get her sister back?

You haven't even tried.

"I don't know how to."

That's because you've eliminated all the possible pathways to remembering everything that matters.

"I..." Her head throbbed.

You hid the memories to help her, but hindered yourself.

She didn't understand any of this. "I don't know what you're talking about."

The snake's forked tongue tasted the air. *Your grief is blinding.*

"I don't..."

... know what you mean.

... know how to remember.

... know if I'm strong enough to keep doing this.

Her eyes blurred with frustrated tears.

A knock at the front door made her gasp in surprise.

The gloom retreated completely into the walls. The snakes slithered around each other in a frenzy, spinning the air until it shimmered and they vanished.

The knock came again.

Peg sucked in a breath and stuck her fingers back into the glove. As she made her way out of the kitchen, whispers filled her ears but only one disentangled itself from all the others.

You need to remember. Everything.

She shivered, getting tired of hearing about her supposed amnesia.

"Yoo-hoo, we're here!" a familiar voice called from outside. "We finally made it!"

"Aunt Eno?" Peg sped up, but paused when a long shadow slithered in front of her.

Remember everything, Pegasus.

The words wound themselves around her ears, sinking into her head. The fact she could now see and hear snakes made Peg feel like a freak.

She shook her head, silenced the voice and stopped in front of the door to stare at the blurry figures on the other side of the frosted glass. Her aunts were here. She wasn't alone anymore. In spite of all the crap she was enduring lately, Peg felt a wave of positivity flow through her.

When she pulled the door open and found both aunts standing on the porch, each dragging a big suitcase, she couldn't help but smile. Their orange VW Kombi bus was haphazardly parked in front of the house. If Mom saw the trails of mud their tires had left, she would freak. Or maybe she wouldn't, since she didn't seem to care about much these days.

"Pegasus, is that you?" Eno said with a vibrant smile. Her face was perfectly made—she always knew how to get those smoky eyes just right—and all the contouring complemented her olive skin. She might have spent hours in a van, but Eno didn't look creased in the fitting black dress hugging her curves and the tall heels. Peg could clearly see the life-like snake tattoo on the outer edge of her left ankle. A tattoo that always fascinated her and Chrysa because all three sisters had the exact one in the same spot.

The twins vowed they'd get one when they were old enough. Now, it would never happen.

She forced a smile. "Yep, it's me."

"You're growing up so fast! And you look more like your mother every time I see you."

She winced, hated being compared to Mom in any way.

"Stop embarrassing the poor girl," Rya said to her sister. Her other aunt was the complete opposite—shorter and athletic—wearing black leggings, a sweatshirt and bright sneakers. "Teenage girls don't want to be compared to their mothers! You're being preposterous."

"I'm being honest, that's what I'm being." Eno pulled Peg into a warm and cozy hug she willingly melted into. It had been a long time since a motherly figure held her close and actually made her feel comfortable. Her aunt's sandalwood scent helped settle her nerves.

All the things she'd hoped to feel from her mother after losing her twin sister—comfort, understanding, support—were now being offered by an auntie she rarely saw.

"Thanks for coming," Peg said as she hugged her other aunt. Rya wasn't as consoling as Eno, but even her awkward squeeze was better than anything Mom bothered to offer nowadays. "Come on in."

She waited for them to step inside and dump their rolling suitcases, before closing the door. "Would you like a cup of tea, or coffee?"

"I would *love* a tea," Eno said.

"I could do with a coffee," Rya added.

Peg's face broke into a smile. "I can make both." She wasn't going to let the rigidness of her cheek dampen her mood. But she did hope her mother was asleep and wouldn't bother to leave the room for now. She had to prep the aunts, make sure both understood how bad things had gotten before Mom soured everything with her presence.

"You really *are* doing a great job around the house." Eno inspected the hallway as she took her time, even checked the corners of the ceiling while running a fingertip over the surfaces of the furniture. She did the same in the kitchen. "Ed doesn't know how lucky she is to have someone who loves her as much as you do. You always were a hard worker."

"I don't like mess." Keeping the place clean and the business mostly afloat made everything appear normal to outsiders. It was more for her benefit than anything else. She didn't want anyone to find out that her mother wasn't coping. The family was already divided, and Peg didn't need any officials butting in to make things worse.

This was all for show and judging by her aunts' approving glances, at least she was doing something right.

"Now, before we go and blast our sister, tell us what's been going on." Eno glanced at the spread deck on the table before taking a seat. "You still reading?"

Peg nodded. "The cards help me stay focused."

"I have no doubt they help center the psychic energy rolling off you, too." Eno cocked an eyebrow, watching her with bright eyes.

"Your power is very intense." Rya stripped off her sweatshirt and flung it over the back of a chair before taking the seat beside her sister. "I can feel the energy from here."

"That's what worries me," Eno said with a shake of her head. "Who else can sense her clairvoyant strength?"

"Don't start with that." Peg was sick and tired of this conversation. *I'm not psychic. Maybe psycho.*

"Peg, you have a lot of psychic energy," Eno said. "And your constant denial won't change your capabilities."

"Anyway, this isn't about me. Like I told you the other day, Mom's acting weirder than usual." She didn't call the aunts to discuss whether she was psychic or not.

Aunt Eno grabbed her wrist. "You shouldn't do that," she said.

"Do what?"

"Shake off your talents as if they're nothing," Rya answered. Her eyes were bright too, but not with amusement. Rya was serious and spiky, got on with life in the most disciplined way she could without needing a partner. Well, her partner was Eno, really.

"I don't do that." Peg hated being scrutinized, but she was stuck to the spot because Eno was holding her left hand. Could her aunt feel the stony surface?

"Yes, you do, but when you come into your own, that'll change." Eno stared at her for several quiet seconds before dropping her grip. "Why don't you read our cards?"

"I need to make a cup of—"

"Nonsense, we're not dying of thirst, we can wait. Can't we, Rya?"

"Uh-huh."

Peg sighed, before slowly taking her seat in front of the spread cards. Without thinking about what she was doing, she picked up the deck and put it aside. Instead, she grabbed the spare one in her pocket and shuffled.

"If all else fails, you can get a job in Vegas," Rya said.

"Good one, Ry!" Eno laughed. "She's very good with the shuffle, isn't she?"

Peg tried not to roll her eyes. Before they were trying to convince her about her *psychic abilities*, now she was amusing the aunties. *Why did I bother calling them?*

She concentrated on the cards. "How about I do a simple one-card reading?"

Auntie Widow and Weirdo shared a quick glance. She used to do the same with Chrysa. Sometimes, a simple look was enough communication between the twins.

I miss her so much.

"What's the hold up?" Eno asked.

She didn't bite this time. "So, who wants to go first?"

"Do Rya!"

"What's your question?" she asked.

Rya thought for a moment. "Can I be trusted?"

Peg thought the question was a bit strange, but held out the cards. "Pick the one that speaks to you the most."

"Ooh, I like your technique." Eno clapped, then elbowed her sister. "Come on, pick one already."

Rya leaned forward and plucked a card with her skinny, long fingers. She took a peek before revealing her pick. "Four of diamonds."

"Stability and security." Peg took the card and added it back into the fold before she started shuffling again. "The cards say that you can indeed be trusted. If you can't trust someone with stability and security, who can you trust?"

Rya's smile was small, but radiant.

"My turn!" Eno leaned over, giving Peg a view of her impressive cleavage. She tried not to stare.

"What's your question, Auntie Eno?"

Her aunt scrunched up her face, as if trying to consider the many possibilities. "What I'd really like to know is if my next Prince Charming is around the corner, but that won't do. We're here to deal with family matters and need you to understand we're on your side."

Peg marveled at her cunning aunties. Their comments about her psychic intuition, how the cards worked, and insisting she do a reading wasn't a way to complement her or have fun. She appreciated the effort and support.

"So, what's your question?" Peg repeated.

Eno sat back and met her gaze. "Okay, my question is... will we find Chrysa?"

Peg's hand shook and she almost dropped the cards as she spread the deck in front of her. She cleared her throat. "Pick a card, any card."

"You really are wasting your talents reading for a bunch of kids and old ladies," Rya said.

"Hey, who are you calling old?" Her sister pouted and made a show of lifting her bosom, while pushing the long locks behind her shoulders. "Ignore Auntie Weirdo."

Peg's stomach fell and she tried to hide her shock.

"Don't look so surprised, we know you and your sister call us Weirdo and Widow," Eno said. "We don't mind. I mean, if the shoe fits, right?" She winked. "Anyway, I have a card to pick." She considered the deck and traced her manicured nails over the spread until she stopped smack-bang in the center.

"Ace of spades!" Eno sang when she flashed her card.

Peg's heart skipped a beat. An Ace—a card with so much potential.

"Well, what's my card say about my question?"

"Um... it's the card of clarity, power and victory." Saying the words made Peg feel lightheaded. Her fingers tingled, and she started speaking before the words were fully formed inside her brain. "According to your pick, we will."

Yet she couldn't bring herself to add *"find Chrysa"* to the end of her sentence.

"Oh, that's fantastic news! Isn't it Rya?"

"It is, but let's not cling to false hope until—"

Eno elbowed her sister to shut her up.

"Now, how about getting your aunts that cup of tea and coffee. Who would've thought that picking out cards could cause such thirst?"

Peg took the card back, slipped it on top of the deck and pocketed it. She tried not to get excited about the potential consequences of Eno's pick.

"Two steaming mugs coming right up!" She pumped as much enthusiasm into her words as she could.

Peg busied herself with grabbing mugs from the overhead cabinets, putting the kettle on and divvying out the correct sugars—one for Eno, none for Rya. Her aunties hadn't even been here for an hour and had already managed to fill her with more optimism than her mother had in months.

CHAPTER FOURTEEN

"T̩ELL US MORE ABOUT E̩D," E̩NO SAID.

It took Peg a moment to get her mind back to the reason why she'd called them in the first place—desperation.

"Well, she won't leave her room, cries a lot, keeps wandering out to the barn in the middle of the night. Weird stuff like that." She paused, sneaking a peek out the window. So much of what had messed up their family had happened out there, and now she'd stumbled on a secret room. Should she tell her aunties? Her heart and mind told her not to. At least, not yet. "And when I ask her to tell me what's going on, she gets upset."

"Ed has reason to be upset," Rya said. "She's always carried the heaviest burden."

Peg didn't know what to say to that. She filled the mugs with steaming water, stirred each one before adding a smidge of milk to the tea and a good dose to the coffee. When she placed the mugs in front of each aunt, they were beaming.

"You remembered how we like our cuppas," Eno said with a smile.

Peg shrugged, grabbed her own mug along with a container full of the choc-chip cookies she'd made with Cal. Thinking about him made her stomach flip. He hadn't texted or called, and she was too nervous to check on him. She hated to think that such a nice afternoon might have been ruined by their stupid kiss.

Maybe he needs a bit of time to sort things out.

She popped open the plastic container.

"They smell delicious." Eno eyed the cookies. "Did you make them?"

"I did, and there's plenty of leftovers." Cookies, cakes and pastries barely lasted a day when Chrysa was around, but now all baked goods lasted most of the week.

Peg sat across from her aunts and realized she'd missed their presence. When she was little the aunts used to stay over a lot during the summer, but that hadn't happened for several years. Aunt Eno was usually too busy in her cycle of marriages, and Aunt Rya too occupied with helping her sister pick up the pieces afterwards.

"I don't know what to do," Peg said, breaking the silence interspersed with the crunch of cookies. "I think Mom needs professional help. I've been trying to put it off until I'm eighteen, but I don't know if I can wait that long."

Eno placed a hand over hers. She almost pulled away, but instead concentrated on staying very still and hoped she wouldn't notice her stony palm.

"I know it must be hard feeling isolated and dealing with a mother who's distanced herself from the world, but you're not alone. We're here now." Her blue eyes were shiny and glowed in the bleak light of the kitchen. "Ed is going through something she's never experienced before. She's always tried to protect you girls from her condition, but after this many cycles, it finally happened. Unfortunately, the Sisters Fate eventually catch up with all of us."

"Cycles?" What was she talking about? *Cycles, condition, fate...* what did any of this have to do with her mother?

"Years," Rya said. "She means years."

"Yes, that's what I meant!" Eno squeezed Peg's hand. "The guilt of what happened to Chrysa has taken over Ed's life and she can barely function. Surely you understand what that feels like. After all, you lost her too."

"Of course, I do. But she keeps talking about a hunter, and how she failed to protect us." Peg didn't want to hold her tongue, wanted everything to be out in the open. Besides, the cards had already confirmed her aunts were going to help. "She went crazy the other night, said someone had broken in and she was hysterical."

"Did you see anyone?" Eno asked.

She shook her head. "I saw some scurrying, but didn't actually see anyone."

Rya's frown deepened.

"I also found her talking to someone she called Athena."

Rya's eyes widened and she looked away, out the window.

"And today, Mom tried to tell me that this Athena isn't some woman who happened to drop by, she's insisting this is the actual *Goddess Athena*." Peg wondered if the owl had spied on her and Belle. "I'm sure you can see why I think she needs help. Talking about a goddess from mythology as if she's real isn't healthy. Maybe it's her way of dealing with things, but it's not mine. I live in the real world."

"That's quite a lot to unpack." Eno drew her hand away and leaned into her chair. She took a sip from her mug. "Do you have an alcoholic beverage I can add to my tea?"

"It's crazy, right?"

Her other aunt silently pondered her coffee.

Eno sipped again, before settling her mug back on the tabletop and running her perfectly manicured nails over the surface. "I wouldn't call it crazy, exactly."

"What would you call it then?"

"The ramblings of a distraught mother," she answered. "A cry for help from someone who has only ever known how to protect and serve others. Ed doesn't know how to reach out for assistance, so it's easier to retreat."

"It's true. Ed has a bad habit of carrying the burden for everyone," Rya added.

A beat of silence filled the kitchen, and neither of the aunts made

eye contact with her. After the card readings and the easy cama-
raderie, Peg didn't understand the sudden awkwardness.

"What aren't you telling me?" She eyed one aunt and then the
other, attempted to read their expressions. Peg had a feeling she
wasn't going to like the answer, but she hadn't reached out to be kept
in the dark. "Has Mom had these mental breaks before? Was she ever
institutionalized? I thought she might have been caught up in drugs
or prostitution, or even the mafia."

Rya snorted, and put her mug down.

"You have such a wild imagination," Eno said.

"Then tell me what you know. If there's something mentally
wrong with her, we can get help," she said. "Mom even started saying
that the people in Minerva hate her, so we can add paranoia to the
list of symptoms. I honestly didn't know she was this bad."

Aunt Eno considered her for a moment. "Why don't you believe
her claims about Athena?"

Peg scoffed and couldn't believe her aunt would ask such a silly
question.

"Because gods, goddesses and monsters of myth aren't real." Yet,
she couldn't help but remember the huge statues in the museum
chamber. How the door miraculously opened after a splinter made
her bleed. The tarnished coin. That there was a statue of Chrysa
and Sword in front of a multitude of others. But how could these
discoveries be answered with something as improbable as
mythology?

"What if they were?" Eno asked.

"Excuse me?"

Eno pressed an elbow against the table and rested her chin on her
hand. "What if all these things we've been raised to believe were
myths aren't stories, but true events about real people?"

"That's not possible." Peg shook her head. Figures from
mythology didn't have a place in the real world. The line between fact
and fiction was one she'd tried to keep firm in her mind since childhood. Even with the gloom always one step behind, and the power
she felt from her cards at her fingertips, she had to reject these

claims. The slow transformation of her hand was another concern, but she couldn't deal with that either.

Not in some strange mythological way.

"But what if it was?" Eno insisted.

"No, it can't be." *If everything is real, what does that mean for me? For Chrysa? For my entire family?* It was easier to reject these fantastical claims.

Eno sighed. "Did you actually see Athena?"

"No, I heard her talking to Mom. The only thing I've seen is a white owl. According to Mom, that's who the owl is. I'm expected to believe that a woman can transform into an owl and back again."

"Athena can transform into more than one animal," Rya said.

"That's great, Ry, but not very helpful right now."

She shrugged and turned back to her coffee.

"How much do you know about Greek mythology?" Eno asked.

"Quite a bit, since Mom read us all those stories instead of fairy tales," Peg said. "And she's got all those books Belle and I like to flick through."

"Then you know Athena is fond of cursing people, especially women." Eno's eyes darkened. "If she heard a rumor or deemed an action as a betrayal, she punished without consideration. This wrathful goddess was especially harsh on the ones who worshipped her." She paused. "Athena was feared for a reason."

"But this doesn't help—"

"You'd be surprised how much blame Athena has to bear," Eno interrupted.

"Understanding Athena's place in the pantheon isn't going to help Mom." Peg couldn't push the frustration aside, and the gloom returned.

Eno looked up.

Rya's eyes narrowed.

"You need to calm yourself," Eno said.

"What?" She couldn't control anything at the moment. All her thoughts were swirling around in a maelstrom.

"Your psychic energy might find an outlet in the cards, but it's not the only way it manifests." Eno was focused on the ceiling. "If you're not careful, you can turn all that power into something very dangerous. Something you won't be able to control once it reaches you."

Peg's pulse sped up. Could her aunties see the gloom too?

"How long has this been happening?" Rya asked.

"What?" She was struggling to voice a single thought.

Eno cocked an eyebrow. "The sweeping darkness, the night sky, whatever you want to call it."

"You can see the gloom?"

"You'd have to be blind not to," Rya said.

Peg shrugged. "The gloom's always been there, in the corner of my eye. But it's gotten worse since Chrysa..."

... *disappeared.*

... *vanished.*

... *faded.*

... *left me.*

"Take a deep breath." Her aunt's voice was soft and calming. "Now let it out, slowly. *Very* slowly."

Peg followed Eno's instructions.

"The way to keep the darkness at bay is to stay calm, don't let yourself get overwhelmed by the night sky." Eno's voice was soft, helped soothe Peg. "And you need to keep an open mind."

"I..."

"Stop closing yourself off because you're afraid of the truth," Eno said. "I know that a lot of what Ed tells you sounds farfetched, but calling her a liar isn't going to help matters."

"I don't call her a liar!"

"But you do," she said. "You just did it to me, when I tried to explain about Athena."

"That's not what I'm trying to do," Peg said, defeated. "To you, or to her."

"I know it's not, sweetie." Eno sighed. "But when you refuse to listen, and challenge every explanation, that's how it comes across."

How could she accept all of this? She shut her eyes for a second and when she opened them, the gloom was gone. As if it was never there.

"Paying attention and accepting the truth, no matter how fantastical it might seem, is the only way we're going to be able to overcome this hardship as a family." Eno's eyes filled with unshed tears. "You want to help your mother, right?

"Yes."

"And believe Chrysa will come back one day?"

She nodded, and said, "I heard her..."

... inside the monochrome woods.

... in my dreams.

... in my nightmares.

... if I listen hard enough.

"You did?" Rya asked.

"The other night, when Mom was in the barn screeching and a green light shot out from her eyes." Her mouth was suddenly dry, but she couldn't bring herself to grab her mug.

"Now I'm positive Athena had something to do with this," Eno added.

"What did Chrysa tell you?" Rya asked.

"She told me to get out of the woods."

"Holy fuck!" Eno stood and her heels clacked against the floor. "She can't be talking about the fabled place where the statues go to rest. I thought it was a myth." She wrung her hands as she paced. "But the bond between the twins must have connected them somehow. This changes everything."

"What do you mean?"

"It means that Chrysa isn't lost forever."

"But where is she, Aunt Eno?" Peg was numb with confusion.

"I don't know."

"None of us do." Rya added.

"But I believe you're the only one who can find her."

"I don't know how—"

"Listen to me, and listen hard." She raised her voice and it boomed inside the confines of the kitchen. "Pegasus, your sister is lost in a place no one knew existed until now. You've uncovered a mythical place that people have only written stories about."

"What good is it if I don't know where it is?" Spending a few seconds inside that cold and monochrome place hadn't provided an exact location.

"You might not know now, but if you're hearing Chrysa, there has to be a way to contact her," Rya said. "A way for you to find each other."

"How?"

"We'll figure it out. Together." Eno stared into her eyes. "That's what families do."

Peg nodded because she wanted to find her sister more than anything, but she was scared. So much about this conversation and the strange things that had been happening inside and outside this house seemed improbable. But she was determined.

"I'm going to find her," she said with a nod.

"Yes, you will, because you're the key," Eno said.

CHAPTER FIFTEEN

"RISE AND SHINE, SLEEPING BEAUTY." AUNTIE ENO PULLED THE COVERS off Mom while Auntie Rya slid the curtains open.

Sunlight added warm light and coziness to the room.

Peg's mind filled with childhood visions of Chrysa and her charging into their mother's bedroom on weekends. How they'd jump on her bed until she woke up laughing and Sword would bark and wag his tail at the display. Mom would tickle the two girls until the twins were an exhausted giggling bundle, and both fell asleep for a few more hours with the dog at the end of the bed. Usually waking after midday, the family would trek downstairs and Mom would make a hearty country breakfast to keep their bellies full until dinner.

"I don't want to," Mom protested. Her words were slurred by sleep and she was curled into the fetal position. The blindfold still covered her eyes.

"Yeah, well, that's too bad." Eno shook her sister's shoulders. "We didn't travel halfway across the country to watch you sleep. We've got things to talk about, stuff to sort through."

"Halfway across the country?" she mumbled into her pillow. The blindfold slipped from one eye.

"Yes, we crossed more stateliness in one day than we've crossed in all our time in this country," Rya said.

"So, it's time for you to behave like an adult again and welcome your sisters," Eno added.

Mom sat up, quickly. "Eno? Rya?" She yanked the blindfold down completely, gripping the scrap of fabric around her neck. "What are you doing here?"

"Your daughter, our very concerned niece, called us." Eno shook her head, and was staring at her youngest sister with a combination of sadness and anger. "She shouldn't have to turn to us for help. Not when she's got a mother who can answer every one of her many questions."

"I can't help anyone with anything."

Peg rolled her eyes. At least she was consistent—acting like a defeated damsel.

"Oh yeah?" Eno sat on the edge of the bed and pushed the knotted strands of her sister's uneven hair behind her ear. "What if I told you that Chrysa is still alive, and we know who can help us get her back?"

"What?" Mom toyed with the blindfold, using it like the lifeline it wasn't.

Eno glanced at the fabric, but didn't comment. "Chrysa isn't dead, she's lost and has reached out to the only person who can find her."

"Who's that?" Her eyes were shiny with tears.

"Your other daughter, of course," Eno said.

Mom turned to stare at Peg as tears slid down her face. The guilt in her stare was so raw that Peg had to look away. She couldn't bear the pain burning in her mother's eyes.

"Sorry about..." Mom whispered.

Peg absently reached for her cheek and shrugged.

"It's good to see you!" Mom turned to her sister and threw her arms around Eno. "You have no idea how much I've missed you both." She reached a hand out and her other sister stepped closer to take it. "We need to get together more often."

"I know, but it's hard sometimes," Eno said.

"Especially when you always have a new wedding and honey-moon to plan for." Mom released Rya's hand and untangled herself from Eno. "Have you set your sights on any new unsuspecting grooms yet? Anyone special waiting on the horizon?"

She winked. "I might have my eye on someone."

"Make that a few horizons," Rya said with a shake of her head.

"You really have to leave some for the rest of us," Mom said.

Peg couldn't remember her mother ever showing an ounce of interest in anyone. Couldn't even recall her going on a single date. Chrysa asked her about her lack of a social life a few years back, but Mom shrugged and claimed she had plenty of time to do that when the girls were grown up.

"Don't you worry. There are plenty of fish in the sea. And you should really be trying to catch one for yourself." Eno patted Ed's arm in the loving way only siblings could do.

Peg missed Chrysa all over again. The loss manifested as a deep piercing pain inside her chest.

"I caught the biggest fish in the sea, and he betrayed me." Mom's smile was sad. "But he did give me two wonderful daughters." Her smile turned to Peg. "Tell me more about Chrysa and Peg."

Peg wanted to know more about this *biggest fish*. Who was he? And why didn't Mom talk about him? Her mother always avoided questions and didn't even provide a name. She was almost eighteen and still didn't know who her father was.

"Peg heard Chrysa the other night."

"I know." Mom's eyes were huge and she was on her knees like an expectant child waiting to hear their favorite story. "But how can that be?"

"You lost control of your power and nearly sent her to the same place," Rya said with a tsk. "That's how it happened."

"No, I..."

"It's okay, Ed." Aunt Eno exchanged a sympathetic glance with Peg. "Because your mistake opened a pathway between the twins."

"I didn't mean to..."

Peg's pulse sped up. She'd seen this obsessive behavior enough times to know losing her was inevitable. Mom would put all focus on the negative and not hear anything else.

"We know you didn't." Rya stepped closer, shadowing Eno.

"I didn't want to hurt her." Mom started rocking back and forth.

"You didn't," Eno said.

"This is what she does whenever I remind her of Chrysa," Peg said. "She eventually shuts down and will rock herself to sleep."

"Not on our watch." Eno grabbed Mom's hands. "Listen to me, Ed. Chrysa isn't dead, she's lost."

"But—"

"We just need to find her."

"But Eno, she's gone forever. We can't find her." Mom shook her head. "It's what happens to all of them."

"*We* might not be able to find her, but I'm sure Peg can." Eno's voice was soft, calming the wretched mood in the room with her demeanor.

"How?" Mom's teeth were chattering. "Hearing Chrysa and finding her are two very different things."

"I didn't think she was this bad," Rya whispered. "We should've come sooner."

Eno gave Peg a sympathetic look and it made Peg's eyes fill with tears.

"We're going to help you get her back." Eno closed the distance further, with both hands still clutching her sister's.

Ed opened her eyes and stopped shaking. Streaks of tears glistened in the sun and it tore Peg's heart in two. Her mother resembled one of those filthy, possessed girls in horror movies—stringy uneven hair, bald patches, sweat-stained nightshirt, gaunt face. It was a horrifying sight.

"We need to talk this through and include your daughter for once. You haven't been honest with her," Eno said. "I know you were doing it to keep her safe. You thought that the less the twins knew, the safer they would be. Well, it didn't work out that way, did it? You've lost one and the other is struggling to understand what's going on."

"It was Athena's idea to keep the twins in the dark, wasn't it?"

Rya's voice carried from across the room because she'd wandered away from her sisters. Peg watched as her aunt stopped in the exact spot where a two-sided mirror used to stand.

Mom nodded. "She said it was best to bind all of their past memories."

"Well, she was wrong," Rya said.

"What you should've done is slowly introduce the girls into the reality of who they are, and where we all come from," Eno added.

"I tried, many times... I told them all the stories." Peg's mom met her eyes.

"You told them stories the two believed to be just that, without once mentioning *they* were some of the players—that we all are." Eno shook her head, frustration evident in her tone.

Her auntie's words made the back of Peg's shoulders itch, just like when she stepped into the statue chamber. She turned away, intending to head for the bathroom to grab the hand-mirror she thought she'd seen in there.

"I didn't want to scare the girls," her mother said.

"You, of all people, should know to never underestimate the strength of girls," Eno said. "We can bear the weight of this world."

"Always have," Rya added.

Peg slowly made her way toward the connected bathroom. She didn't want to interrupt the ongoing conversation. When the sun's rays glossed over the closet, her gaze snagged on the half-open door. *What's that inside?*

As she neared, Peg frowned. She tried to make heads or tails out of what was inside.

"I know that," her mother continued. "But when I confided in Athena, she thought it was best to let Chrysa and Peggy live their lives like mere mortals."

"But they're not," Eno said.

"You should've spoken to us about this," Rya added. "Athena isn't the most trustworthy goddess."

Peg edged closer to the closet. While her mother was concentrating on the aunts, she closed the distance and took a peek. Her heart skipped a beat.

The way the sun was shining on the hidden object in her mother's closet revealed exactly what it was—or who. She'd noticed him checking her out enough times to recognize the curve of his wide shoulders, the way his hair was styled, all the way down to his sneakered feet. This was a statue of Ira Danae.

He was frozen in time, like Chrysa. Who made this? And why was it here?

Mr. Danae's accusation shot through her mind. He'd asked her about his son, claimed he would find out the truth one way or another. At the time, Peg had no clue why he was asking *her,* or what possessed him to think she would know anything about Ira's whereabouts. *What does that teacher know that I don't?*

Her head was pounding and she wished she'd never spotted this statue. The throbbing in her temples was loud, and she hadn't realized the conversation had stopped. Silence filled the room. Sweat beaded down her back, and her shoulders itched so much she wanted to tear her skin open.

Peg spun around to face the bedroom and found all three sisters watching her with such intensity, her skin crawled. She fumbled to say something to break the awkward silence, but struggled to come up with anything worth voicing.

Mom, Eno and Rya stood motionless.

When did her mother get off the bed? Wasn't Aunt Eno sitting on the bed consoling her while Rya looked around the room? And why were all three looking at her like that? She opened her mouth, but still nothing came out.

The three advanced together, seemed to glide instead of walk. The gloom curled along the walls behind them, crawling faster than usual.

What did her aunt tell her earlier? She had to calm down, don't let the obscurity reach her or something bad would happen. That was it, right?

She took a slow breath, but struggled on the exhale when the three women she'd known all of her life morphed before her eyes.

Mom stood between her older sisters and her skin shimmered, a new layer of emerald scales chased over her pale skin. Her hair grew longer and the strands were replaced with actual hissing snakes. Eno was on the left and deep blue iridescent scales spilled over her skin until she was covered from head to toe, and wore a crown of multi-colored serpents. Rya's legs joined to become one thick tail as scales took over her body too, and more snakes joined this horror show.

All had glowing eyes—blue, green, blue.

"No," Peg whispered. "This isn't happening." But it was. The time of denial was over.

The three women wore hissing serpents on their heads.

Peg dashed for the bathroom. She slammed the door shut and flipped the lock, before taking several steps back. She didn't take her eyes off the flimsy barrier. What was going on? Had she really found the statue of one of her classmates hiding in her mother's closet? And were there three snake-women standing in place of the mother and aunts she'd been talking to only minutes ago? The women trying to make her understand myths and legends were real? The same ones who'd insisted a goddess able to shift into an owl was a frequent visitor to their barn?

When something slammed against the door, she jumped. A gasp escaped her, and she felt like a foolish child.

"Pegasus, open the door." That sounded like her mother's voice, but she couldn't trust her ears. Not when her eyes were obviously deceiving her.

"There's no need to be scared," Eno said.

"Come out here," Rya added.

Had Peg really imagined her family turning into scaly reptilians? *What are they—Sirens, Lamia, Echidna?* The answer was skating her mind, but the sudden pain stopped her from making the connection.

She winced, pressed both hands against her temples while trying to quiet the turmoil inside her skull. She'd always wanted answers to her many questions, but now she wasn't sure if she was ready for the truth.

Another knock, much louder this time.

"Come out, we're not going to hurt you." Yet, the way the three sisters spoke in unison turned her blood to ice.

Peg took shallow breaths and was about to switch on the light when she decided she didn't need it because she could see well enough. A slithering sensation around her ankles made her gasp.

There's no need to be scared. This was definitely the snake she'd spoken to in the kitchen. *You need to remember who they are as much as who you and your sister are.*

"I can't!" She was determined to cling to denial for as long as she could. "I won't!"

The knocking continued, much louder.

A wave of dizziness swept through her, so she reached for the vanity. It helped keep her upright, but her hand also found the hand-mirror.

Peg wrapped her fingers around the bright handle and couldn't remember ever seeing this before. Where did her mother find this antique mirror? The disturbing feel of snakes sliding over her feet made her take a step sideways and she caught the shimmer of the mirror.

She'd expected to find her reflection, but instead found trees and fog. Peg had only seen this once before, but it was etched inside her brain. She angled the mirror and focused on the trees. Wide black trunks were everywhere, spreading to menacing branches. A thick fog rolled around the bottoms, twisted all the way to the top. She noticed something else—something moving in the distance, to the right.

Her heart sped up when a hooded face appeared. She shrieked and dropped the mirror.

Fuck.

The last thing she needed was seven years bad luck. Didn't she have enough of that already? Peg kneeled, picked up the mirror and found the tiled floor was obscured by a multitude of shadowy snakes.

She couldn't see the white tiles beneath because there were so many. Were these the snakes she'd felt earlier? The ones coiled under the kitchen table? She shook a few off the mirror's surface.

At least it didn't break.

Her heart was beating fast when she raised the hand-mirror in front of her. How could a mirror be a window to some other place? The scene was now static, like a picture. Trees, fog and more trees, but nothing shifted.

The pounding on the door had become a murmur to this new madness, hardly registering. Shadowy snakes slid over her hands and made her skin crawl. She rose to her feet and the mirror slipped from her grasp when she faced the wall and found the bathroom mirror exposed. The tape she'd used to cover the surface hung in torn uneven strips, revealing enough to see who was there.

"Chrysa."

She raised her left hand to the cold surface and a cool mist curled around her fingers, snuck under the woolen glove until it was sucked into her stone palm.

The slithering snakes rose up her leg.

The door exploded behind her.

But Peg didn't break eye contact with her sister.

IN THE BLUR

"Bait."

"You're bait."

"Bait."

Chrysa refused to become bait.

"Rest."

"You need to rest."

"Rest."

Chrysa refused to rest.

"Sleep."

"Sleep is the only way."

"Sleep."

Chrysa refused to give into the sleep threatening to drag her down.

The endless whispering cycle stabbed into her brain like a thousand splinters. Splinters capable of tearing her apart, from the inside out if she let them. She knew she wasn't back in stasis, but her mind was still at risk of being overtaken. And she wasn't going to allow that to happen.

"Get out of my head!" Ira yelled beside her.

"Whatever you... do... don't. Fall. Asleep," Lovey called out to him, or to Chrysa, or maybe to anyone who could hear her. But she sounded a lot weaker.

How are we going to get out of this?

Chrysa refused to give in.

It wasn't just Lovey's instructions that pushed her to fight back. This was the stubborn streak she'd always embraced. How many times had she had a fight with her sister because she'd refused to admit she was wrong? How many times had Cal ended up apologizing after a silly argument because she'd refused to?

At least, for once in her life, the refusal to give up or give in might actually pay off.

Chrysa shut her eyes tightly, until all she could see were explosions of color. Instead of being annoyed or worried, she concentrated on how these small fireworks exploded in what could easily be the night sky.

She would *not* fall asleep.

She refused to slip into the safe and warm place the voices were telling her to fall into.

She refused to lose control again.

Had Chrysa been stuck in this damn place weeks, months or years? She didn't know, but would never forget how awful it felt to sink from one incoherent dream into another. She would never let reality get out of reach again. Or allow dreams to become her only reality.

She wasn't going to fall back into nightmares.

"Chrysa, don't you... dare... fall asleep." Lovey's voice sounded thinner.

"I'm not," she whispered.

"Open your eyes," Ira said.

"I don't need to open my eyes to stay awake." Did they think she was sinking into unconsciousness? They were both wrong.

Her eyes filled with bursts of yellow and blue, white and pink, green.

Chrysa's heart skipped a beat.

Green. There's something dangerous about the color green.

She couldn't remember why, but knew it was somehow attached to how she ended up in blur. Lovey and Ira knew how she'd gotten here. Both pointed a finger at her mother. Claimed her mom was responsible for this place, and for Chrysa's captivity by these monsters. But how was that possible? Mom was just an average woman who didn't have any connection to gods and goddesses. Not in the way Lovey kept implying. And she wasn't evil, not like Ira told her from the beginning.

Chrysa refused to accept her family's part in any of this.

All she had to do now was stay awake. Keep her eyes closed so she couldn't see the horrors trying to pull her under.

Stay awake, awake... *awake.*

She shook herself before it was too late. Before she slipped away completely. Before the veiled could reclaim her.

Chrysa flexed her fingers, tried to get the blood flowing again.

She tried to stay conscious and aware, but it was getting harder.

Her body felt rigid, and the sharp roots digging into her skin were slowly tearing the fabric of her clothes. Some of the sharpest points had already broken through, and she could feel the tips burrowing like parasites into her body. Trickles of blood made her shudder.

She felt useless.

"I need to stay strong." The whisper slid between her lips.

I need to get home.

How much time had ticked over at the farmhouse?

"You're not strong enough."

She clenched her jaw. "Yes, I am."

"You're bait."

She gritted her teeth. "No, I'm not."

"You are."

She wanted to hurt someone. "I'm going home."

"You are home."

Chrysa attempted to shake her head and entangled her hair in the roots instead. "This is not my home."

"You are bait."

"Who am I bait for?" she screamed. Her voice shook the leaves high in the trees.

"Don't scream," Lovey said. "Or more will... come."

"How many are there?" Frustrated tears pushed past Chrysa's closed eyelids.

"Countless... she's been doing this... for a long... time."

It was on the tip of her tongue, to ask who. But she didn't. Didn't dare, because in her heart she already knew the answer. These two had already told her, but she couldn't bring herself to accept such a horrid truth about a woman she'd loved since birth.

"Chrysa."

The voice was so unexpected, so familiar that her eyes snapped open.

She blinked away the tears and glared past the faceless horrors hovering around the cages. These freaks were focused on her that their forms wavered. The veiled were using all of their energy to keep the trio stuck in this position.

Chrysa heard her name again.

Her vision cleared and in her prone position, past the shrouded figures of her tormentors, the sky above was filled with her sister's face. She was looking right at her. It didn't make any sense, because Chrysa could see her.

"Peggy?" The name made her heart beat in a way she hadn't felt before inside this wretched place. Was it a shudder of hope, or despair? Both, she suspected.

"Where are you?"

"I'm trapped," Chrysa whispered. Cleared her throat and added, "I'm lost."

Peggy's eyes were wide and she raised a hand.

Where was her sister? How could they see each other?

"What are you doing inside the mirror?" Peggy asked.

Inside the mirror? She tried to shake her head, again forgetting she could barely move an inch in either direction. "I'm in the blur."

"Where?" Peggy asked.

"In the forest..."

"On the other side... of the... statues." Lovey's whisper was barely there but she heard her.

"Who said that?"

"Peggy, you have to find me—us."

"I will."

"Please," she cried. "Before it's too late."

Peggy pressed a hand against the sky and the world above quivered like water. *"How do I find you?"*

"Mirrors," Lovey said.

"What do you mean by mirrors?" Chrysa asked. "Lovey, does that make sense to you?"

"Lovey?" Peggy echoed.

"Yeah, she's here and so is some guy called Ira."

Peggy's hand remained pressed against the sky and her eyes widened as if she was in pain.

"What's wrong?"

"Nothing," Peggy said. *"I'll find you."*

Chrysa knew her sister was lying. How could anyone find her in this improbable blur after all this time? But she didn't question her.

The veiled multiplied, closing in fast, trying to block the sky while stealing her breath.

"Chrysa, I can't see you!"

"I'm still here."

"Damnit, where are you?" Peggy leaned forward and a thunderous crash filled the forest.

And just like that, her sister disappeared.

The sky fell, crashing down in fragments.

As the pieces rained down around her, Chrysa felt an array of stings where the pinpricks caught her skin. The veiled contorted, folded into themselves as their pained shrieks surpassed the uproar of the shattering heavens.

The raining jagged pieces hacked at the roots that formed the cages until the wood creaked.

Chrysa wanted to be free, but not this way and not from this height.

She tumbled through the air, reaching out for the spot where her sister had been only seconds ago. Vertigo engulfed her as she plummeted with the veiled robes that were now nothing but floating, scattered fabric.

Chrysa was falling amongst ghosts.

CHAPTER SIXTEEN

"CHRYSA, I CAN'T SEE YOU!" A COMBINATION OF PANIC AND ELATION tied Peg's stomach in a tangle of knots.

"I'm here." Chrysa's voice sounded soft, pained.

"Damnit, where are you?" Peg leaned closer to the bathroom mirror. Although the edges were still filled with trees and fog, the scene in the middle was concealed and she couldn't make out what was hiding her sister from view.

She couldn't see her anymore, which was both a good and bad thing. A good thing because she didn't have to see her trapped inside some weird looking cell. A bad thing because the connection had been severed.

The broken door was lying halfway into the shower cubicle, blocking off her mother and aunts. But she could hear the screeching and hissing, the trio were trying to shove the block of wood out of their path.

Something slithered up her legs and torso, wound around her stomach.

The surface in front of her was getting misty, but it wasn't from this side.

"No! Chrysa, where are you?"

Peg smashed her left hand against the bathroom mirror. The reflective surface shattered into smithereens when her stony palm slammed into it. Some shards sliced her face and hands, but most ended up on the countertop, sink and floor.

A sob crept up Peg's throat as a snake slithered around her neck, causing a wave of weakness to wash through her body and slowly paralyze her limbs.

Grab the mirror.

"What mirror?" She stared at the sharp pieces, her mind not seeing past the destruction she'd caused with her damaged hand.

Peg was surprised when her fingers curled around the snake hugging her neck.

Fighting against me is futile.

"Then get off me!"

I've got to make sure you remember. And this is the only way. The snake's head was directly in front of her eyes, the cold orbs piercing deep into her soul like the jewels on her bracelet. *Grab the hand-mirror.*

"Why?"

Stop fighting me as hard as you fight the truth, and listen. You're going to need that if you want to keep track of where she is.

"I don't—"

You have to trust me.

"Why should I?" Everyone else was concealing truths, keeping secrets and dishing out small doses that didn't amount to anything. How could she trust a shadowy snake?

Because you want to know the truth, and I can give it to you.

"How?"

I can show you all of it.

"Can you do it without strangling me?"

This is the only way.

She shoved the mirror into her back pocket, concealing it between jeans and hoodie.

"Who are you?"

Someone who's going to guide you.

"How are you going to guide me?"

By making you remember.

The snake slithered along the side of her neck before slipping into her ear. She howled in pain. The length of the sleek body slid down her eardrum and she felt every excruciating inch before the creature burrowed into her brain.

She doubled over. Her fingers clenched around the edge of the vanity even though she wanted to stop the warm trickle from her ears. Shards of glass were embedded into her woolen gloves, some tearing her right hand.

"Get out of there." She let go and slapped her ear with the hard surface of her left palm.

"What's happening to her?" someone asked.

"I don't know, but she made a mess."

"What's happening to my daughter?"

Mom!

But wasn't she some hideous beast with snakes for hair and glistening eyes? They all were—the trio of freaks. Her relatives were monsters, which made her one too. Otherwise, how could she have seen her sister inside a mirror as if she were looking out a window? And then her stupid stone palm went and wrecked everything by smashing it to pieces. Had she ended up hurting Chrysa instead of helping?

She'd promised to find her but still had no clue where she was.

No, that wasn't true, she was lost in the ghostly woods. *On the other side of the statues* was what Lovey had said. Lovey, who was apparently there too, with Ira. The guy who was a statue inside her mother's closet. None of this made any sense.

It will soon.

The whisper inside her head made her flinch, so she stopped pounding against her ear.

"Peg, sweetie, step away from the broken mirror."

She made a move to turn, but at the last second faltered. Her feet slipped on the scattered shards and she couldn't remember if she was wearing socks or shoes. She slipped and landed on her back. The air gushed out of her. Her spine took the impact seconds before the back of her head.

"Oh, my goddess, is she okay?"

Peg blinked and saw Eno standing above her.

"She's still breathing."

Peg blinked and saw Rya there too.

"What's happening to my baby? Why is her ear bleeding?"

Peg blinked and found Mom.

The three were looking down at her.

"You're not snake-women anymore," she said, but outside her head the words were nothing but a garbled mess. Was she choking on her own blood? Had the snake lied and was killing her?

No, you're choking on your memories, the snake whispered. *The real ones. The ones you've been missing, neglecting, and will never doubt again.*

The sudden surge of pain was tremendous. Peg's eyes rolled into the back of her head and the three Ceto women faded away.

Remember...

A scalding sensation flowed through her body, made her fingertips buzz and her shoulders itch until the pressure exploded out of her chest. A powerful shockwave spread from the Ceto property and into every corner of Minerva.

For the first time, she was awakened and understood the truth entirely.

No more denying the obvious.

I am Pegasus.

Daughter of the Stone Maiden, Medusa.

Sister of the Golden Warrior, Chrysaor.

Niece of the ferocious Gorgons, Stheno and Euryale.

Eternal companion of the heroic, Bellerophon.

CHAPTER SEVENTEEN

CONSCIOUSNESS RETURNED PAINFULLY SLOW. ALONG THE WAY, PEG revisited the many non-linear lives she'd inhabited. Starting with her mother's initial tragedy, and followed by the shocking revelation that every person in her life had existed countless of times in this human world, as both past and future versions of themselves.

Her brain skated over a myriad of memories, until her eyelids flickered. At first, her vision was veiled, and for a horrifying instant she wondered if knowledge had come at the expense of her eyesight. But several frantic blinks later, the familiar ceiling took shape.

The gloom was coiling around the edges, waiting to drip down the pale walls.

Send the night sky away. The whisper was accompanied by a sting on her leg.

She sat up in bed and rolled the hem of her jeans over her left ankle, where she found an identical version of the coiled snake tattoo her mother and aunties all wore in the same spot. One of Medusa's spectral serpents had initiated her road to recollection by drilling into Peg's brain, and now she was marked. She was finally a member of their club.

A very freaky club.

Peg still couldn't believe her mother was Medusa. The beautiful maiden cursed to become a hideous monster whose deadly stare was forever feared by men. Yet another woman tormented for sins she didn't commit but carried for a man.

She'd never considered herself or her family to be normal, but this was a hell of a lot more than she'd ever expected. Though it did explain a lot of things she'd taken for granted, hadn't noticed or escaped her attention.

We're mortals with an endless cycle of lives that always end the same way.

Her heart dropped, because she finally understood what was going on. How Chrysa's disappearance had sparked a chain of events that would lead to the end of this cycle.

But I'm not ready to move on.

Their creation began with betrayal, ended in tragedy and propelled everyone on a never-ending cosmic existence guaranteed to lead to the same *unhappily ever after*. A reality she didn't want to face yet. Not when it felt like things were just getting started. Besides, she wasn't going anywhere until she got her sister back.

The truth might be depressing, but she was determined to face whatever came their way head-on. The time for confusion and denial was over.

Night had completely engulfed the ceiling, was dripping down the walls and had nearly reached her feet. The gloom obscured most of the room and was creeping too close for comfort, but she knew how to deal with it now.

"I'm not ready for you yet." She finally understood what the gloom really was, and she wasn't prepared to accept her ultimate fate.

Peg closed her eyes to the gloom's oily fingers slinking over her skin. She willed the searching darkness to recede back into the night sky, where it belonged. When she snapped them open, her bedroom was back to normal. Everything was back in place and her ultimate destination to become a constellation was completely gone.

The sky would never stop searching for Pegasus, but she could keep it at bay.

She raised her hands and noticed cuts on her right hand from the mirror she'd shattered inside her mother's bathroom. Her left wasn't damaged because most had already turned to stone.

Her back was also sore and something was stabbing into the base of her spine.

When she reached back and pulled out the small mirror, she gasped. She'd stuffed it into her jeans, and although the pearl handle had snapped off completely—which was what had stabbed into her skin—the surface remained intact.

Peg's heart raced as she prepared to peek into the mirror. The forest was quiet. Static. Foggy. It could be a painting instead of a mirror that served as a window. How could she use this to find her way to Chrysa?

Her thoughts and memories tangled together. How had she survived so many varied lives all over history, and forgotten about them until now? *Athena.* Of course. The binding Mom mentioned several times was what kept Peg and Chrysa's brain separated from the horrors of their true existence and past lives.

She sighed because something else dawned on her. She hadn't hidden or covered the mirrors inside this house because her mother might attempt to slash her wrists to cut away the agony of loss. She'd suspected that would happen because she'd been looking at the situation through human eyes, but even then, her subconscious knew Mom might attempt to turn herself to stone by staring at her reflection.

A piercing pain tore through her brain and Peg was suddenly somewhere else.

Her mother runs back to the house after turning Chrysa to stone. Peg ran after her and ends up in her bedroom. Mom stands in front of the swiveling two-sided mirror. Her eyes are shimmery, a green beam starts up. She howls in pain when the color intensifies.

Peg shoves her out of the way before the reflection changes her.

She coaxes her sobbing mother back to bed and covers her eyes with a bandana sitting on the bedside table. The one Mom uses to hold her hair away when she deals with rusty things.

Peg falls asleep beside her because she doesn't want to leave her alone.

The next day, all Peg can remember is that Chrysa disappeared, and that her mother is so lost in grief she has given up on life, is borderline suicidal, and refuses to function.

"How could I forget all that?" The sound of her own voice shocked her out of the disturbing reverie. Mom tried to destroy herself with her own reflection, because while Medusa's stare couldn't hurt others via a reflective surface, it would destroy her. Mom knew this, and had been prepared to terminate herself and possibly everyone tied to her.

A selfish act of grief.

Peg considered the small mirror in her hand. Mirrors were the answer, but now that the only large mirror left in the house was smashed, she knew she had to go to the ones she'd stored—hidden—in the barn.

She jumped off the bed but paused when she got to her feet because both of her hands were exposed. A detail she'd noticed minutes ago but didn't even think about until now. The stony surface of her palm was spreading and now engulfed her knuckles. Her thumb was covered up to the bottom of her nail. The back of her hand showed traces of gray. Would the stone eventually extend all over her body? And if it did, what did *that* mean?

None of her recovered memories helped solve this mystery.

A ding caught her attention and she grabbed her phone sitting on the bedside table. There were several unread texts. All from Belle.

OMFG PEG I REMEMBER EVERYTHING!!!!! <3

And?

need to cu

She considered what to say because as much as she wanted to see Belle, there was too much going on at the moment.

Can you come over tomorrow?

4sure xxx

XXX

She pocketed her phone, packed an extra deck of cards in her pocket and tiptoed to the closed bedroom door. When she couldn't hear anyone outside, she ducked out. Taking very small and quiet steps, she made her way across the hallway and peeked into her mother's room.

Peg didn't dare go inside to check the closet or the bathroom, only wanted to see if her family was there. But the bedroom was empty.

Staying close to the wall, she descended the stairs and didn't find anyone in the living room, or the kitchen. She wasn't sure where Mom, Eno and Rya might have gone, but was glad they weren't around.

She opened the back door and snuck outside.

The night air was cool against her face, but she welcomed the sensation on her heated skin. She stepped into her boots and fast-walked across the long grass, slipped into the relative safety of the barn. With eyes narrowed, she checked the eaves and the tops of the shelves for any sign of the owl. But the snowy bird was nowhere to be seen. Did she know what had happened in the house earlier? Surely Athena would know when one of her bindings was severed.

A crash in one of the aisles made her freeze, her breath quicken.

Maybe the owl is here, after all.

It took her a moment to regain her courage before stepping between the shelves to head toward the noise. No matter what her past had revealed, her family's demise was always one step away. She snuck glances all around, expected the owl to have knocked over a rusty ornament as its claws landed on the top of the shelving.

When her shins knocked into something and she lost her balance, shock flowed through her. Peg stumbled, hit the metal shelf on the other side and sent a bunch of vintage cans crashing to the ground. The sound ravaged the silence she needed. Still, she'd managed to stay on her feet and when she looked down, found Eve cowering at her feet.

"What the hell are *you* doing here?"

She didn't respond, only covered her head with her hands.

"Eve, what are you doing here?"

"I, uh, I was looking around for..."

"What are you hoping to find in *our* barn?"

"Uh..." Her hair was in a ponytail but the elastic was struggling to hold the curls.

"Is that the best you can do?" Peg crossed her arms. "It's the middle of the night, on a weekend. What are you doing on our property, rummaging through our things?"

"I wasn't trying to steal anything, I promise."

"Then what *are* you doing?" Eve was the last person Peg had expected to find in here, because she didn't fit into any of her rediscovered memories.

"I'm looking for something."

She shook her head. "I thought we already established that whatever it is you're looking for, you're not going to—"

"But I have to!"

"What is this mysterious thing you're looking for, anyway?"

Eve's hazel eyes were glossy in the dark and she seemed close to tears. Whatever she wanted to find must be gnawing at her day and night. On some level, Peg understood what this girl was going through, but to break into someone else's property was pathetic. Was Eve the reason her mother went crazy the other night because of an intruder? Mom also mentioned the hunter—*heroes*—the ones Peg now understood would forever pursue their kind. She was well aware of who would be hunting Medusa, but hadn't been able to identify who Perseus was in this town yet. And that baffled her.

She surveyed the girl she hardly knew. Eve was annoying as hell and started loitering around as soon as she came to their school and was suddenly everywhere, always hounding Peg to read her cards. What if her intentions weren't pure? What if *she* was the one hunter?

"Well, what is it?" Peg asked.

"Okay." Eve licked her lips, pouted. "I've already told you I'm looking for someone."

Someone? Thought it was something.

Peg's heart sped up. "Oh yeah, and who did you expect to find in our barn?"

"I..." She shook her head and the apple charm she was wearing sparkled.

"I think you better leave before I call the police."

"But I'm on a very important mission. It's why I traveled halfway across the world to come to this shitty town in the middle of nowhere."

Peg stepped closer. "And when you find whatever, or whoever, it is you're looking for, what do you intend to do?"

"What do you mean?"

"Are you going to kill them?"

"Kill them?" Eve sputtered and her eyes widened. "Why would I do that?"

"Isn't that why you're here, *Perseus*?" She added pressure to the name. The one she'd had such a hard time spitting out in class because of reasons she hadn't understood then, but fully realized now. This girl, with her smooth brown skin and cute curls could be the one trying to jeopardize everything.

"Don't come any closer," Eve said.

"Why, are you going to stab me?"

"No!" Eve appeared shocked. "Will you stop talking about killing and stabbing? I don't want to kill anyone."

"Then what *do* you want?"

"Pegasus, are you in here?"

"Damn." *Talk about bad timing.*

Eve's annoying charm was glowing. "Your name is short for Pegasus?"

Embarrassment chased up Peg's neck and face, warming her skin. She'd always hated her full name and sought comfort in Peg being such an average version of an otherwise jarring given name. Little had she known that the answer to all of her questions had been in front of her all along.

"So, what if it is?" she said with a scowl.

Eve smiled. "I knew I was right!"

"Peg?"

"Yeah, I'm here, Aunt Eno!" She headed for the end of the aisle and popped her head around the side.

"I need to speak to you," she called from the open barn door.

"Okay." Peg had to get rid of Eve, and quickly. But when she turned to tell the girl to get the hell out before her aunt saw her, she was already gone. She couldn't worry about her now, she had to deal with her aunt.

Peg headed down the aisle and kept her eyes on the woman who was now back to being her attractive human self, and not the monster Gorgon from mythology. Aunt Widow had changed into a lowcut black sweater and tight faded jeans tucked into heeled boots.

"There you are," Eno said with a soft smile. "I've been looking everywhere for you. I was worried."

"I needed some air." Peg avoided meeting her gaze. After all, she now knew her stone hand was a side effect of staring directly into her mother's eyes.

"I don't blame you. After what you went through, it's under-standable."

"How's Mom?" Even now, she couldn't help but worry about her, wonder if she'd freaked out and lost it when she found her daughter collapsed in the bathroom full of mirror shards, spectral snakes and blood.

"She's okay," Eno answered with a sigh. "She wanted to see if you were here, but I told her it might be best if I checked."

"Oh, yeah, why's that?"

Aunt Eno paused under a shaft of moonlight and an ethereal glow made her skin shimmer, illuminated the scales beneath the surface of her skin. "I know how confusing this might seem to you. You're angry about all the secrets, and probably with us too, but she —we—didn't do any of this on purpose."

"I know, you did it to protect me." She kicked at the dusty floor. "To protect *us*."

"Everything Ed does is to protect those she loves," Eno said. "You need to remember that."

Peg met her aunt's blue eyes. "I know everything now."

"And it's about time." The smile twisting the side of her mouth was cunning, maybe even a little wicked.

"It doesn't change the fact you freaked me out, though," Peg said with a nervous laugh. "I wasn't expecting that transformation." Or her own, really.

"I'm sorry, that wasn't our intention, but when you discovered the statue in the closet... we couldn't stop our *reaction*." She was quiet for a moment. "Peg, what happened in the bathroom? It was more than getting your memories back, wasn't it?"

Peg took a shallow breath and when she exhaled, it came out shaky. "I saw Chrysa in the mirror and then shattered it with this." She held up her stony left hand.

"Oh."

She couldn't help but smile. "Yeah."

"So, you've got the tattoo now, right?"

"I do."

Eno's eyes sparkled. "And how are you coping with everything?"

"Well, I'm out here hoping to run into Athena and I'm still determined to find Chrysa, so not too bad." The sudden weight of the Medusa coin in her pocket calmed her. "I just don't know what's going to happen next."

"What happened to Chrysa has never happened before and now that the cycle is nearing its end..."

"I know." The thought of everything she knew ending terrified Peg. She wondered what would happen if she didn't get Chrysa back in time.

"You're the only one who can get her back." Eno frowned and nibbled on her thumb. "But hold on, let's back up a bit. What do you mean you saw her in the mirror?"

Peg pulled out the broken frame and showed her. "I saw where Chrysa is in here, and then spotted her in the bathroom mirror too."

Aunt Eno bent closer and her eyes widened as she inspected the surface. When she jumped, Peg knew one of those cloaked creatures must have appeared.

"What—or where—*is* this?"

"I don't know, but I found this mirror in Mom's bathroom. And she's not supposed to have access to any mirrors."

"Athena must be responsible." She shook her head in disgust. "Her magic is turning a darker shade with every new cycle."

A glowing owl swooped from the ceiling, her wings vanished as quickly as her beak and she grew taller. One second, she was a snowy hooting bird, the next a beautiful woman with honey-colored hair, wearing a white dress with gold trimming. A golden breastplate protected her torso, she had a matching helmet on her head, and a lance and shield clipped to her back.

"Good to see you, Stheno," Athena said.

"Wish I could say the same to this unpleasant surprise." Eno didn't hide her distaste.

"You always were the comedian of the trio."

Peg recognized the voice. This was definitely the woman her mother had spoken to the other night.

"We're not a band, or a group for you to toy with," Eno spat.

"I don't and never have toyed with anyone. I helped your sister keep her children safe," Athena said with a self-satisfied smirk. "Isn't that the deal we struck? Isn't that why we ensured the history books were incorrect and made me sound a lot worse than I really am?"

"Oh, they weren't wrong about *that*. You still thread your wickedness into every single one of your supposed best intentions."

Athena shrugged. "Comes with the territory, unfortunately."

"If your delusions help you sleep with a clear conscience, keep believing they're true."

"My conscience is always clear."

"What do you want?" Auntie Eno crossed her arms under her ample bosom. "We're having a private family discussion."

"I'm as much a part of this family as you are."

"Not by blood."

"If that helps *you* sleep at night, then keep believing it's true."

Peg watched the exchange between the two beautiful women. She couldn't hide her amusement. To watch a goddess and a monster fighting it out with cruel words was quite an impressive display.

She knew all about Athena, the Maiden Goddess. The daughter of Zeus and goddess of wisdom, patroness of intellectual activities, the protector of Athens. The forever virgin who sought revenge on every woman who dared go near any of her husbands. Her wrath was well documented in history books. What wasn't, was how she cursed mortal women but afterwards secretly plotted against the men who did her wrong. In an act of sisterly solidarity, Athena cut deals with the other maidens. Offered the chance to exist in non-linear life cycles enabling victims and their direct families, lovers and associates to exist in an endless parade of lives. While these opportunities enabled these women to travel through past and future, their enemies and foes always came along for the ride.

And this was why the Ceto family was tied to this goddess. She was the one responsible for their multiple lives. Out of a tragic murder came an unexpected birth, and Athena offered a way to keep their existence alive. But every new chance at life eventually came to an end, and it was always for the same reason.

Perseus, the hateful *hero*.

"I'm tired of this banter," Athena said. "Must we always fight?"

"Yes."

"We are true sisters if we squabble every time we meet." The goddess chuckled and the sound wrapped itself around Peg, drawing her closer. "I hope you finally understand that binding your memories wasn't something I did to cause any harm or heartache. It was an essential request your mother has made time and time again. She didn't want either of you to live with the burden of what you are until it's essential."

"Yet, somehow, it always ends up being essential," Eno said.

"It's true, as much as Medusa wishes you could all go through at least one full cycle without having to deal with any of this, Perseus eventually finds you. I send him to the opposite ends of the Earth every time, yet he somehow finds his way back to her. The connection is strong," Athena said. "After he killed her the first time and their blood mingled, it was inevitable."

Peg hated this particular truth. Didn't appreciate that nothing about their lives was done with total freewill. Chosen directions and paths were somewhat varying, but never truly their own. What was the point if everything always ended up in the same vicious sequence of destruction? And if Perseus had found her mother, this meant her family would soon be dead. To be reincarnated in another time and place. To become other people.

But Peg wasn't ready to leave this life behind. She hadn't even finished high school. Hadn't gotten the chance to tell Belle how she really felt. She didn't want to end up somewhere else before exploring her heart's desire with her best friend.

"You understand that, don't you, young Pegasus?"

She released her burdened thoughts. "Don't call me that."

"Peggy, then."

"Not that either."

Eno laughed.

Athena considered Peg for a moment, glanced at the hand-mirror in her hand and smiled. "I see you've found the looking glass."

"I have, but it's useless."

"It's the map to the place you want to find," she said. "I hardly think *that's* useless."

"I want to find my sister."

"Exactly."

Peg's attention was perked. "Do you know how I can use this?"

"I believe you already have."

"Not intentionally," she said, starting to understand Eno's frustrations with this goddess. Her way of answering direct questions was already getting tiresome.

"Whether intentional or not, you know what you have to do," Athena said.

"The bathroom mirror was the one that..."

... revealed Chrysa.

... confirmed she was alive.

... showed me she's suffering.

... changed everything.

All those thoughts amounted to one thing—in order to actually see Chrysa, she needed a bigger mirror.

"What is it?" Eno cocked a brow at Peg.

"I think she's starting to understand," Athena said with a knowing grin.

"What're you thinking, Peg?"

Her mind was racing, thoughts tumbling over each other.

"It's a good thing she's finally figured this out," Athena said, and yawned.

"Why's that?" Eno asked.

"This particular cycle is drawing to an end, and there's nothing any of us can do to change that. But due to such unforeseen circumstances, if Chrysa isn't found and returned before Perseus arrives, she will cease to exist."

"What?" Peg couldn't believe her ears.

"Don't be so surprised, young one. I know you overheard me tell your mother the other night." Athena narrowed her eyes. "If you've located where she is, you better try to get her back as soon as you can."

"Are you sure there's nothing we can do to stop this?" Peg had to know, or at least try to find out. The weight of what their destiny entailed smacked her hard. This world wasn't perfect and she'd experienced many sad days, but she wanted to survive until life ended naturally. And she couldn't fathom the possibility of living another lifetime, somewhere else without her twin.

I can't let this happen.

"Well?"

Athena stayed silent.

"Are you seriously not going to answer?"

"The only thing I'll confirm is that her disappearance made it easier for Perseus to locate you," Athena said. "All of you."

"Now you know why I can't stand this schemer," Eno said.

"I'm no schemer."

Eno scoffed.

Peg was starting to understand the dynamics between these two a lot more, but she didn't need Athena for what she had in mind. "We need a bigger mirror."

IN THE BLUR

CHRYSA'S SCREAM CUT OFF ABRUPTLY.

The jolt of impact against the unforgiving ground reverberated through her spine, sucking the breath from her lungs. A shot of pain surged along her legs and made her arms numb. At least she wasn't dead.

Could anyone die in this place? Watching the last of the bloody robes tumble around her like limp parachutes answered the question.

She stared at the sky, once again barely visible through the grayish canopy of trees.

How had her twin sister ripped away a section of this reality and stared down on them? And where did she go? The sting of losing her all over again hurt more than the physical onslaught she'd taken after landing.

A groan to her left made her startle.

A moan to her right got her blood flowing.

"Lovey, Ira?" Her voice sounded mechanical, and a spasm tore through her spine when a coughing fit forced her to sit up.

"Take it... easy." Lovey still sounded weak.

"What the fuck just happened?" Ira asked with another groan.

Chrysa tried to swallow the coughs, but couldn't. She rode each breath-strangling exertion until she was able to get some sense of control back. Her throat burned and her chest felt compressed. Everything was aching, but she was alive. And that was more than she could say about the veiled. So many of the leaden cloaks, mostly torn into scraps, littered the area. She couldn't believe this forest could accommodate this many freaks.

A crashing echoed through the trees and made the ground rumble.

"What the hell was that?" Ira asked, looking around.

"The blur is... eating itself."

Chrysa stared at Lovey. "What?"

"When your sister..." She took a slow and sharp breath. "... touched this place, the destruction began."

"So, you saw her?" The words snuck out before she could stop them. *If we want to get out of here, we have to work together. Stick together.*

After seeing Peggy, she was more determined than ever to get the hell out.

"Yeah, I saw her." Ira sat up and winced. His face and hands were cut, tiny pinpricks of red covered the exposed skin of his forearms and neck.

He didn't look as bad as Lovey, who was sickly pale and had a lot of weeping gashes everywhere. The long, dark branch sticking out of her side had turned the surrounding skin black. At least her ankles were free.

"We all saw Peg," Lovey whispered.

"Can you get up?" Chrysa asked.

"No chance." Her breathing was labored and she was pinned to the ground by the root branch sticking out of her torso.

Chrysa checked her own body, flicked away the cracked roots stuck to her clothes and skin. None had penetrated deep enough to affect her, but her exposed arms and legs were streaked with bloody lines from the shattered sky. It was shocking to see this much red in a place leeched of color.

"Are you going to be okay?" Chrysa needed to know.

"I'll be better when... this fucking tree... is out of me."

"Woah, that's no language for the *Goddess of Love.*"

"Shut up, Ira." Even though it obviously took a lot of energy, she gave him the finger.

"I'm curious. Who told *you* who Lovey is?" Chrysa didn't appreciate being left out of the information loop.

He shrugged. "I know a lot of things."

"I bet you do."

He responded with a smirk. "Maybe I'll let you in on some of those things."

Even injured, Lovey scoffed. "You're wasting... your time. Her heart belongs to someone already, and she doesn't have room for anyone else."

Cal's face appeared in Chrysa's mind, and she tried to take comfort in his good looks but a wave of sadness swept through her. He'd gone to so much trouble to find her, and she might never see him again.

"Everyone's got a little room for Ira," he said.

"Not everyone," Chrysa spit back.

"So, how are you going to get that out?" He glossed over her comment and pointed at Lovey's injury.

"I can't." Lovey wrapped a hand around the intrusion but was too weak to make much of an impact. "You guys... have to do it."

"No way, I'm not touching that," he said with another shake of his head. "It's enough that I was trapped by those things, and now I'm all carved up. I'm not going to wrap my hands around that toxic crap."

"I'll do it." Chrysa ignored the dull throb at the small of her back. The creaking bones and aches weren't going to stop her. "I understand that you're a weak-ass boy and can't be bothered helping anyone but yourself."

"Hey!"

Lovey flashed a toothy grin and there was blood on her teeth.

She managed to get to her knees with the intention of crawling closer to Lovey, but a fragment of sky caught her eye. It couldn't be!

She leaned over and gasped when she caught sight of herself. Not because her hair was a tangled mess and she was bloody, but because she realized she was staring into a mirror.

How had the sky turned into a mirror?

Nothing about the blur made any sense.

"What's wrong?" Ira asked.

"The bits of sky, they're mirror shards."

"What?"

"The sky was a mirror," she repeated.

He crouched beside her. "No wonder our skin is sliced."

"Yeah, so the sky shattered... like a mirror..." Lovey's voice trailed off. "But are you removing this before... the destruction... reaches us?"

The earth rumbled and the canopy overhead wavered.

"Whoa. You know what I don't get?" When no one answered him, Ira continued, "I don't understand why you can't heal yourself? You're a goddess, doesn't that warrant instant healing powers or something?"

"Not when you wander into this place... and draw blood." Lovey scanned them both, sucking in air. "It's one of the first things the... veiled do." She sucked in a breath. "They take blood. Let it seep into the roots and the earth. It's how they trap you. Not even Chrysa's psychic power... can manifest in here."

"I don't have any psychic power."

"You do," Lovey panted. "Mommy Dearest just didn't tell you." She paused. "If she'd been honest... you wouldn't have... ended up here." She looked at Ira. "You shouldn't be here either. It's your father who should... Why did you take his... place?"

"I didn't." Ira scoffed, running a hand through his black hair and sending a spray of mirror and root shards flying. "I decided to scope out the farm and she caught me. The freak lost her shit and before I knew it, I was inside this forest prison. I feel like I'm trapped in a really bad horror movie with two girls who aren't anywhere near good enough to be final girl material."

"Maybe *you* can be the final... girl," Lovey snapped.

"Hell yeah, I'll take that title any day."

"Guess that means you're a virgin."

"It's all about the cliché with you," Ira said.

"Stop!" Chrysa's voice echoed through the trees, catching in the branches and slinging the word back into her ears like an endless echo.

Lovey and Ira stared at her.

Chrysa sighed, and even though her knees quaked and her feet were rubbery, she gritted her teeth and stood. She made her wobbly way over to Lovey and kneeled beside her. The action shook her insides all the way to her teeth, but she didn't care.

"Are you ready?" The impaling was worse up close.

Lovey sucked in a breath. "I don't think so."

Chrysa wrapped both hands around the branch and slipped when the ground shuddered.

"It's getting worse," Ira said.

She tried again and the tiny thorns stabbed into her fingers, but she held on tighter. No wonder Lovey was in pain, these branches were barbed. At least her feet weren't caught by roots anymore.

"Tell me when you're ready."

Lovey opened her mouth to reply, but Chrysa yanked before she got the chance. The blonde howled and the branches twitched. Her spine curved, helping the intrusive branch slither out.

Chrysa's hands were covered in blood and Lovey's gaping hole dribbled crimson like a leaky tap. "We need to stop the bleeding."

"Here, use this." Ira thrust a strip of gray fabric in front of her face.

She took the wad and pressed the scrunched-up mess against Lovey's wound. She flinched, but Chrysa didn't falter. She wiped away as much blood as she could, before shoving the fabric into the gaping hole. Blood dribbled from the edges, and the strip was already red, but she didn't know what else to do. When Ira tore and offered longer pieces, she tied the bits around Lovey's slim waist and created a makeshift bandage.

"At least these assholes came in handy for something." Ira raised a cloak and scowled. "What're they even made of?"

"They used to be skin and... bones," Lovey said. She seemed to be sitting straighter, and getting a bit of color back on her pale face.

His eyes widened, before returning to the lifeless robe. "The veiled were people?"

"They were the people Medusa turned to stone," Lovey said, pausing for breath. "The longer they stayed here, the more... they subsided."

"But, what about the statues?" *Medusa.* Chrysa chose not to focus on the name because the realization hurt too much. "Are you saying we would've eventually become like them?"

"That's exactly what I'm saying," Lovey said. "First, you're a statue, then your insides wither away... until the stone turns into... that."

"But what's underneath?" Ira asked, glaring at the material in his hand.

"Whatever tattered piece is left of your soul." Lovey sat straighter. "The veiled feed on rage... and confusion. They make sure no one escapes their shells until the soul is almost completely... gone."

"And my mother did this?" According to Lovey, her mother was Medusa. How was this even possible?

"Well, technically it was Athena. She's the one who created the loophole for those your mother turns to stone. Better to end up here than to be dead, I suppose."

"But they're all dead now," Ira said.

"The mirror shards must have destroyed them," she said. "Severing whatever small pieces were left."

"So, they're completely gone?" Tears blurred Chrysa's vision. "These people who once existed died because of my mother." *Because my mother is freaking Medusa.*

"Well, your sister broke the sky," Ira said. "If I get out of here alive, remind me to never go anywhere near your family." He shook his head. "I can't stay away from you freaks! Not even after we get out of here. Damn it!"

Chrysa considered the mirrored pieces, seeing herself multiplied in tiny fragments while trying not to think about the veiled who used to be living, breathing people. The anger she felt towards her mother was savage.

"Hey, I don't need your anger," Lovey said. "I need your love."

"What?"

"I can't help much like this." The blonde held out a hand. "I need your... help."

Chrysa didn't understand. "I don't—"

"Give me your hand... and you'll see."

She hesitated another second before placing her bloody hand in Lovey's. "Why do you need my hand?" Her mouth felt dry.

Lovey curved her fingers around hers, caught her gaze. "Think about Peg, and how she reached out."

Chrysa's heart swelled at the thought of her sister never giving up on her. That she was still out there looking, even after all this time. That Peggy told her she'd find her.

"Think about Cal... summoning the goddess of love because... he can't live without you."

Lovey's voice was soft and warm, like a comforting cozy blanket.

Cal's handsome face filled her mind. How Chrysa loved staring at his strong forearms in summer, that he hid away in baggy hoodies in winter. Warmth crept up her neck and her face burned when she relived their more intimate moments together. He was the best boyfriend, but he was also a kind and wonderful person.

"Wow... that should do it."

"What the hell are you doing to her?" Ira asked.

Chrysa's head felt light, her chest full of the love she felt for Peggy and Cal. Sword's smiling pooch face flashed inside her head too. Her mother's warm smile reminded her of relaxing weekends. Aunt Widow's easy grin. Aunt Weirdo's rigid ways. Belle's cheeky look every time she claimed she didn't have a thing for Peggy.

Her hand was blazing in Lovey's.

Everyone she loved was far away, out of range.

Except for Sword.

He was here, and she'd left him behind while trying to escape the veiled. He was alone, probably scared. She could feel his puppy love from here. Heard his whining in her ears. If the blur was falling apart, she had to get him.

"Are you stealing love from her?"

"That's not what I'm doing, Ira. I'm tapping into the overabundance she possesses."

Chrysa heard the exchange, but all she could do was swoon. Her body was full of love. The need to see the people she cared about the most morphed into an agonizing ache.

Aphrodite is sucking the love out of me.

She shook her head, cleared away the cloud of affection and tried to pull her hand back. But Lovey tightened her grip.

"What did you do to me?" Anger coiled in the pit of her stomach. Anger, love, confusion, horror. She was exhausted, suddenly craved Peggy's choc-chip cookies.

"You helped me heal."

"I thought you couldn't heal yourself while we're in this dump?" Ira said.

"Not while that thing was stuck inside me, slowly poisoning my blood and leaking all the love from my veins."

"So you took mine?" Chrysa scrutinized Lovey and some color had returned to the blonde's cheeks. Her hair was glossier, and she didn't seem as weak. Her grip on Chrysa's hand was definitely harder too.

"I don't *take* love." Lovey shook her head. "I share the love, and the love returns to me if I need it."

Chrysa fought against the anger. It wasn't worth getting upset and jeopardizing an escape out of blur. Now that she'd glimpsed her sister and remembered the love she was missing, she wanted it back. And for that, she needed Lovey.

She met her shiny gaze and nodded. She was at least glad that her guide looked a lot healthier than she had before. "Fair enough."

"Thank you."

"Yeah, okay." She made a move to pull her fingers back.

"I mean it." Lovey squeezed again. "Thank you for removing the root and allowing me the privilege of sharing your love. With that much to go around, I'm glad Cal's determination nudged me to find you."

The anger dissolved like dust. How could she be mad with her now?

"Whenever you two are done with this tender show of affection—which by the way, is a total turn-on—we need to figure out what we're going to do next." Ira said with a small grin.

"I didn't realize you were such a jerk," Chrysa said.

He shrugged. "I learned from the best."

"He's not as tough or crude as he makes out," Lovey said. "Ask his guardian."

"Whatever you reckon, Blondie." But color rose in his cheeks.

"Ira's right about one thing, though," Lovey said. "We need to move."

"But where do we go?" Chrysa asked.

Lovey was thoughtful for a moment, and finally released her hand. "You mentioned mirror shards, and that has to mean something important..."

"Important how?"

"Mirrors can serve as pathways," Lovey said. "If Peg used one to find you, we might be able to do the same to find her. After all, you know what they say about everything a Pegasus touches."

"No," Ira said. "What do they say?"

"When Pegasus paws the earth with a hoof, a spring of water forms."

"How does that relate back to us?" Chrysa knew the myth of Pegasus, but didn't understand what a mythological story had to do with her sister.

"Are you still in denial about the truth?"

"I don't..." Medusa was her mother. That meant Pegasus was...

"You're both forgetting one very important detail," Ira said, considering the reflective pieces on the ground.

"What's that?" Lovey asked.

"We're in the middle of a freaky forest, so where are we going to find an unbroken mirror? Because I doubt these pieces are going to help us."

Lovey considered the shards spread over and under the discarded robes. "Maybe if we find a piece that's big enough?"

"I guess," Ira said, though he didn't sound convinced.

"Why don't we take a look before we give up?"

"You think one of these pieces of sky might lead back to Peggy?" Chrysa asked.

Lovey nodded.

The question of how was at the tip of her tongue, but she wasn't ready to admit the connection that was already fully formed in the back of her mind. Instead, she said, "Let's find it then."

"This is an *impossible* task," Ira whined. "A waste of time."

The three crawled around the wreckage, trying to find a single shard that didn't reflect their surroundings or their faces. Time turned differently inside this forest, but Chrysa could feel the seconds ticking away. Every piece she found reflected her haggard face, reminded her of the truth. But it didn't mean she wanted to accept any of it.

But the longer the trio searched, the more the ground shook beneath them.

"Think I found something!" Ira crouched, grabbed a piece and squinted. "Is that a house?"

"Let me see." Chrysa snatched the piece from him.

"Hey!"

She didn't care that the edge was sharp, only wanted to catch a glimpse of the farmhouse or her sister. She peered inside, but all she could see was a wall. Her enthusiasm deflated. "That's not my house."

"Pass it over."

She gave it to Lovey, who closed her eyes.

Chrysa and Ira exchanged a look. He seemed as confused as she did.

When Lovey opened her eyes, she said, "It's some sort of storage room."

"Well, that's not going to help us. It could be the basement or the attic. And no one ever goes to either of those."

Ira sighed. "I think we should get moving. Can you guys feel the air shifting?"

The crashing vibrations were getting louder, and branches were snapping above their heads.

"I agree." Chrysa stared at the forest floor, lamenting their inability to find a miracle way home. "If only we could find Dorothy's silver slippers and could wish ourselves back..." But even Dorothy had to go through many trials before the shoes worked.

"Weren't they red?" Ira asked with a scowl. "Dorothy had ruby shoes."

"That's in the movie," Chrysa said. "In the book, they were silver."

"A fictional character's footwear doesn't matter," Lovey snapped. "Focus!"

Ira lowered his head and continued searching. "Hey, there aren't any *silver* shoes, but maybe we should put these on." Ira grabbed one of the discarded cloaks, shook the shiny fragments off, and held it out. "Don't just stare, take it."

Chrysa took the offered robe, but handed the horrid thing to Lovey who was leaning against a tree. She made a move to help her slide into it, before she remembered the blonde had healed completely and was more than capable now. She took another from Ira and threw the fabric over her head.

"Let's go," Lovey said.

"In what direction?" Chrysa asked.

"Does it matter?" Ira answered.

She supposed it didn't.

"So, what's the plan, Lovey?" he asked.

"Mirrors aren't always made of glass," Lovey said, thoughtfully. "Remember what I said about Pegasus?"

"What the hell are you talking about?" Ira asked, shaking his head.

Chrysa's mind filled with a childhood memory. After a particularly wet winter, huge puddles spread all over the property. And every time her sister touched the water, the pool widened and the twins made funny faces at their reflections.

That's because my sister is Pegasus. "She means that a body of water can be a mirror."

"Exactly." Lovey winked at her.

"I hope you two don't start finishing each other's sentences next," Ira said.

Chrysa took a step, but paused when three old ladies appeared out of nowhere. Crones with hollowed eye sockets, toothless mouths, haggy skin and tattered rags hanging off their skinny bodies.

"What the hell?" Ira said, taking a step back.

"Direction always matters," the three crones said in unison.

Chrysa didn't move, couldn't take her eyes off their raised wrinkled palms as a single eyeball rolled over each hand like an electric orb. A snaggle tooth roved in the opposite direction, and both items stopped in the middle woman's palm.

She opened her mouth and said, "We see what no one else does, hear what others do not."

"And what do you see in our path?" Lovey maintained a fair distance, but seemed as transfixed as Chrysa.

"We see trials and trouble."

"Do you see us getting out of here?"

"Yes, Aphrodite."

Chrysa's heart soared.

"How?" Lovey asked.

"To escape the forest before the void swallows it up, you must find the lake."

"How do we find the lake?"

"Wait a minute, what void?" Ira said.

"The lake can only be found by the golden weapon, the golden familiar."

Lovey looked thoughtful for a second and finally nodded, as if she'd solved the riddle.

"What void are these old women talking about?" Ira repeated.

"The void is where everything fails to exist," the woman said.

"What the Pegasus introduced when she touched this forbidden place."

Chrysa didn't like the sound of that. Was Peggy responsible for all of this pending destruction?

The eyeball and tooth shifted to the lady on their left. "The void is where we're all headed if we remain here."

The eyeball and tooth traveled to the lady on their right. "The void is where you will go if you don't escape."

"Does anyone understand any of this?" Ira asked.

Lovey nodded. "Thank you, my dear Graeae."

"The void threatens the other side too," all three said at the same time.

Chrysa blinked and the women were gone.

"That was some freaky shit right there." Ira yanked the cloak tighter around his body. "All this talk about a void is making me sweat."

Lovey stepped away from the tree and considered their surroundings. "It'll do more than that if we don't find the lake."

"Who were they?" Chrysa asked, even though she already knew the crones from mythology. She also couldn't help but think about her elderly aunts. The three she never saw because they lived on a remote island in Greece and refused to travel anywhere—Dina, Enya and Pem Grae. But they couldn't possibly be the same women. Or could they?

After everything she'd seen, learning her mother turned people to stone, and her sister had apparently created a void, she supposed anything was possible.

The time for denial is over.

"The all-knowing Graeae sisters. Derno, Enyo and Pemphedo are the Graeae and can see what the rest of us can't." Lovey's brow furrowed. "If they say we're headed into deep trouble, we have to pay attention."

"Where did they come from though?" Ira's eyes were too wide. "And why would they help us?"

The thunderous roar under their feet made Chrysa jump.

"Come on, we have to go." Lovey led the way into the trees with Ira close behind, but Chrysa remained.

"If this place is going to implode, I need to find Sword." She'd promised to go back for her companion, and she wasn't going to leave him behind.

"Who the hell is Sword?" Ira asked.

"My dog."

The air wavered.

Something was coming.

"We're not wasting time or risking our lives for a pooch," he said, disgusted.

"I'm not leaving him behind."

"Your dog?" Lovey turned to face her with a glimmer in her eyes. "The golden retriever?"

"Yes."

"Chrysa's right, we can't leave without him."

"What?"

"Sword might be our way out," Lovey answered.

The ground shook and fog poured between the trees.

"I'm not going anywhere without him, so..." Chrysa might not fully understand what Lovey had suddenly realized, but she was glad because she refused to budge on this. She'd already left Sword alone for too long. He was her loyal companion—followed her around everywhere, slept at the end of her bed, insisted she pat his head constantly.

I won't leave him.

"That's just fucking great." Ira kicked at the discarded bloody cloaks like a toddler. "As if we don't have enough crap to worry about, now we're going to rescue a dog."

The forest floor trembled, but Chrysa stood her ground.

CHAPTER EIGHTEEN

"Now what?" Athena's hands were on her hips as she contemplated the dusty storage room packed with mirrors, but Peg ignored her. "How vain are you people? Why do you need this many mirrors?"

"Some aren't ours. They're pieces Mom was going to sell. Actually, I've kept the listings open and have sold quite a few already." Peg didn't want to reveal too much about their personal situation. She didn't know what this woman could use against them. She considered the many mirrored frames propped against the shabby wooden walls. "Besides, I wasn't going to take any chances with Mom."

"Peg, what're we doing here?" Eno stood by the door, eyeing the room but not daring to step inside.

"We need a big mirror to reach Chrysa, I'm sure of it." The small hand-mirror might be helpful as a map, but it wouldn't get her where she needed to go.

"You think Chrysa is trapped inside a mirror?" Eno asked, resting her hip against the uneven wooden doorframe.

"No, I think a bigger mirror can serve as a proper pathway." Peg instantly thought of the double-sided mirror that used to sit in her mother's room until she'd removed it. But where was it? Where did she put it?

"So, we're hoping to find her *inside* one of these mirrors?" Eno asked.

"Yes, we are." At least, *she* was.

"What do we do if she *is* inside one of these?" her auntie asked. "How do we get her out?"

"I don't know that yet," Peg admitted.

Eno cocked an eyebrow. "Maybe Athena can shed some light on the matter."

"I can't reveal any more than I already have."

"You haven't revealed anything," Eno snapped.

"I've revealed enough."

"Clearly not enough to help in any useful way."

The exchange might have been cute back in the barn, but not while Peg was trying to think rationally about such an irrational situation.

"Okay, guys, this isn't getting us anywhere." She didn't want to be rude, but these two were acting ridiculous. "Instead of bickering, could you help me figure this out?"

"I already told you, I can't."

Auntie Eno snorted.

Peg sighed, wandered deeper into the room while trying to find some kind of inspiration. A spark to ignite a solution inside her mind. Her head was packed full of knowledge now and she hoped this would help find a way to get her sister back.

Her aunt was right, though. What happened if she found Chrysa inside one of these mirrors? How would she get her out?

"What's showing in the small looking glass?" Athena sidled up beside her, the skirts of her outfit swooshed against the floor, stirred a cloud of dust that tickled Peg's nose.

She held the mirror up. The forest was quiet, too silent. "Nothing much."

The image flickered like a rickety camera that had been jolted by some unseen force.

"What was that?" Peg asked.

The tall trees shook, branches snapped off several trees.

"There's something malicious emanating from that image." Athena closed her eyes and rubbed her forehead. "Things aren't going well on either side."

"What does that mean?"

Her brow furrowed, and her eyes remained on the reflection. "I'm not sure."

"What's going on?" Eno remained outside the storage room.

"The trees are shaking," Peg said. The ground seemed to rumble, like the footage she'd seen of earthquakes. "Something's definitely going on."

Peg placed the hand-mirror on the floor and went about pulling the coverings off one dusty frame after another. She held her breath every time, hoping to find her sister on the other side. Instead, she could only see herself. When she'd uncovered every single one, she stepped away, until she was standing in the middle of a hall of mirrors, surrounded by her own reflection.

She spun around in a circle, and felt so alone in that moment. Alone in this dusty room with too many versions of herself. Alone in her search for answers. Alone in this quest.

Peg tilted her head to the ceiling, watched the gloom lengthen and stretch. The darkness dripped down the walls, but she didn't close her eyes. In this murky space, she could see the shine of stars—blinking diamonds sewn into black velvet. Every single one a constellation awarded by Zeus.

For just a second, she considered giving in.

A hand on her shoulder jolted her and she closed her mind to the gloom, sent every shady piece back to the bleak corners.

"Don't lose yourself yet," Athena whispered.

"You're right..." *I need to find her first.* But there weren't any answers in these mirrors. If only the solution was written on the wall.

Her heart stuttered.

Words on the wall.

There *were* words on the wall, but not on this one.

Peg pulled her phone out of her pocket and went straight to her gallery.

"What are you doing now?" Aunt Eno, still at the entrance, sounded concerned.

"I'm looking for something." She scrolled through the pictures she'd taken of the symbols, disappointed to find none of the pictures had turned out. Instead of the sections she clearly remembered were covered with inscriptions, she found blank screens. Even her sister's statue was nothing but a blur. "The photos didn't turn out."

"What photos?"

"The photos I took in the statue chamber."

The air quivered and she found Athena staring at her with narrowed eyes. "Have you been inside the forbidden chamber?"

Peg swallowed. "Why?" For the first time since she'd crossed paths with this woman—goddess—she felt a worm of terror. The way the ends of her hair floated as if she was under water was unnerving, especially since her clothes remained still.

"Answer me. Did you enter the chamber?"

"Yes, so what?" Her mouth was dry and she wanted to flee from Athena's proximity.

"You disturbed the order of things, didn't you?"

"No, I didn't." But she remembered the statue she'd bumped into, how the heads rolled everywhere. And that something definitely scared the hell out of her and she'd left in a hurry.

"Peg, tell me you didn't go down there." Eno was now in the room, and both women stood in front of her with matching frowns.

"I found it by accident." She thrust the phone in front of her. "I snapped some shots of the walls, hoping to translate the symbols. And there was a statue of Chrysa down there."

"You shouldn't have gone inside," Athena said.

"Maybe those symbols will help us—"

"No, Stheno," Athena said. "It's too dangerous. The monstrosities below cannot be unleashed into this world. If we do that, we will cause a catastrophic event."

"I have a feeling we're not getting out of this without some sort of catastrophic event." Eno's hands were at her sides, clenched into fists. "We might as well go out fighting."

Peg's heart was beating fast.

"If you do this, you're on your own," Athena said.

Eno shrugged. "Just the way we like it."

"Very well." The goddess stepped away from the confrontation. Faster than the eye could see, she morphed into the snowy owl and soared out of existence.

"I thought she'd never leave," Eno said with a sigh. "She's almost as exhausting as all these mirrors." She grabbed Peg's arm. "Pegasus, are you ready for what lays ahead?"

"As ready as I'm ever gonna be."

CHAPTER NINETEEN

THE DOOR HAD NEVER APPEARED THIS MENACING. EVERY SPLINTER ON the wooden surface suddenly resembled jagged bamboo strips threatening to stab beneath her skin. Thirsty for her blood.

Athena's words had alarmed Peg, but she pushed them aside.

Her skin buzzed with the need to reach out, but the thought of what might have changed since the last time she'd escaped the chamber frightened her. Someone—or something—had stalked her from the shadows. And she couldn't forget about the multi-headed statue she'd accidentally tipped over.

"Hey, are you okay?" Aunt Eno tapped Peg's shoulder.

"I'm fine." She found strength in her aunt's concern. "Never imagined any of this would happen."

Eno sighed. "That's on us, we should've told you before it got to this."

"No, I'm glad you didn't." Now that she knew everything, the weight of knowledge clouded Peg's mind. She couldn't imagine what it would have been like to learn about all of this when she was a kid, or even a few years ago. The truth of who her family was would have been too much of a burden. "It would have made life a living hell."

"It's what Ed always said." Her voice was low, softened when Eno spoke about her youngest sister. "She wanted you girls to enjoy your lives without the baggage."

"Yet, she carried it on her own."

"That's her way. She's the protector, and has always carried the true weight of our problems."

"Well, it's time for me to shoulder some of that weight."

"And you think the walls in the chamber will provide the answers you need?" Was that doubt in her voice, or hope?

"That's what I'm hoping." *More like wishing.*

"It doesn't hurt to hope." Eno squeezed Peg's shoulder before dropping her hand. "Whenever you're ready, I'm right behind you."

Peg instinctively extended her left hand, but faltered when her palm rebounded against the surface. She'd forgotten about her stony hand. She wasn't wearing her gloves, and didn't even care.

"Peg," Aunt Eno said.

"Yeah?"

"Ed did that to your hand."

She considered lying, but what was the point? "When I found Mom screaming in the barn the other night, she looked straight at me and my palm turned to stone."

"But you didn't tell her?"

"I didn't have to. She knows, but didn't want to talk about it."

"When you fainted, I asked Ed about your hand," Eno said. "She's really sorry, but I guess we all know how the pathway between you and Chrysa opened up."

"I guess." Peg's chest constricted because she hadn't thought about that until now. She placed her right hand on the door and when the sharp prick on her skin struck, she gasped. The door clicked open, a gush of cold air rolled out from the darkness, and her breath misted in front of her.

"It's freezing in there," Eno said, rubbing her covered arms.

"I know." Peg stepped inside and turned to face the closest wall. The inscriptions no longer appeared to be symbols, but were clearly words in an ancient Greek dialect. She recognized a lot of the characters, but still couldn't make heads or tails out of a single line. Why couldn't she decipher this scrawl? She stepped closer, holding her phone up to shine a light on the surface.

"Well?" Eno asked.

"I still can't understand any of this."

"I can." Her aunt dipped her fingertips into the indents carved into the wall. "It's an old script we made up. No one can understand it but the three Gorgon sisters."

"What does it say?"

"Nothing that will help with this situation."

"Who put it there?"

"Your mother, I suspect." Eno sighed. "It's mostly rantings about safeguarding this space to keep people out." Her fingers traced the surface. "The remorse of what she's done because of the curse. It's the sad script of a tortured soul."

"I finally understand why she didn't share her secret, but I wish she would've lightened the burden somehow." Peg's chest ached at the thought of Mom suffering this deeply and keeping so fucking much inside. No wonder she could barely leave her room.

"You know what she's like, she bottles everything in."

Peg opened her mouth to respond but was interrupted by the unexpected echo of voices from below.

"There's someone down there," Eno whispered.

Peg's pulse quickened. She switched off the phone light and descended the marble steps with her auntie by her side. She tried to calm her breathing, but by the time she reached the bottom, her heart caught in her throat.

"Mom?"

Her mother jumped, turned away from the statue she was helping Rya position beside Chrysa's. The base screeched when she dropped her end. "You scared me!" She looked past to focus on Eno. "How did you two get in?"

"Down the stairs," Peg said with a shrug.

"What stairs?" Mom's hair was a disheveled mess, but she was actually dressed in a pair of faded jeans and an oversized woolen sweater. She might not be the dependable and safe mother she used to be, but this was the most put-together she'd looked in ages.

"The ones leading down from the barn," Eno answered.

"There aren't any stairs in the barn." Mom stepped away from the statue, but Rya continued to scrape and shove until Ira's statue was straight.

Ira Danae, in statue form, sat next to her sister.

"Peg, there aren't any stairs," she repeated.

"The other night, I found a door in the barn, and an old coin." The coin in question still burned a hole in her pocket.

Mom shook her head, the confusion obvious.

"Ed, the stairs are right *there*," Eno said. "Opens up into walls full of your carvings."

Mom shook her head again. "I don't remember..."

Peg couldn't take her eyes off the statue. "How did you get him down here?" If her mother didn't know about the secret door inside the barn, how did Mom and Rya bring Ira's statue down here?

"The only way to reach this chamber is via my closet." Mom's eyes were wide and bright. The compulsion to shy away and conceal her gaze seemed to have vanished. The blindfold she'd kept permanently around her neck was gone, too. "There's no other way."

"Ed, you're wrong, there is." Eno grabbed her younger sister's hand. "There's no point in arguing. Let me show you."

Mom let Eno lead the way and Peg turned to watch the two disappear up the marble staircase, only to return a few seconds later.

"I had no idea." Mom rubbed her temples. "I shouldn't have let things get so out of hand." She met Peg's gaze. "That door must've always been there for you. Maybe even for your sister. But that script... I etched that somewhere else."

She didn't know what to say, so she nodded.

"You shouldn't be so hard on yourself," Rya said, coming up beside Mom.

"What were you doing with him?" Peg pointed at Ira's statue.

"Putting him where I should've put him days ago."

"He was skulking around the other night, wasn't he? He's the one who made you scream. The reason why I've got a shitty piece of rock for a hand." She held up her palm.

"I'm so sorry." Her mother pulled her into a tight hug. "I really am, honey. I didn't mean to do that to you. I would never do that intentionally. I—"

"Mom, I know." Peg found it hard to breathe because Mom was holding on tight, but she was afraid to say anything. And didn't want to lose this connection.

"Ed, you're smothering her," Rya said.

Mom loosened her grip and reluctantly stepped out of the hug. She took Peg's stony hand. "This must be your connection to the other side. To the place I feared I'd created but never knew for sure. Not until I struck you." She considered Peg's hand for a few seconds. "Were you wearing your bracelet that night?"

"Yeah, why?"

"That's probably why I didn't turn you into a..." Mom glanced at Chrysa's statue. "Your sister wasn't wearing hers..."

Another mystery solved. But she didn't want to focus on that.

"Mom, what is that place?"

"It's where all the people I turn to stone end up," Mom answered, and her face paled. "For many years I believed I'd killed every person who suffered my stare, but as the cycles passed, I started to consult the oracles. Heard whispers about the possibility of the victims being frozen in our world, but physically sent somewhere else. I tried to reach out many times, to find out if it was real or just a myth."

"Why?"

Her eyes shone with tears. "I wanted to find a way to release everyone."

"But weren't these people bad?"

"Not all of them," she said. "As you've seen for yourself, I can't control my power if I'm mad or overwhelmed. My overprotective nature pushes me into a rage and I lose *total* control."

"But what happened to Chrysa has opened up new possibilities," Rya said.

"You've confirmed that everyone I've ever transformed really goes somewhere else." Mom squeezed Peg's hand before letting go. "It might be too late to save the many ancient souls I've sacrificed along the way, but I can try to save my girl."

A wave of determination swept through Peg as she considered Ira's statue, while doing a quick sweep for Lovey. She'd heard her sister mention the girl's name, yet there wasn't a statue of the blonde anywhere. Maybe she was somewhere else, but she didn't have time to search. The only thing she wanted to do was get Chrysa back.

"I'll figure this out," she whispered. "I promise."

"Honey, it's not your burden to—"

"According to Athena it is," Eno said.

"What do you mean?"

"That pesky bitch thinks Peg is the only one who can break through to the other side and find Chrysa."

Something caught Peg's eye. On the shiny floor, in front of where Chrysa and Sword's statues stood, was the engraving she'd noticed the other night. It was etched into the marble. She bent closer as her mother and aunts debated the merits of Athena's prediction.

Peg narrowed her eyes and couldn't believe she actually understood the engraving. She couldn't read it before but now, the words were clear. She wasn't sure if it was in Greek or some other dialect, but she finally understood what it meant.

Her legs almost collapsed beneath her as she deciphered the line. *A double mirror is the way through.* Her head spun with the realization. "A double mirror is the way through."

"What did you say?" Aunt Eno was the first to respond to her outburst.

"I need to bring the mirror down *here*." Peg's thoughts were racing, getting ahead of her. Hadn't she been thinking about the two-sided mirror more than usual lately? But she hadn't found it, or searched properly. "And not just any mirror, your two-sided mirror!"

"What is she talking about?" Rya asked.

"Peg, speak to me." Mom grabbed her arm, attempted to get her to stand. "What are you saying?"

"I know what we have to do."

"You do?"

"What is it?" Eno asked.

"I'll be right back." Peg tried to shake out of her mother's strong grip, but she held on tight.

"Pegasus, tell me what's going on."

"I'll do better than that, I'll *show* you," she said with a smile. "But I need to get something first."

"Peggy."

"Please Mom, let me explain later. I need to do this. Now."

She reluctantly released her and Peg gave her mom a quick peck on the cheek.

"Do you need any help?" Aunt Eno called after her.

"Not yet."

"Be careful," her mother said.

"I'll be back soon." Peg raced up the stairs and came dangerously close to slipping several times. But she didn't, because the itch between her shoulder blades had returned and somehow helped her keep her footing when her feet failed.

As she stepped around the half-open door and dashed into the barn, she turned a corner too quickly and smacked into someone.

"Fuck!" Her spine connected with a shelf and several items tumbled around her. The sound reverberated through her bones, and the ease she'd felt within the chamber was gone. Peg was back to being clumsy on her feet.

"Whoa, I didn't see you there. Are you okay?"

She recognized the apologetic tone instantly. "Cal?"

"Hey, yeah, I popped in to speak to you about..." The apology was already in his expression.

"I don't have time to talk right now."

His eyes twinkled under the dim light. "Look, I'm sorry about what happened the other night."

Cal reminded her of a lost puppy. She had the impulse to hug him, but didn't want to venture into those dangerous waters again. "I really can't get into this at the moment."

"Peg, I have to tell you—"

"What is it?" The seconds were ticking away and she was losing patience.

"When I woke up this morning, I... uh, my head was full of memories I didn't recognize, or understand."

She met his eyes. "You remember everything?"

"*Everything* about *everyone.*"

"That's great, Callirrhoe. But you could've texted or—"

"I did! I tried to call you and texted, but you didn't respond."

With everything that was going on, Peg wasn't surprised she'd missed the notifications. "Sorry about that, it's been a bit busy around here."

"Um, there's something else."

"If this is about the other night—"

"I did a love spell."

"A what?" For a horrifying moment Peg thought Cal meant he put a spell on her or himself, and that was why they'd kissed. "On who?"

"Well, it was more like a summoning of love ritual."

"I have no clue what that is."

"I tried to summon the goddess of love," he said, avoiding her gaze.

"Aphrodite?"

"Yeah."

"And what were you hoping that would do?" She knew how much Cal loved Chrysa, but Peg never would've guessed he would do something this extreme.

"I asked her to find and protect Chrysa."

"And did it work?"

"I knew you'd think I was being an idiot."

"I didn't say that," Peg said.

"You didn't have to."

"Come on, Cal, that's not what I meant." She attempted to soften her voice, and hide the relief of knowing she wasn't part of his love spell. "Tell me what you did."

He hesitated for a moment. "I called on Aphrodite to find Chrysa, and to guide me to her. I had to burn a rose wrapped around her photo. When it burned out, I was supposed to get an image of where she was."

"And did you?"

"Her photo was replaced by this barn."

"So, that's why you're convinced there are clues we missed on the property?" Her heart skipped a beat. She couldn't believe his summoning had somehow worked. *He* might not understand what the barn's significance was, but she certainly did.

"Exactly," he said. "But I've already checked the barn a thousand times, and there aren't any clues here. The spell didn't work."

"I think it did," Peg said before she could stop herself.

Cal's eyes widened. "What?"

"She's not exactly *in* the barn, but..."

"What are you saying?" The nervous energy was bouncing off him. "Did you find her?"

"Sort of."

Cal's stormy eyes were huge and shiny. "Have you contacted the police and told them?"

"No, they can't help us. Have you?"

"No."

"Good."

"Peg, tell me what you found." His fingers dug into her arms. The sadness, confusion and the excitement of possibility were all shimmering inside. "You better not be messing with me, that would be cruel."

"Trust me, I'm not."

"But what you're saying doesn't make any sense."

"At the moment, nothing around here makes any sense." She sighed and decided to let him in on the big secret. Besides, she needed someone to help her carry the mirror downstairs. "Cal, I'm not lying and I'm going to prove it to you. But first, you have to help me find a double-sided mirror."

"A what?" His grip loosened.

"Come on, let me show you."

IN THE BLUR

"DO EITHER OF YOU KNOW WHERE WE'RE GOING?" IRA GRUMBLED WITH every step. "Doesn't it feel like we're going around in circles? I could've sworn we passed this line of trees a few minutes ago."

His annoying complaints were mostly drowned out by the tumbling branches and endless tremors beneath their feet, but his attitude added to the stress. And even though neither Chrysa nor Lovey bothered to answer his useless questions, he kept asking.

Chrysa was caught in her own cycle of mental pain with the same set of thoughts spinning around.

She would never see Peggy again.

Cal would be left to mourn her forever.

Mom would never get over the guilt.

So, if there was a way to get back to her family—even the slimmest chance—Chrysa wanted to try. That time was running out, and she didn't have a clue about where to find the lake the Graeae mentioned, didn't deter her. And she trusted Lovey—Aphrodite— might be able to swoop in and save the day. She *was* a goddess, after all. A goddess who'd shown a lot of weakness and only survived because Chrysa helped her.

Concentrate on the positive.

"Is anyone going to answer me?"

A thick branch cracked above their heads and struck Ira, knocking him to the ground.

As Chrysa and Lovey pulled the branch off him, she ignored the gash on his head. She wondered if this strange forest was getting sick of his endless ranting too.

"Are you okay?" Chrysa asked.

"Yeah." He rubbed the back of his head, but seemed able to stand on his own.

"Maybe you can shut up for a while now," Lovey said, getting back on the path. "And I know exactly where we're going, it's where I found Chrysa."

"But how much longer do we have to walk around this maze?"

Lovey pointed ahead. "Not much longer, actually."

Chrysa looked up, and even with the fallen branches in the way, she spotted Sword and sprinted ahead. She leaped more than ran over the debris, but nothing was going to get in the way of reaching her trusty companion.

"Sword, I'm here, buddy." She dropped to her knees and was surprised to find patches of stone had already broken off him. His brown eyes were glossy inside the stone encasing his shaggy face, and his whine echoed past what was left of his rock prison. "How do I get him out?"

"Do what you did before," Lovey said.

She stared at her, confused. "What?"

"Share your love."

Chrysa turned back to face her dog. The companion who trailed after her wherever she went. She cradled his muzzle as she met his gentle eyes. "Come on, boy, I need you to break out of this."

The ground rumbled, and thick branches collapsed nearby.

"Can you speed it up a bit?"

She ignored Ira, took a deep breath and pressed her forehead against the top of her dog's head, let all of the warm memories wash through her. Sword running beside her, throwing a stick or a ball for him to fetch, feeding him his favorite food, sneaking a snack after he performed a silly trick, how she shared her meals with him, that he liked to sleep at the end of her bed every night, the way the golden retriever always forced his way in between her and Cal when they tried to kiss.

All of these thoughts brought a smile to her face. Her chest filled with warmth, and the love flowed through her and into the canine statue. She could feel the heat leave through her fingertips. "We have to get out of here," she whispered near his shaggy ear. "Please break out before it's too late."

One ear twitched.

She kissed the top of his head, and the stone crumbled beneath her lips.

"Man, that's gross," Ira said.

"Good boy." Chrysa stared deep into his lovely doggy face. His tail was wagging and he threw his paws over her shoulders. When she hugged him back, he whined some more, yapping near her ear before falling back on all fours.

He barked and took off.

"Sword, wait!"

"Where the hell is he going?" Ira turned to watch him go.

"We have to follow," Lovey said. "Come on."

Chrysa didn't need further encouragement. She took off in the direction he'd gone, trying to avoid the endless rain of branches and the trees now plummeting in her way. The treacherous path made her more determined.

"This is getting really bad." Ira missed a step when the ground broke underneath his feet.

Chrysa grabbed his forearm a second before he slipped between the crevice, and pulled him up. She caught sight of what lay beneath—total blackness. An endless void like the blind sisters warned.

"Thanks." He seemed embarrassed.

Sword's barking echoed through the trees.

"I think he found something." As much as the broken terrain frightened Chrysa and filled her with an endless sense of doom, she didn't give up hope. She didn't miss a step, jumped over a huge fallen tree, with the top half already plunged into the earth.

"It's the lake," Lovey said. "I was right!"

Chrysa rushed to Sword's side. He was pacing back and forth in front of a frozen surface, barking. She patted his back and focused on her reflection. It was smudgy, but when Lovey stood on her left and Ira on her right, their reflection was in the lake.

"What do we do now?" Ira asked, reaching out.

"Don't touch it!" Lovey said. "Not yet."

"How did he know it was here?"

"Because, my dog's the best."

"No, it's because he's the golden weapon, the golden familiar—the *golden retriever*," Lovey said with a smile.

"He's the one the Graeae were talking about," Chrysa said. Of course!

"Aren't you glad we found the dog?" Lovey teased Ira.

"I'm glad, but if we don't know what to do, what good is it?"

"You did good, boy." Sword bumped his wet nose against Chrysa's hand. "When we get home, you're going to get a very special treat."

He licked her hand, and plunged into the lake.

"No!"

CHAPTER TWENTY

"Now what?" Cal stood beside her, staring into the full-length mirror they'd managed to drag down the marble stairs and positioned in front of Chrysa's statue. It took a while to find this particular mirror hidden behind a bunch of other frames, but it was narrow and swiveled on a stand. Trying to keep a tight grip while ensuring that neither reflective side smashed against something on the way down was tricky.

"I'm not sure." Peg considered the reflective side in front of her and hoped their discovery would offer the pathway home her sister needed.

"Nothing's happening," he said.

"I can see that."

Mom appeared on her other side. "There's got to be something we're missing."

"Of course there is!" Aunt Eno approached from the shadows. She'd been inspecting the other statues while Peg did a crappy job at explaining everything to Cal after he'd placed the freestanding two-sided mirror in front of Chrysa and Sword's statues.

"What is it?" Rya was next to the ruined pieces of the statue Peg broke the other night.

"*You're* missing!"

Peg stared at her aunt, confused. "What?"

Eno gripped her shoulders and forcibly positioned her in front of the mirror. "*You* need to touch the surface."

"Are you sure?" *It can't be that simple.* Then again, she'd expected her sister to come through by simply placing the mirror in front of Chrysa's statue.

Aunt Eno raised Peg's left hand, which was now gray stone all the way to the wrist. "I'm sure that if you touch the mirror with *this*, you'll open up the pathway."

"The last time I touched a mirror with this hand, it shattered." The thought of going to this much trouble, only to break their only way to get Chrysa back made her sick to the stomach.

"Darling, you have to try."

"I don't want to undo everything we've done...." Her heart was already beating too fast. "What if I shatter this mirror too?"

Mom wrapped an arm around her waist. "Honey, I think your aunt might be right. Your hand is the key. You have to at least try."

"But what if I break it?"

"You won't break it."

"You don't know that."

"Listen to me, Peg." Mom released her grip and cradled her face. "I don't think you realize how strong you are, or how important you are to this family. The fact you were able to see the forest and set all of this in motion confirms you're the only one who can do this. At least Athena was right about that."

Eno snorted.

"Now, please, touch the mirror."

Tears slid from Peg's eyes and her mother cleared them away.

"Only you can do this," Mom whispered. "Chrysa needs you. I need you."

The words sunk in, racing over Peg's skin and sinking below the surface. After Chrysa vanished months ago, Peg never gave up hope that her sister would return one day. *This* was the day she could finally put all of that energy into motion.

Peg took a deep breath, nodded and her mom stepped aside, unblocking her view.

"I can do this." She considered the mirror, surprised to find it wasn't her reflection staring back. It was her sister's. Chrysa's long brown hair was tangled and dusty. Her clothes were dirty and torn, her skin paler than usual and cut in several places, but she would recognize her twin anywhere.

"Chrysa," Cal whispered.

Peg raised her left hand and slowly reached out. Even without touching the mirror, an electric current flowed from the other side, and washed over her calcified skin.

Chrysa, if you can see me like I can see you, come home. Please.

She pressed her fingers against the cold surface and tapped her sister's image with her stony fingers. The sensation reverberated all the way up her arm, but her twin's reflection didn't mimic her actions. Why wasn't the mirror reacting?

Defeated, she dropped her hand.

"Don't give up now." Eno's encouraging grip was back on her shoulders.

"You can do this." Mom wrapped an arm around her waist again.

Using the strength of her family, she extended her hand again and whispered, "Here goes nothing." This time, when she pressed her palm against the smooth surface, a blast of cold air filled her lungs. Mist caressed her face as her fingertips dipped past the mirror and into molten ice. Garbled mumblings filled her ears.

Peg watched her sister's reflection and could make out two other shapes next to her. They weren't as clear as Chrysa, but she knew who they were. The deeper her hand slipped through, the more mumblings she heard, but still couldn't understand a single one.

A cracking sound tore through her and she thought something was suddenly broken inside her.

"Chrysa," she said. "I'm here, where are you?"

The full-length mirror vibrated and her hand dipped deeper, until she actually came into contact with something on the other side. She instinctively pulled her hand out of the molten surface and noticed her skin was back to normal. The mirror had somehow washed away the stone completely. But how?

"You did it!" someone cheered, but she didn't know who. All she could focus on was the turmoil inside the pathway, the thunderous rumblings. Trees and branches were falling everywhere, and the ground was trembling. What was going on over there?

Peg watched the mirror's surface quiver like water.

Barking echoed from the other side, followed by a loud, "*No!*"

Before Peg could get out of the way, something shot out of the mirror and landed on her. The impact sent her to the floor and stole the air from her lungs. A wet tongue lapped at her face. It took her a moment to realize who it was. "*Sword!*"

The dog whined and wagged his tail, sending a cloud of grainy sand into the air. His once golden fur was now caked with a fine layer of dust.

"It's really him!" Cal said.

When Sword heard him, he leaped off Peg and went to him.

"What did you guys see?" Peg wiped away the crumbling dust the dog had scattered on her. She desperately wanted to know if she was the only one who'd seen the turmoil seconds before Sword came through.

"When he came through the mirror, his statue crumbled," Rya said. She was inspecting the spot on the other side of the frame, where Sword had sat faithfully beside Chrysa. All that was left now was a neat pile of stone dust.

Peg stood as the sound of crumbling stone echoed around the chamber. "What was that?" she asked, her voice barely a whisper.

"It looks like Sword isn't the only statue waking up," Mom said.

IN THE BLUR

"Where did he go?" Chrysa's heart sank. Only minutes after getting him back, Sword had disappeared into the lake.

"Wait a minute," Ira said.

"What?"

"That's not your reflection in the water."

"What're you talking about?"

"Look for yourself, you've become your reject emo sister." Lovey was staring into the water, too. "And the lake is liquid again."

Chrysa bent closer and found her reflection wearing her sister's short hair, black skinny jeans and an oversized hoodie. If she was looking at Peggy instead of herself, did that mean this really was their way home? Was that why Sword jumped in, to lead the way?

The sound of breaking branches and crumbling trees escalated. The earth was crumbling, but she didn't dare check the damage or proximity over her shoulder.

"We have to get the hell out of here," Ira said. "And fast, because the void those weird old chicks were talking about is headed right for us."

Chrysa touched the surface of the lake and dipped her fingers into the cold water. "You're right, it's completely melted."

"I'm going in." Before she could stop him, Ira dive-bombed into the middle of the lake, but there was no splash. He simply fell through—was there one second, gone the next.

"You did it, we're actually getting out of this depressing place." Lovey's smile was wide, and her pallor was as close to healthy as the colorless blur allowed.

"I didn't do any of this." Peggy and Sword were the ones who should get the credit. Even the Graeae. "I don't understand how this happened..."

"Isn't it obvious?"

"Not as obvious as it should be, apparently."

"It's quite simple, really." Lovey shrugged. "Whether she realized it or not, as soon as Pegasus came in contact with this forest, she infected the blur with her darkness. And when she touched it a second time, not only did she make the sky fall, but she created this lake." The goddess pointed at the still water. "But what's even more important is her connection to you, because that's what ultimately opened up the pathway."

"Yeah, you're right. It all makes perfect sense now."

"Really?"

"Of course not," she snapped. "Nothing will ever make sense again." Yet, a warm glow filled her heart. After being stranded in blur for what felt like forever, she'd thought her family might have forgotten her. Or given up hope.

Thunder rolled closer, but so did something else.

"What's that?"

A swarm of color burst from between the trees and flew past her, hovered above the lake. A multitude of butterflies beat their wings over the reflective water, shedding radiance into this monochrome hellscape.

"I'll be damned," Lovey said.

"What are these butterflies doing here?" In all her time here, she'd never seen an insect or an animal. Asides from Sword.

"These are the souls of the veiled. Looks like some survived after all."

"What do they want?" Chrysa asked, mesmerized by their fast-beating wings.

"They want to go home."

"Is it safe for them to go through the lake?"

"Of course," Lovey answered. "Once these souls get out, each can cross into the Underworld."

A rumble shredded the earth nearby and a chunk crumbled into the growing nothingness.

"You better go through before it's too late," Lovey said. "The void is near."

"Wait, how do we make sure these butterflies come with us?"

"I can take them through," she said.

"You have to go first, then."

"I'm not leaving without you," Lovey said with a shake of her head. "Cal summoned me to find and protect you, and that doesn't end until we're safely on the other side."

"You won't be leaving me. I'll be right behind you. I just want to make sure all of these souls get out safely." She didn't want a single living creature to get left behind in the blur. Especially since her mother was responsible for sending them here.

Lovey's eyes were bright. "You're a lot braver than I thought, and selfless. Are you sure about this?"

"I'm positive, just take them," she said. "Hurry!"

"You'll be rewarded for this, I assure you." In that moment, Lovey abandoned the pretense of being a teenage girl. The cloak fell off her body. Her platinum blonde hair grew as long as Rapunzel's and cascaded around her shoulders, the strands winding themselves around her breasts and hips, enough to modestly cover some of her nudity. Her bare feet floated a few inches off the ground and her skin glowed. All traces of blood and injury were gone.

Chrysa was suddenly blinded by emotion.

"Come to me, my lovely psyche." Aphrodite spread her arms and a rush of multicolored butterflies emerged from every direction to join the others. The goddess floated above the lake with a tornado of vibrant wings.

"Stop showing off and go already," Chrysa said.

She smiled and melted into the lake with the butterflies swirling around her radiant body.

The crash and rumble of the forest shattered too close to where Chrysa stood. She took a moment to study the swelling blackness raging forth faster and stronger than a tsunami. The darkness would engulf her and the lake if she didn't leave.

She was about to dive in when she spotted the flutter of blue wings on a branch. The butterfly struggled to get loose, but was stuck.

Chrysa rushed over and found one wing was caught between two branches. With the void bearing down on her faster than a giant wave of doom eager to take her under, she released the trapped appendage.

The butterfly sat on her palm as she raced back to the lake.

She watched the reflection of her sister for a moment. One that was as familiar as her own. She could see the ominous wave's reflection bearing down, ready to engulf her if she didn't get out of the way.

Chrysa dived into the lake and out of blur.

CHAPTER TWENTY-ONE

"Where's my sister?" Peg watched the new kid step through the mirror as his statue shattered behind him.

"It's nice to see you too."

"Where is she?" She tried to push him out of the way, but he wouldn't budge.

"Relax, she's on her way."

Peg ignored him and stood in front of the mirror, but had to duck when a huge cloud of beating wings rushed into the chamber. At first, she thought this was a swarm of bees and wondered if these insects were responsible for the indecipherable murmurs. But as the cloud rose around her, she noticed the butterflies encircled a blonde figure.

A surge of shattering statues echoed all around the chamber, filling the place with piles of dust.

"What the hell?" Peg covered her nose and mouth until the residue settled. The others did the same, though someone was coughing.

"Don't worry, Peg," a familiar, bittersweet voice said. "Those are the statues of the released souls shattering. They're finally free."

"Lovey?" She recognized the girl in the center of the butterflies. But why was she hovering in mid-air? And why wasn't she wearing any clothes? The only thing offering any cover was her super long mane of hair.

"That's Aphrodite to you," she said with a grin. She turned her attention to Cal. "I answered your call, and she'll be here shortly. After all the trouble I went through, you better cherish Chrysa the way she deserves."

"I will."

"I have some souls to direct to Hermes." Lovey floated higher, taking the colorful butterflies with her. "You too, broken one."

Peg and Cal followed her gaze and were shocked to find Chrysa standing in front of the mirror with a butterfly resting in the middle of her palm. The bug flew around her face before soaring to join the others before vanishing in a rush of wings and color.

"You're here!" Peg was paralyzed to the spot. After all the crying and hoping, the endless sadness and grief, she didn't know what to do.

"Thanks to you." Chrysa's smile was small and tentative, but one Peg had missed.

Peg ran to her sister and hugged her, tighter than ever. She was a scratched-up mess and as dusty as Sword, but Peg's twin was finally back. She glanced in the mirror and for a second, couldn't understand what was happening.

"The gloom," she whispered.

"What?" Chrysa leaned back, holding her at arm's length.

"The gloom is in the mirror."

"No, that's the void."

She couldn't take her eyes off the raging storm. There might be a barrier between them, but she could feel the gloom calling her.

"Peggy?" Her sister was trying to get her attention, but her voice sounded far away.

She'd already convinced herself she would never give into the night sky, that she wasn't ready to allow the gloom to consume her. So, when Chrysa squeezed her arms, Peg was grateful to be tethered back to reality.

"Hey, what's wrong?" Chrysa asked.

"It's nothing, I'm glad you're back."

"Chrysa."

"Cal!" Chrysa threw herself into her boyfriend's open arms.

Peg wanted to give the couple some privacy and turned back to the darkness now engulfing the entire mirror. She could feel the weight pressing against the other side and knew the gloom—or void, as her sister called it—would eventually smash through if she didn't do something to stop it.

"Watch out!" Aunt Eno shouted.

She ducked out of the way a second before the giant ox statue was thrown into the mirror and swallowed up by obscurity.

"What're you doing?" Peg asked.

"Throwing the monsters in before they get a chance to wake up." Aunt Rya shoved a large dog with two heads into the full-length mirror and it disappeared, before Mom added another creature.

Peg slowly realized these monsters were feeding the expanding darkness.

She stood in front of the black surface, ignoring the calls for her to get out of the way.

I have to stop this, she wanted to say. But all she could do was concentrate on the swirling mess, and understood it was her duty to calm the turmoil she'd experienced since first coming into contact with this double-sided mirror.

Peg stared into the violent whirl and identified a pair of eyes caught in the center of the maelstrom. She gasped, and it took her a moment to realize they were her own. She wrapped her hands around the sides of the mirror and watched as the gloom licked her skin with cold, hungry tendrils.

"I won't let you come through."

The gloom extended past the edges, wrapped itself around her fingers and threatened to engulf her. She didn't want this darkness anywhere near her, but at the same time had to fight the need to give into the comfort of oblivion. She'd spent much of her life fighting the darkness that always seemed one step behind her, and wasn't about to give up now.

Not after everything. Not when Chrysa was back.

She was well aware of the Pegasus myth and how the night sky would be her final resting place as a beautiful constellation in the heavens one day, but not today. She wasn't going to let this comforting darkness consume her.

Peg fought against the pressure and pushed the mirror, watched as the long reflective construct crashed against the marble floor and shattered into a thousand lethal pieces. The gloom was trapped in individual sections of glass, unable to grow or rejoin. As she stood in the middle of the mess, Peg stared as the bits of gloom faded like smoke until there was nothing but shattered reflections left behind.

"What just happened?" Chrysa asked, coming up beside her.

"I had to destroy it..."

Her sister's eyes were shiny but she nodded, as if she understood. Maybe after the nightmare she'd survived inside that freaky forest, Chrysa truly understood the weirdness.

She wondered when her sister would get her memories back.

"Kids, we have to get out of here!" Mom yelled.

"What about the other monster statues, we can't leave them here," Peg said. She recalled this threat was the reason Athena had refused to help.

"We have no choice," Aunt Eno said. "Come on!" She rounded up Ira and Cal, led them towards the bottom of another staircase Peg was sure hadn't been there a second before.

Chrysa took her hand and led her away, but Peg tripped and lost her grip. Her sister stopped when a huge monster stepped between them.

"No!" she yelled. "Peggy!"

Peg tilted her head and found a gigantic creature towering over her. Not just any monster—the Chimera.

The hideous Chimera was the stuff of nightmares—one body with two heads and a snake tail. The horned goat head spewed fire from its massive, razor-toothed mouth and missed her only because she rolled to the side at the last second. The lioness made a swipe in her direction and sent her skidding along the floor.

"Let me go, I have to help her!" Chrysa struggled against some-one, but Peg couldn't see who. She was too busy trying to dodge the monster.

"Just go," Peg called. "I'll get out the other way and meet you at the house!"

"No, I won't go!"

"You have to! Run!"

"Peg, make sure you seal the door when you get up there!" Aunt Eno yelled over the commotion, because other monsters were cracking out of their statues. "It's the only way to trap them!"

Was the void responsible for these monstrosities coming alive now?

"Okay!" She rolled to her feet and barely avoided another swipe from the Chimera, before having to dodge another line of fire She sputtered and tripped several times but finally charged up the now familiar marble stairs, her heart beating and breath catching. She somehow reached the door at the top, with the heat chasing her all the way.

As she stepped into the barn and slammed the door behind her, the lioness smacked through and splintered the wood in two. The huge snake tail tasted the air with its forked tongue but made no attempt to attack her.

"Shit!"

Peg ran between the aisles, lost her footing and fell to her knees. She got right up when she spotted Belle standing in front of the open barn doors.

"Get out of the way and run!" she yelled.

Belle looked confused, didn't budge.

"What're you doing? We have to get out of here, come on!"

"Pegasus. I'm not going anywhere." Her friend's eyes glowed too brightly behind her glasses. "You know I was born to battle the Chimera."

CHAPTER TWENTY-TWO

"W<small>HAT</small>?" P<small>EG</small> <small>ASKED</small>, <small>BUT OF COURSE SHE WAS WELL AWARE THAT</small> Bellerophon was the hero who killed the Chimera.

"I've got this." Belle stepped forward. "Stand behind me."

"Are you sure?"

"Yes." Her friend stood her ground, legs bare because she was wearing a black denim skirt and boots. Her pink bubblegum hair was swept up in a high ponytail. She pulled her glasses off with her free hand and threw them aside.

Belle was a total badass, holding an old, long-barreled gun.

"Nice gun."

"It's one of Pa's most treasured toys." She admired the weapon with joyful admiration, as if there wasn't a monster already pushing its way out of a tiny doorway at the end of the barn. "It's vintage, a Colt Buntline revolver with a 12-inch barrel and *lead* bullets."

Peg slipped into the adjacent aisle and winced at the screeching Chimera. "If we weren't in a life and death situation, I might find your knowledge of this phallic symbol somewhat arousing."

"Good to know." Belle's grin was wicked sexy. "What do you think you're doing? I told you to stay behind me."

"I have to close the door so nothing else comes through!" Peg wound her way across the barn, avoiding the random shots of flame. If this monster cracked free of her stone prison and figured out how to escape, others would eventually do the same. She couldn't risk another grotesque slipping through. The aunts and her mother might have sent a few of the beasts into the void, but there were plenty left.

When she reached the shattered door, she couldn't believe Eve was peeking inside.

"Hey, get away from there!"

Eve spun around to face her. "I, uh... I hated how things ended before. I want to come clean."

"In case you haven't noticed, now's not a good time." At least the Chimera was on the other side of the barn, and nothing else had crawled out of the door yet.

"What is this place?"

Peg was about to slam the door when a massive claw-tipped paw swiped at Eve. She screamed, tried to get out of the way but the tip snagged her curls.

"Fuck!" Peg searched the assortment of junk until she found a small metal sign with a jagged edge. She grabbed it, hoped she wouldn't get tetanus and charged the paw. She hacked and sliced, didn't stop until the appendage was severed completely, and a deafening squeal of pain echoed from the womb of the chamber.

Eve screamed and stumbled forward, ended up on the ground. She squirmed and struggled to pull what was left of the claw from her hair.

Several growls joined the squeal and Peg dumped the sign.

"Eve, grab that side of the door!"

"What?"

"Grab that side of the door and I'll deal with this one. Hurry!"

The nuisance struggled to her feet before lumbering to the left side of the gaping darkness. She wrapped her small hands around the wooden mess and Peg did the same.

"Let's press them together!"

"Like this?" Eve's voice quivered, as she pushed.

"Yes!" Peg dug inside her pocket with shaky fingers and eventually found the Medusa coin. "Press a bit tighter, so I can slip this in."

Eve nodded but she looked scared and jumped when something smacked against the other side.

"Don't let go!" After a few misses because her hands were sweaty, Peg jammed the coin into the slot. The two sides melded together before vanishing completely.

"What just happened?" Eve's eyes were wide and she was visibly shaking.

She didn't bother with an explanation as she gritted her teeth and struggled to drag the huge sign back into place. When she was done, she was sweating profusely, her hands were red, and she was breathing hard. But at least the chamber was sealed and nothing else could escape.

A line of fire blasted up the middle aisle before smoldering to smaller flames.

"Damn it!" She'd almost forgotten about the Chimera. At least Belle was taking care of that hideous thing.

Eve seemed a little unsteady on her feet. "Seriously, what's happening?"

"I've already told you! This isn't a great time. Why don't you do your disappearing act again so you don't get hurt?" She really didn't want her here. And this time, it wasn't because Eve was a pain. She genuinely didn't want her to get hurt.

"But I *really* need to talk to you."

A roar filled the barn and the blood froze in Peg's veins.

She backed Eve up against the shelf. "Are you here because you want to kill my mother, *Perseus*? Because I won't let you. We've been through enough shit already and—"

"I'm not Perseus, and I don't want to kill anyone!" Eve yelled in her face.

"Then what do you want?" The weight of the cards inside her pocket reminded her of where this all began—in a classroom with an innocent reading. "What are you looking for that involves me?"

"I've sent you countless of emails, but you never responded to a single one." Eve's voice rose and fell. "If you had, I might have been able to warn you without all of these—"

"Games?"

"Yes."

"What emails are you talking about?"

"I, uh, the subject was A Friend from Africa."

"That was *you?* I thought they were spam."

"It was my attempt to reach out and warn you."

"About what?"

"Not what, *who.*"

A bleat echoed from across the barn, followed by more fire. But the shelves kept them mostly hidden for now. Soon, Peg would have to join the action, but first she needed to get Eve out of the way. And she didn't want to waste time chatting about emails.

"Who were you going to warn me about? In case you haven't noticed, we're running out of time!"

Eve glanced at the ceiling and winced. "At first, I didn't understand why I had the compulsion to find my relatives, but I knew it wasn't right for him to take all those weapons with the intention of murder." She paused for a second because she was speaking too fast. "Still, I didn't fully get it. Not until Chrysaor disappeared, that's when everything started to come together. And now, it all makes perfect sense." Her necklace shimmered.

"*Who* wanted to come here to murder someone?"

"Perseus! He took the weapons from the Garden of Hesperides with murder in mind. Even though the other hero tried to talk some sense into him, he wouldn't listen."

Between these fairy tales and the monster rampaging through the other side of the barn, she couldn't connect the dots. Who was the other hero? She knew, but couldn't think straight. Not when Belle was battling a monster. Not when she shouldn't be wasting time on a silly conversation that was going nowhere.

A deeper, louder screech followed by the sound of gunfire cracked through the stifling air.

"Look, I don't have time for this right now!" She glared at Eve. "You have two seconds to tell me what you really want."

The girl rolled up her sleeve and flashed a silver snake bracelet, with two rubies for eyes.

"What the hell?" Her eyes widened. "Where the hell did you get that?"

"It's a family heirloom. We've all got one," Eve said. "We don't want to become statues and get lost in that dreadful forest, do we?"

There was a lot to decipher in that one statement, and Peg didn't know how to respond.

Eve snuck a look over Peg's shoulder. "I came all the way from Africa to tell you about Perseus because you're my cousins and you were in danger... but I was scared to tell you the truth."

"That's what happens when someone comes on too strong." She couldn't believe this girl was her cousin. "Where did you say you were from?"

"The Garden of Hesperides."

"Oh, right." Yet, she hadn't remembered a single thing about Hesperides. As far as she knew, the Garden of Hesperides wasn't a usual player in this game. So, why was Eve really here? She sure as hell didn't warn them about Perseus.

"It's in Africa."

She checked over her shoulder but the metal shelf was too packed with junk and she couldn't see a single thing that was happening on the other side.

"Peg!" Belle yelled and her voice echoed around the barn. "I need a boost!"

"You need to go now!" When she turned back, Eve was gone.

The sound of Belle's voice got her legs pumping. Peg took a sharp turn around the next corner and a strange sensation flowed over her body. She didn't stop but reached for the cards inside her jeans pocket. She knew that wouldn't be enough, so she also grabbed the second deck tucked into her hoodie pouch.

Peg held a black deck in one hand, red in the other. She threw the cards high into the air and the two colors combined, but one card stood out the most.

Three of spades.

The assortment fluttered above her head to form a mosaic of face and deck cards, then plunged edge-first into her shoulder blades, tearing through her hoodie as easily as razors. The cards dug into the spots along her shoulders that itched so badly for days, connected deep beneath her skin before fanning out into a unique wingspan. One very different from what she'd proudly sported when she'd had real wings with white feathers and Bellerophon rode her during a similar battle.

She found Belle ducking behind a shelf, barely concealed from the fire-breathing monster. Belle cocked the gun. "Are you ready for me, Peg?" When she caught sight of the playing-card wings she whistled. "Wow. They're beautiful."

"Thanks." The cards were embedded deep into her flesh, and she could feel the warm blood trickling down her back. But it wasn't painful. "Are you ready?"

"Always." She stood. "Come and get me, Pegasus."

Peg stepped up behind her friend, wrapped her arms around Belle's midsection and willed her new wings to take flight. The cards took a moment to respond before whipping against the hot air and taking them high into the rafters.

"Hold on tight, the recoil's going to be a bitch." Belle expertly held the Colt in her right hand, and pointed the long barrel in front of her.

"I won't ever let you go," Peg whispered in her ear.

"Good to know."

Peg held on tight and watched the spectacle over her friend's shoulder.

"Take us closer."

The monstrous Chimera straddled several shattered shelves. The snake tail hung uselessly behind her, and the lioness swayed blindly because Belle had shot out both of her eyes. The goat's horns were destroyed but she still drew her head back, preparing to take a flame-fueled breath. While the lioness roared her frustration, part of the roof caved in.

The goat opened wide to exhale.

Belle was quick and shot two lead bullets straight into the goat's gaping mouth. The creature bleated and screeched when the flames were stifled. She attempted another exhale but the lead was already poisoning her and she fell sideways. Before the monster hit the ground, all three parts of her dissolved into ash.

"You did good, Pegasus."

"So did you, Bellerephon."

"I'm glad we finally remembered everything."

"Yeah, finally." Peg lowered her friend to the ground but Belle jumped before Peg could join her. She dumped the gun on the ground, as if it was poisoned now.

"You better be careful with that or—"

"This might be his pride and joy, but you're mine." Belle grabbed a hold of her hands and lowered her the rest of the way until Peg's feet touched the ground.

"What happened to your spear?"

Belle shrugged and was so magnificent in that moment, practically glowing like a true hero after a huge conquest. "Who needs a spear when you have a gun?"

Peg smiled, and Belle squeezed her fingers.

"Those wings of yours really are amazing."

"Thanks," she said, blushing. "Listen, Belle, I need to tell you something."

"Oh yeah, what's that?"

"I, uh, I kissed Cal."

Her eyes widened. "You did?"

"Well, he kissed *me* and I... I let him. I pushed him away eventually, but we got caught up in a weak moment of grief." She watched for a reaction, hoping Belle wouldn't be upset.

She seemed disappointed when she said, "Isn't this something you should be telling your sister?"

Peg stepped closer. "It's something I need to tell you because I want us to be honest with each other. No secrets."

Belle sighed. "Well, I've been keeping a secret too."

"You have?"

"Every time I told you that messing around between guys was enough, I was lying."

"You were?"

"Yeah, I enjoy having you to myself because somewhere along the way, I fell in love with you." Belle looked away, avoided her gaze.

Her heart soared at Belle's confession. "Me too."

"Really?"

"Yes!" Peg pressed her body against Belle's, wanted her to feel how fast her heart was beating. Needed her friend to understand how happy this made her, because having Belle by her side was what she really wanted. She wasn't going to lie to herself or to Belle anymore. "I've wanted to be more than best-friends-with-benefits for a while now."

Belle's eyes sparkled. "What're you saying?"

"I'm done being quiet about how you make me feel. I want the world to know."

"Are you sure?"

"Positive."

With multiple fires burning inside the barn and bent metal shelves all around, the two heroes kissed with the heat of mutual passion that had chased them through history.

"We've always been tied together," Belle whispered when they drew apart.

"And always will be." Peg stared into Belle's pretty eyes and watched a slideshow of the many times they'd fallen in love through their shared lifetimes. "I'm ready for whatever the future brings."

"So am I."

As they kissed, the card-deck wingspan collapsed behind Peg.

"So, you finally found me?" The sound of her mom's voice outside the barn pulled her out of the kiss. She grabbed Belle's hand and led her to the door.

FREE FROM BLUR

RUNNING.

The dark chamber full of crumbling statues haunted her, but all Chrysa could do was run. Her legs burned. Every cut on her face, hands and legs stung. Ever since returning her dulled senses had escalated from zero to a hundred miles in a matter of seconds, making every one of her injuries hurt like hell.

"We can't leave her there." How many times had she said this already? But no one was listening. "I have to go back for Peggy."

After being away from her twin sister for so long, she couldn't bear to be separated this quickly. Not after everything Peggy had obviously done to make this possible. Why was the void connected to her? Lovey tried to explain it before, but it still didn't make any sense.

"She'll be fine," Aunt Widow—or Aunt Weirdo—said. They were different and she usually had no trouble telling the two apart, but both were running ahead of her and she couldn't see anyone clearly.

Cal gripped her hand too tightly. "Peg can take care of herself."

She couldn't help but glance at him. Chrysa wanted to bathe in the glory of having found her way back to the boy who loved her enough to summon a goddess to find his lost love. His hair was longer and tumbled over his forehead and into his eyes. And when he smiled, the claustrophobic staircase seemed to light up.

Where are we going?

The roaring inside the chamber was fading fast, and she prayed her sister would be okay.

Her sister.

Her twin.

The one who made sacrifices to reach her. How could she ever repay Peggy and Cal for their loyalty and love?

She couldn't.

It would take many lifetimes to do so.

"Come on!" Mom pushed the door at the top of the staircase and Sword rushed through. The aunts went next, Cal and Chrysa followed and when Mom shut the door, she realized this was the inside of her mother's closet. How many times had she hid amongst the hanging clothes and coats, the shoes and random boxes hoping Peggy wouldn't find her? Not once had she thought there might be a hidden door leading to a secret place.

Cal dragged her with him into the bedroom beyond, but before they could leave together, Mom stopped her. She released his hand and he frowned.

"It's okay, follow my aunties downstairs and I'll be there shortly."

He didn't seem happy about going without her, and she didn't want to leave his side either, but she needed a moment alone with her mother. He nodded, kissed her cheek and stepped into the corridor.

Mom pulled her into a hug, but Chrysa let her arms hang at her sides. She could blame this reaction on sheer exhaustion, but one thing she hadn't been able to shake was the anger she felt towards her mother.

"I've missed you so much," Mom cried into her hair.

"You're hurting me."

"Oh, sorry." Mom released her and made a grab for her hand, but Chrysa pulled away. "I never meant to... I'm so, *so* sorry for what happened, I—"

"Did you know I would end up inside that forest?"

"I didn't even know it was you I was staring at until it was too late." Tears shone in her eyes.

"That's no excuse. What about all the other people?" The butterflies were one thing, but when she'd seen how many statues crumbled as a result, that truly broke Chrysa's heart.

"I couldn't control myself, the rage—"

"You could've warned me—warned *us*." How much did her sister know about any of this? She didn't know half as much as she wanted to. Only managed to put together the pieces Lovey and Ira threw her way. Still, she knew her mother was Medusa and she was the reason why so many souls were trapped in the blur.

She suddenly realized that Ira hadn't ascended the stairs with them.

Mom shook her head. "I wanted to protect you."

"Yeah, well, you didn't protect me in the blur. Did you, Medusa?"

She flinched. "In the blur?"

"That's what I called the forest... Never mind." She stepped back and didn't say another word for a while. The uncomfortable silence settled around her and Chrysa could hear the murmur of commotion outside the house.

Still, she couldn't bring herself to speak.

"Oh, baby, I really am sorry," her mother finally said. "Was it... was it really bad?"

Chrysa focused on her for several loud beats of her heart. Her mother was different somehow, worn around the edges with more wrinkles on her usually youthful face. Her hair was messy and she had bald spots. She was also wearing one of the sweaters Chrysa had given her. That almost melted her resolve, but she held onto the anger. It wouldn't last forever, but she wanted to make her mother suffer for a bit.

For what she was and all the lies she wove around Peggy and her.

"How long was I gone?" she asked, because she didn't know what else to talk about.

"Over three months."

She'd lost that much time? And now she was losing even more

trying to avoid having a real conversation. How many minutes—that felt like hours—had passed inside this stifling room?

"Chrysa, I'm going to make it up to you." Mom took a strand of Chrysa's dirty hair between her fingertips. "We have to get you cleaned up, make sure these cuts don't get infected."

"Mom! Can you stop fussing and really look at me?"

She dropped her hair, hand falling to her side. "Chrysa, you were gone for months and until the other day I was convinced you were dead, so no. I can't stop fussing over you, I won't." Her unevenly chopped hair shifted around her face and Chrysa wanted to step away because she wasn't ready to see this truth. Couldn't bear the thought of snakes manifesting in her mother's hair.

"I—"

A loud screech cut into whatever her mother was about to say.

Mom's eyes widened. "She didn't lock the monster inside."

"What does that mean?"

"We have to help." She dashed past her and left the bedroom, thundered down the stairs so loudly Chrysa could hear her footsteps from where she stood.

So much for her attentive mother.

She sighed and when she was about to step into the corridor, Cal walked back into the room. He smiled, a small tentative spread of his full lips.

"Are you really here?"

Chrysa's lips quirked in response, because she couldn't speak. She closed the distance and rushed into Cal's arms. Their mouths moved fast and hard, trying to make up for lost time with a single kiss. All the words they could be saying were delivered via their eager lips, and her heart swelled.

She pulled away, breathless. "I can't believe you summoned Aphrodite for me."

"I would summon the devil for you." His thumbs caressed her jaw, his eyes intent on hers and dark with longing. "I've missed you so much."

"I missed you every single moment."

"Now that you're back, I'm never going to let you go," he said.

"Good, because I don't want you to."

He was quiet for a few seconds. "Chrysa, while you were gone... I missed you a lot, but something happened with—"

"I don't need to know." She caressed his lips with her fingertips to stop whatever confession he was about to make. "Whatever happened while I wasn't here doesn't matter. I want to pretend none of this ever happened. Make myself believe that it's the next day after the last time we saw each other. As if we were apart for one very long night." This wish was easier said than done, but she didn't want him to feel bad about anything.

He nodded and kissed her again. Chrysa got lost in the moment, gave herself to the real sensation of his mouth against hers and his hands running up and down her back. Cal didn't care that she was a total mess, he still held her the same way he always had. Was helping to bury some of the worst memories she'd carried over.

Time meant nothing, but she didn't mind.

The commotion outside eventually became too much to ignore.

"Seriously, what's going on out there?" Cal said, caressing her face.

"We should check, to make sure this nightmare is really over." Even though she didn't want to leave the comfort of his embrace, Chrysa slid out of his arms and made her way to the bedroom window. Her mom and aunts were standing in the yard between the house and barn. Ira loitered a few steps behind them, slowly making his way toward Peg and Belle, who were walking out of the barn hand in hand.

Her sister seemed wilder, more untamed animal than girl.

Belle, an action hero with a gun hanging at her side.

A crackling energy flowed around the two.

Chrysa couldn't help but smile. She'd known they were messing around ever since she'd found them kissing in the barn last summer, but she hadn't said anything.

"What's going on?" Cal asked, standing behind her.

"I don't know, but we should get down there." She leaned closer to the window. "Hey, who's that?" A man she didn't recognize was running down the driveway, and he was carrying a large weapon in his hand. "Maybe he wants to sell that relic to Mom..." Enough random people popped in and out of their property with junk to offload.

"Wait, is that Mr. Danae?"

"*Who?*"

Ira rushed forward, seemed to be calling out while waving both arms above his head as this strange man approached.

"He's our new history teacher," Cal said.

Ira's father. The teacher didn't slow and leaped impossibly high into the air, landing in front of her mother.

Chrysa's breath misted the glass. The disgusting taste of acid rose up her mouth, and she tried to swallow down the nausea.

Ira stopped in front of him, still shouting something she couldn't hear. The man swung what Chrysa now clearly identified as a sword. The sharp edge carved the air in slow motion. The shine of the rising sun glossed over the blade like a line of fireworks, and when the sharpest edge sliced her mother's head off in one clean swoop, she screamed.

Her mourning wails were echoed below.

The Ceto sisters—both pairs—wept at the sudden loss.

The window shattered in front of her.

Cal pulled her back and his mouth was moving, but Chrysa couldn't understand a single word. All she could hear was the constant cry she couldn't stop. He covered his ears and she dislodged from his grip. Raced out of the room and didn't stop until she was outside.

Cold air rushed into her lungs, but she still couldn't stop screaming.

CHAPTER TWENTY-THREE

THE BARN WAS A TANGLED MESS. HALF HAD BEEN BURNED BEYOND recognition because the metal shelves had melted, and the other was full of twisted, toppled shelving and destroyed junk. But Peg felt invincible.

Her heart beat loud and strong and with her hand blazing in Belle's, she thought they could rule the world together. Not that she wanted to. All she cared about was having her sister back, defeating a few monsters and getting the girl.

"Are you ready to face the world?" Belle asked as she scooped up the discarded gun.

She met her gaze and smiled. "With you by my side, always."

The girls stepped out of the ruined barn and into the rising sunshine of a new day. The air was stained with smoke, but she didn't care. Mom, Eno and Rya stood on the long grass between the barn and house. Sword was sitting in front of the backdoor, and Ira was rushing up behind them. He was screaming something the wind stole from her ears.

Peg turned her head and spotted Mr. Danae, sprinting down the drive. He was holding a huge sword with a curved blade that reminded her of a scythe. Sweat prickled the back of her neck, slid down her spine and made her shiver. Stung the points where her playing-card wings had pierced the skin.

None of that mattered as much as what was happening in front of her. "What's he doing here?" she asked, feeling a sense of emptiness settle over her.

"Shit, what's he going to do with that?" Belle added.

"No, stop, *don't!*" Ira rushed in front of Mom, waving his hands.

This man who'd taught lessons about ancient Egyptians, the similarities between the Romans and the Greeks, how Norse mythology varied from Celtic, had also goaded her to remember who Perseus was and what he was celebrated for. And now, he was on their property carrying a sword.

In that moment, the truth rushed into her head. Mr. Danae was Perseus. Danae—he'd used his mother's name.

As he closed the distance and leaped into the air, he faded from existence for a second before dropping in front of her mother.

Mom turned to face Peg and her eyes shimmered with tears.

"No!" Peg wanted to take a step but couldn't. Could only watch as Mr. Danae swung the scythe and sliced through Mom's neck in one sharp and smooth motion, sending her head rolling off her shoulders. The snakes that had been masquerading as hair writhed in pain.

The horrifying reality of what he'd done smacked Peg square in the chest. A shriek she couldn't control, driven from the deepest recesses of her core, tore out of her mouth. It was echoed from inside the house, as well as from Aunties Eno and Rya.

The four screamed and screamed, unable to control their grief.

Perseus considered the decapitated body and dropped the sword.

"What have you done?" Ira cried. "Didn't you hear what I was saying?"

He shook his head. "I did what I had to, what I'm eternally destined to do."

"But they helped me," he said. "They got me out of that place!"

"*Ira?*" The teacher's eyes seemed to clear. He blinked as he realized who was talking to him. "What're you doing here? She killed you..."

"No, she didn't, I was sent to some weird forest. Why did you kill her?"

"She's not dead, she never is." He made his way towards Mom's head and when he dug his hands into her snaky hair and lifted her off the ground, her face was caught in the same frozen yell as her sisters and daughters. The combination of short and long vivid colored snakes didn't stop shifting. "I'm going to get rid of all the monsters."

"No!" Ira stepped in front of the aunts. "Don't!"

"Get out of my way, son."

"I'm not your son," he spat.

"Ira, get out of the way!"

"No."

"Have it your way." Perseus held Medusa's head in front of him and although her eyes lit up with a shimmer of emerald, no one turned to stone. He frowned, seemed genuinely confused about his son not turning to stone. "Why didn't it work?"

"I tried to tell you. The other side is gone now, she can't hurt anyone anymore."

"I don't—"

"It was destroyed!" Ira yelled. "You killed her for nothing! Are you happy now?"

Hatred coursed inside Peg's veins, sending a bout of toxic blood through her, strong enough to force her into action. Her hand slid from Belle's and she took her time across the expanse of grass. Every step got her closer to the killer and his apprentice, who were still lost in chatter. One trying to understand why Medusa's glare wasn't working. The other trying to convince him what he'd done was wrong. The older man was still holding Mom's head while pointing at his winged shoes, probably trying to make a quick getaway.

I won't let him.

Peg spotted her sister running out of the house with Cal trailing close behind. The wails were still spilling from all of their mouths as

Peg leaned over, wrapped her fingers around the hilt of the sword and winced at the burning pain. Harpe—the weapon Perseus used to kill Medusa—burned her palm, but the sting was nothing compared to everything else. She'd suffered a stone palm, and had a snake burrow into her brain to reveal the truth of her many pasts. She'd challenged the hall of statues and got her sister back.

A melting hand was nothing. Not even the smell of burning flesh stopped her.

Peg raised the sword, surprised at how heavy it was. As she swung the long blade, she caught sight of a snowy owl and an ebony crow sitting on the fence post. She faltered for a moment, but swung the scythe hard enough to slice Perseus's head clean off his shoulders.

The owl became Athena and the crow a slight woman she didn't recognize.

Mr. Danae's head rolled on the grass. His body collapsed but his fingers were still tangled in Medusa's snakes.

The wails stopped abruptly as the remaining Ceto women shut up instantaneously, leaving a buzzing silence in their wake.

Peg wanted to drop the sword, but she wasn't done yet. She held the tip against Ira's neck. The apprentice had to die too. She couldn't leave anyone else to destroy her family. Refused to.

"No, Peggy, don't do it!" her sister called.

"He's the son of Perseus, he has to die."

"He wasn't my dad, I tried to tell you that already." Ira's voice trembled and he shut his eyes, held both hands over his face as he cowered. "Please, I tried to stop him. I never wanted anything to do with his crusade. But I had no choice. My mother made him my guardian." He opened one eye. "I had no choice."

She pressed the blade into his skin and a tiny bead of blood spilled down the side of his neck. Now that this guy was back, she knew who he was. Another worthless hero—Hercules.

"Peggy, listen to me." She hadn't seen her move, but Chrysa was suddenly standing beside her. "Don't do this. That man deserved what he got, but Ira hasn't done anything to deserve this."

"I have to destroy the heroes." Her arms were shuddering from the strain and her hand hurt like hell. "I need to end this."

"It's already ended," someone else said.

Athena and the other woman made their way across the yard.

"Listen to your sister, this is over." Athena's eyes were on her. "Coronis, take him to Hermes."

The brunette kneeled beside Perseus's head and petted his hair. "Such a waste."

Peg stared into Ira's now open eyes and moved the sword away from his neck. He collapsed onto his knees. She couldn't let go of harpe because the weapon was stuck to her palm. As if she sensed this, Chrysa took the pommel. A line of smoke lifted from Peg's hands, but her sister managed to pull until the skin tore from Peg's palms and the sword was lying on the grass.

Athena stared at the blade with distaste.

Coronis cradled Perseus's head. "I've got him."

"You can't take him." Aunt Eno stepped forward. "He's not supposed to move on, none of us are."

"Yes, well, that was before your niece took his head." Coronis held the severed cranium like a puppy and when she touched the headless body with her fingertips, it rose beside her. "Now he's mine to do as I please. Before handing him over, of course."

"But that changes everything," Aunt Rya said, confusion etched on her face.

"It does." Coronis kissed Athena's cheek as she passed her by. "I'll see *you* later."

Athena smiled. "You most certainly will."

No one said anything as the woman dressed in black trudged across the grass with a head cradled in her arms and a headless corpse shambling in her shadow. When she reached the fence post, the woman and the dead hero vanished into mist.

A crow cawed and flew into the sky.

What did this all mean?

Peg turned her attention to her mother's severed body and her legs crumbled beneath her. She reached out to touch her mother's face. At the last second, as the tears began, she decided to lay out her body and positioned her head where it should be. Mom might not be back together and her eyes were closed in death, but she finally looked peaceful.

Chrysa dropped beside her. On the other side, Aunt Eno and Rya did the same. Cal kneeled between Chrysa and Eno. Belle fell next to Peg. Ira closed the circle beside Belle and Rya. Even Sword was there, close to Chrysa.

"You might as well join them," Athena said.

"Oh, I don't think so." Eve, shy as ever, was suddenly there.

"You should," Peg said, looking up. "You're family. Isn't that what you were so keen to tell me?"

The curly-haired girl offered a rueful smile and crouched between Cal and Eno. "I wanted to warn you about all of... this. But as usual, I failed."

"You have to bring her back." Peg didn't pay Eve any attention. She was talking to Athena. The one responsible for setting these cycles in motion. "You have to fix this."

"I'm afraid I can't do that."

"But Perseus is gone," Peg insisted. "Doesn't his death change everything?"

"I don't understand what's going on." Her sister's voice was weak and filled with confusion. "What's all this talk about cycles?"

"There's no time to explain." The Goddess Athena raised both arms and reached for the sky. The clouds shifted faster than they should be able to, changing from white to bruised and ready for a storm. "Perseus isn't the only one who'll be moving on."

Peg's heart sank. "What do you mean?"

"We're all going to the Underworld," Eno answered.

"The cycle is finally complete," Rya added.

"It can't be." Peg refused to believe that. "After we got rid of the gloom—void. After everything we've suffered? No, we deserve another chance."

"You don't deserve anything but what I give you." Athena's eyes glowed amber, and Peg realized it was *her* who'd stalked her on the way home. Her, who was constantly keeping an eye on the family. Her, who was aggressive and manipulative. The goddess was responsible for every tragedy from the start, and this wasn't any different.

"You did this," Peg said. "You planned *all* of this."

"I was growing tired of this endless work." She shrugged, shaking her fingertips to ignite lightning bolts that she fired into the sky. "Baiting Medusa was always easy. And having one of her daughters vanish at her hand highlighted your location to Perseus."

Every time Athena fired another shot of lightning, Peg felt the pain slice through her stomach. *She's stealing my lightning bolts, the ones I hold for Zeus.* Was there no end to her cruelty?

"Stop that," she whispered between clenched teeth.

"You all get the chance to enjoy multiple lives, but I don't," Athena said. "I'm destined to be a voyeur. Always waiting until the hunter finds you, lobs off Medusa's head, before a new cycle begins somewhere else in time. Blah, blah, blah."

"These are our lives you're toying with." Eno looked ready to pounce, but Rya grabbed her hand to keep her steady. "You have to honor what—"

"I have to honor *nothing!*"

Thick raindrops fell from the dark sky and lightning struck in the distance. Thunder rolled nearby strong enough to make the ground rumble.

"You're a disgrace." It was Eve who voiced what everyone was thinking. "I was raised in the garden to respect and worship many goddesses, and there was none I admired more than you."

Athena laughed. "Your opinion means nothing to me. Why did you leave your garden of peace anyway?"

"I wanted to help my family."

"No one can help your family!" She shook her head. "You're all getting bolder with every cycle, the curiosity is too great. I can't allow this to go on. Adding new players to this tragedy was never part of the plan. Yet, here we have a Nymph from Hesperides and Hercules." The goddess's rage intensified the storm. "I won't allow it!"

"You might not, but I will."

Everyone turned in time to catch Lovey's approach. She was still naked but her long blonde hair concealed most of her body. She glanced at Cal and Chrysa, smiling broadly. When she met Peg's eye, she winked.

"You have no say in any of this, Aphrodite," Athena spat. "You think that befriending this family gives you the power to do anything?"

Lovey chuckled. "Maybe I don't have the power, but *he* does."

A new player appeared. He was a golden man with bleached hair and dark roots. He had a trim swimmer's body and was wearing nothing but white trunks. He was riding a huge wave in the sky with a surfboard made of clouds, in an ocean that formed out of nowhere.

Peg recognized this man. He'd come in and out of their school. A substitute teacher who'd specialized in sports and coached the swim team. Most of the girls had crushes on him, including Chrysa. Which was awkward now that she knew he was their father, Poseidon.

Athena glared daggers at Aphrodite. "Who asked you to involve *him*?"

"I don't need anyone to prompt me to do anything. What you want to do is savage and cruel," Lovey said, looking bored as she consulted her fingernails. "These daughters of Gorgon helped release thousands of souls."

"That their mother put there."

"Because you cursed her!"

"I won't allow this," Athena said.

"You're not in charge anymore, and we all know you can't say no to dear Poseidon."

Poseidon didn't bother to land, instead floated in the sky on his cloud surfboard with the impossible shifting wave beneath him. His eyes were bright and aquamarine as he considered the group beneath him, and especially focused on Chrysa and Peg. A small smile curved his full lips, made the sky brighten.

"They deserve to have a choice." His voice boomed like thunder.

"But, Poseidon, they killed Perseus."

"I never cared for him, anyway."

Athena crossed her arms but the cracks in her demeanor were already spreading. "What do you want me to do?" she finally said.

"Give them a choice." He circled over their heads, expertly riding the wave for all it was worth as lightning struck around him and thunder roiled violently.

"What kind of choice?" She narrowed her eyes and pouted, which seemed out of character for the warrior goddess. "After they changed the game—"

"Ask Love herself," he said, flashing out of sight. He zoomed back in, on the other side of the sky, now above the barn. "I'll know if you don't honor their choice and will deal with you accordingly."

Poseidon wiped out, taking the waves and storm with him.

"Typical of him to come and go so quickly," Aunt Eno muttered.

"Hush," Rya said.

Lovey—Aphrodite—was all smiles and seemed flushed with happiness.

"What is it you want me to grant these useless mortals?" Athena spat.

Lovey said, "Give them the choice to live out this cycle until they each meet their individual, but natural end. Only then will all the souls crossover to the Underworld. *Or,* they can choose to start over somewhere else one last time, without all of these painful memories."

"I have to admit, I like these odds." Athena appeared lost in thought, either considering the options or how to get revenge. "Either way, I win. I want this exhausting cycle to be over." She glared at everyone, saving a scathing glint for Peg. "So, what will it be?"

"Do we get our mother back?" Chrysa asked, and there was a certain sadness in her teary eyes.

"Yes, the only one who won't come back is Perseus," Athena said. "But your sister has awakened all the gods and monsters, so everyone in town will be subject to your decision. Whatever you choose, it will affect all of Minerva."

"What?" Chrysa looked confused.

"I'll tell you later," Peg whispered.

"Sure, we can do *that* and involve everyone in our messy business... but there's always *this* option." Eve slipped the necklace over her head and the apple charm morphed into a large golden apple.

"Those apples aren't yours to offer," Athena said, appalled. "You shouldn't have smuggled one out—"

"Relax, will ya?" she said with a cheeky grin. "I'm one of the guardians of the Garden of Hesperides and can do what I choose with this particular apple." Eve turned her attention to Peg and the curls swirled around her face. "So, what's it going to be? Live out the rest of this lifetime, begin one final existence somewhere in time, or accept immortality without all those pesky cycle restraints? One bite is all we need, and there's plenty to go around."

"What about Mom?" Chrysa asked.

"Yep. Even Medusa can—"

"But how will she take a bite in her... condition?" Chrysa's eyes were shimmering with tears.

"Don't worry, Athena will help with that."

The goddess groaned, but reluctantly nodded.

"And Sword?"

"Of course."

Peg couldn't help but grin at the girl she'd found annoying and tried to avoid. "You know, Eve, I'm really glad you found what you were looking for."

"Me too, cousin." She returned the smile. "And I'm glad the cards were wrong."

"Cousin?" Chrysa echoed. "Someone better tell me everything I've missed."

"We will, but first we need to make a choice." Peg took her sister's hand in one of hers, and Belle's in the other.

"Well, girls and boys," Auntie Eno said with a flourish. "What's it going to be?"

"Yes, make this quick." Athena crossed her arms and was positively fuming. "I haven't got all day."

When she met Belle's glistening eyes and her girlfriend nodded, Peg knew what her choice was going to be.

She hoped everyone else would agree.

ACKNOWLEDGMENTS

It's no secret that I love writing horror tales that bleed into other genres. I also love to have fun with tropes. One of my favorite things to do is to weave folklore and mythology into the tapestry of my stories. Sometimes it's a small ingredient. Other times, it's the main focus, but I like to twist the familiar into a modern retelling of my own.

Meg and Chrysa's story was a family tragedy from the very beginning, and was based on one of the tales that has always fascinated me. The maiden. The sister. The mother. The monster. A woman who suffers for the sins of a man and is cursed by a woman. Only to be hunted down by a hero, with the help of the gods. The ones responsible for turning her into a monstrous being in the first place.

Yeah. I like to explore injustice in my fiction.

I'd like to thank Tony Anuci for believing in my weird little novel about a cursed family who might be doomed, but never stop believing in each other. I want to thank Adrian Medina from Fabled Beast Design for the fantastic cover that fits perfectly! Also, thanks to Katarina Yerger.

And of course, I want to thank my very awesome husband for his endless support. For listening to my ramblings while I try to sort through my endless thoughts and ideas out loud.

Plus I'd like to thank YOU. For reading my nightmarish tragedy.

ABOUT THE AUTHOR

Yolanda Sfetsos lives in Sydney, Australia with her awesome husband and spends a lot of time daydreaming about dark ideas. Or actually writing them.

When she's not taking notes on her phone or sitting at her desk with her laptop, she loves going for long walks and is sure to be reading something. But if she's not reading, she's definitely buying new books to add to her HUGE TBR pile or checking out cute Squishmallows. Maybe she's even playing a cozy game or two on her Switch Lite.

http://www.yolandasfetsos.com/